I0654937

Walking on Water
&
After All This

Two Novellas By

Thom Nickels

(Revised and updated from the original book published
by Banned Books, Austin, Texas, 1989)

Herndon, VA

Published in the United States by STARbooks Press

PO Box 711612, Herndon, VA 20171

Many thanks to graphic artist Emma Aldous:
www.arthousepublishing.co.uk

Printed in the United States

Herndon, VA

Contents

Part I. Walking on Water

Chapter One

Dennis left the subway singing a Latin hymn that a friend and he usually sang while walking back to Dennis' Harvard Square rooming house. He hummed "Veni Creator" and thought it rather good. In the back of his mind, he could still see himself as a priest.

He put his hands in his pockets and walked along casually. No one else was on the street, though there were lights on in the various rooms of the university dorm on Kirkland Street. He looked for a shadow or profile behind the shades and curtains, but only saw desk lamps. He walked briskly now, taking quick glimpses at the porches on those houses he passed everyday. There were feral cats peeking out from under automobiles and one of them stampeded across his path as if being chased.

"Veni Creator…" he hummed a little softer now and climbed the steps of Kirkland Manor. He thought to go to bed since it was very late, but once inside, he decided to go downstairs to the communal kitchen to see if any of his roommates were around.

At the bottom of the stairs he smelled a foul odor, much like a rotten piece of fruit. There was a slight buzzing sound from the overhead neon light, which cast everything in a depressing glow. Ashtrays were scattered over the kitchen table and filled with candy wrappers.

Dennis turned back quickly and walked to the first floor corridor. He didn't want to go to bed. The day, and now the night, seemed to "want" something else. He went upstairs to his room and sat at his desk. He folded his hands on his lap and let his mind wander –thoughts of the Cambridge Common near the Square, the long sofa that was the best piece of furniture in his room. He often thought it strange that this room was in the shape of an L, the alcove reserved for the bed almost hidden from view when he sat at the desk.

He turned around. What good were those silly motorcycle photos tacked up by the mirror above the fireplace, he wondered?

Sometimes when he was alone like this, it was like his room was cut off from the rest of the house and set adrift in the sea –when it was so dark outside you couldn't see a thing and the blackness might as well have been the view from a ship's porthole. When it was sleeting out and the weather was cold, he would picture the black hull of a ship cutting through the miserable weather with slow, unfeeling precision. His mind wandered with thoughts of the sea...

# # # # #

There was something to be said for the little rowboat outside the house, roped to a small dock that ran alongside the first-floor window. It wasn't so new anymore, what with patches of chipped paint and pieces taken out of the sides from various accidents. The boat would sometimes appear older and even, on some days, seem to have changed shape. Its usual high hull, remembered from the evening before, would shrink and, when he'd come to fetch the morning paper, Dennis would see a much smaller boat. It was as if the old one had been traded during the night. Although he much preferred the elegant white boat, he knew it was necessary to go along with the adjustment. Besides, what could he do? He couldn't remember when he resigned himself to finding a different boat on occasion, nor could he remember exactly when the changes occurred. But he did know it was some sort of miracle.

# # # # #

The river that flowed beneath his window narrowed considerably at the rooming house. At least it was like that on most days. Other days it would change just as the size of the rowboat changed. He would wake up to find not only a different boat, but a wider river like the Charles –perhaps stretching far out to the horizon so that it looked like the sea. Sometimes, but only on rare occasions, it *was* the sea. On days

2

like this, Dennis would leave his house with more than an ounce of terror in his soul because, when the river became the sea, it was rarely calm and picturesque. When the river changed to a much wider river (perhaps the size of a bay), he saw islands a couple of miles out.

Naturally, these changes of scenery had an affect on him. He wasn't adept at handling them all the time and if, on walking one morning he saw that nothing but swamp lands surrounded Kirkland Manor, he would go back to bed.

On the thirteenth of October he remembered rowing out into the wide river. He had gotten up very early. For the last two days he couldn't bear to leave his room, the river being so wide. He was used to a small stream, almost a creek, with great trees hanging over the house and big boulders showing up out of the water. When he first saw the creek he thought he was stuck. There seemed no way of rowing through it, so he went back to bed. He woke up once more and went outside to walk around it.

He knew it was a brief respite when he could take his shirt off and lie on the grass. The rowboat looked ridiculous; it was so large for the creek. Also its faded brown color made it look like trash, especially with nowhere to go. He had to wait for rain and then he was only able to row a few yards.

But with the river there was a different challenge. It had to be met and not sloughed-off. Sloughing-off meant only that the scenery never went away until whatever was "out there" was rowed into. The sea or a river or bay – whatever it was – would remain until he rowed out into it and faced it head-on. Before long, he would get sick of the scenery, besides feeling trapped. There would only be change after an attempted rowing excursion.

# # # # #

He sang his Latin hymn again, and got down into his rowboat to row out into a land mass. The river was rough; there were all sorts of ripples coming from somewhere and he really had to work. As he rowed, he could feel the sun on his face. Periodically, he would turn to see whether he was heading for the island and then turn back again, his eyes on the ever-shrinking rooming house.

He was surprised when he pulled the boat up on the island beach. Not only was there a Trappist monk standing on the shore, but recognized the monk as Thomas Merton, author of a number of books on Catholic spirituality.

# # # # #

He was a fan of Thomas Merton's writings. Before he came to Cambridge, he bought books by Merton and stayed up late nights reading the monk's diaries and autobiography. Thomas Merton and Nikos Kazantzakis kept him going the long hot summer he worked as a laborer for a cruel and tyrannical landscaper. After a full day of shoveling gravel or planting bushes he'd come home sunburned and take a shower, then fall on his bed and think about the two hours of reading he was going to do that night. He would review the previous night's reading; try to picture Merton as a twenty-six-year-old novelist living in New York, working at odd jobs while trying to be devout. The picture fascinated him. There was some sin in Merton's life, or so the dust jackets read, but as far as Dennis could see they were only drunkenness and a few allusions to women.

But he loved reading about how Merton wrote letters to numerous monasteries then went to retreats and observed the monks in white and black robes kneeling in semi-darkness.

"I will become a monk!" he said to himself, lying in bed, every muscle strained from the day's labor.

# # # # #

Dennis was flustered. He had almost forgotten about Merton. "I know who you are, I think," he said.

"Who am I?" the monk said, placing his hands on his hips.

"You are Thomas Merton, though I don't know how this could be."

"Where are you from?" the monk asked. Dennis looked out over the water to where the roof of his rooming house was visible. As he pointed, the sun seemed to come out from behind the clouds and the water shimmered.

4

"I've seen you pass several times before. Of course it might not have been you. There was a family cruise ship that passed along here, and then a lone boy in a rowboat. I've seen that boat anyway...and your red hair! Welcome to the island!"

"Father Merton, I was really startled to read about your electrocution in Bangkok. It came during a religious conference, didn't it? Do you know that after your death there were people who said that you died because you were getting too involved in Zen Buddhism and forgetting Catholicism?"

"Oh, I know, I know," Merton said, dismissing this with a flash of his hand.

"How come you didn't dry yourself when you came out of the shower that day in Bangkok? Tripping over a fan when you're soaking wet usually means automatic electrocution."

"Well, obviously it was my time. Something inside drove me to do it. I was unaware of danger."

"Do you still keep your vow of celibacy? Your diaries indicate you had that affair with a nurse." Dennis watched as the wind ruffled the end of Merton's robe, revealing a pair of bronzed legs.

Merton was silent a moment. "This island is very conducive to celibacy, however we also preach the Theology of the Body. But if you want to know the truth, I milked a cow this morning and got very horny."

"What's the Theology of the Body?" Dennis asked.

"The cosmic mingling of sexual love with the love of God; it's a totally subjective, individual experience, you know."

Merton and Dennis looked at one another until the monk grabbed hold of the hull of the rowboat and pulled it ashore.

"We're due to get heavy rains this afternoon. And wind. I'll help you carry this up the side of Saint Benedict's Hill. Say, you're not going to leave – you will stay awhile?" he asked.

"Sure," Dennis said. "I've been wanting to meet you for a long time."

In Merton's stone kitchen, Dennis sat a wooden table. Merton was bent over a little Franklin stove stirring some oatmeal and raisins and preparing to cut some freshly baked bread. On the wall was a modernist drawing of Christ riding the subway; He was holding onto a handrail and being squeezed in by many people. A small halo over Christ's head also served as a lasso a cowboy was twirling in a liquor ad on the train wall.

"I like that picture," Dennis said.

"Ah yes, *Christ of the Speeding Subway*. It was drawn by one of the Council fathers at Vatican II. It represents the opening up of the Church to the modern world."

"I've always wanted to become a monk," Dennis confessed suddenly. "When I was seventeen I thought of writing your Abbey in Kentucky and seeing if I could come and make a retreat. But then, you know, something always happened. My vocation would deflate and I'd get interested in something else, like life's pleasures, and then think, how could I ever want to go there..."

"Hmm," Merton reflected, spooning raisins over his oatmeal.

"I really thought for a long time that I wanted to be a priest or monk. It was an obsession and it kept me going for a long time. I didn't talk about it much to my parents. I was a little embarrassed about it because somehow I thought that other people thought there was something pale and weak about wanting to join a monastery."

Merton rolled the arms of his tunic up around his elbows. Dennis could see he had muscular forearms and thick calloused fingers with nails cut evenly across.

"My rooming house is a kind of monastery – and I live sort of like a monk, except that I am not celibate. I could never be celibate. A friend of mine says I'm much too hyper for that. And I am. I think, Father Merton, if I was to keep a vow like that I would turn mean, or at least I would really suffer and tremble at night. You seem not to have been very sexual; at least when I was reading *The Seven Story Mountain* that was not one of your preoccupations...so perhaps it was easier for you to take the vow. I know much of that has changed with the Theology of the Body and Vatican II: New Mass, new laws, a big sense of freedom. Why become a monk today at all?"

They both ate the oatmeal, Merton making loud slurping noises. They drank coffee from earthenware mugs. Dennis kept looking at Merton's thick fingers.

"Do you think they'll canonize you?" Dennis asked,

"Oh!" Merton laughed, putting his spoon down. "They can do whatever they want. Actually I've had calls from many people to come to them as a vision, to appear and perform miracles, but I don't believe that anymore. I prefer my quiet, lost Limbo; my reincarnation. With you here now, though, it's a little less lost. I guess the minute you get back you'll write a book about me."

Merton chuckled, but Dennis felt offended. "No Father, I couldn't do that; you see each day I wake up in my rooming house, there's been this new landscape outside my window. I'm never in one place, either. I mean, there are always shops around where I live and things like that, but whenever the water changes, I board my boat and take to it and row. Then I come to the shops and all of that. So even if I were to write something about this, I would never be somewhere long enough to give it to anybody to read. I've never yet rowed to a modern city like the one I used to live in."

After a while, Dennis asked if there were other monks on the island.

"Two," said Merton. "Novices from Colorado. Both youngsters a little younger than yourself. Will you join us for Compline?"

Dennis agreed and Merton led him outside and down a cobblestone path to a tiny white church, much like the kind you would see in Greece. Entering the chapel, Merton rolled down his sleeves, bowed, put his thick fingers into the holy water, and crossed himself. Dennis did the same, watching Merton the whole time.

Merton went up the center aisle and to one of the wooden chairs set before a simple altar table. Behind the table was a massive scar on the wall of the church as if something big and solid had been ripped out. Two candles on the table were lit, and a twisted crucifix with an elongated Jesus about eight feet high was suspended from the ceiling with the kind of thick rope Dennis had seen tied to boats at various docks. Two hooded figures to the side knelt silently, one taller than the other, a cord tied tightly around the tall one's waist, accenting his broad

7

shoulders and manly figure. The other monk was a smaller version of the first, but was wearing glasses and had his head turned slightly away from his companion. Dennis could see a little bit of his lips; they seemed to be drawn downward in a pout.

Merton began the prayers. The face of Christ on the cross, at least what could be made of it, was etched in terrible pain. The mouth was open, there were tears carved in the face about the cheeks, and the gash at his side was very wide, at least a couple inches across. The inside was painted a bright red. There was a loin cloth which folded gracefully and which came down in one sash, touching one knee. The physique was excellent, the artist having rendered a particularly potent abdominal area, the navel being perfectly oval and having a series of circular bands inside it.

Dennis looked at Christ's face just as one of the novices began a prayer. The legs were crossed and there was one nail through both feet. Dennis often thought about having a nail driven through both feet and he wondered which was the worst punishment, having it done this way or having a nail driven through each foot with both legs hanging flat.

If only he could meet Padre Pio as well as Thomas Merton, but one cannot be greedy, he thought.

"Offer up your prayers in the morning, at the third hour, the sixth, the ninth, the evening, and at cock-crowing..."

The smaller monk said this, and each word was pronounced so correctly that echoes of the crisp-sounding syllables turned the prayer into a rich chant. Dennis watched Merton. Merton seemed to be in a trance, his eyes closed, his lips moving. At the end of the prayer, the taller monk stood up and went to the table to extinguish the candles. In the glimmer of the candle light Dennis could see that the man was quite good looking.

Auburn hair came down over his forehead, and he had an aristocratic profile. His high cheekbones caught the glow of the second candle as he blew out the first. Dennis looked hard. The monk's hood was halfway off and was falling slowly with every move he made. Turning around to bow before the table, it fell off completely and the shock of hair sprung out like autumn leaves from a bushel basket.

Merton seemed less involved in the litany now, as was Dennis. Merton had his hands folded under his chin and seemed to be watching the young monk through half-closed eyes. The other monk stood up just as the first extinguished the remaining candles. The chapel was now in complete darkness except for the tiny votive lamps. Dennis could only see the tall monk's shadow as he glided past his chair. When he was gone there was a distinctive smell of talcum powder in the air.

Dennis was to sleep in one of the monk's cells. Merton led him to the small room at the end of a line of rooms on the second floor of the dormitory. The bed was only thirty-six inches wide and very hard, though it did have a mattress and the sheets were very clean. The cell window was right out of picture book monasteries; crossbars going lengthwise on a 12x12 square. Merton was very ceremonious leading him to the room. He spoke to him in whispers, telling him there'd be a hand bell rung at four the next morning and that he should be up not long after it rang.

The two monks followed Merton and Dennis and when the smaller one opened his room door, Merton turned around quickly and said, "Good night, William," and the taller one continued on to his room. Merton turned to him and said, "God bless." Dennis's room was next to his, and he made a point of looking at the monk as soon as he grabbed the doorknob. They looked into each other's eyes, and Dennis thought he felt something. Merton quickly ushered Dennis inside his room. He turned on a lamp beside a writing table for him and then left. The door was closed and nothing could be heard except the swish of Merton's robes going down the hall.

Pretty soon, Dennis thought he heard a sheet ruffling in the next room. He listened again. The sound was more distinct, as if the monk next to him – Brother Rudolph – was turning over in bed. Dennis imagined him fluffing out his pillow. He got to wondering other things too. He thought about underwear – monks in underwear. He wondered whether Rudolph was lying in bed in his underwear. He must be, he thought, because the rooms were so stuffy. If he was in his underwear, then, did he masturbate when he got erections at night, or did he suffer? Dennis tried to picture the monk, and he saw him fondling himself, muffling his voice into the top sheet. If this was the case, a voice or other told him, then how far was it to other things. That was impossible, he convinced himself. That Brother Rudolph looks so

9

strict! He had fanatical fire in his eyes. But the ruffling sound came again, only this time it was prolonged like it was being deliberately staged. He was secretly overjoyed, even if a part of him was shocked...he didn't expect...not here...in a monastery. After a few more seconds of quiet, an unmistakable noise, much like the sound somebody makes when the breath is held too long and then released, a frantic red-in-the-face blow, loud enough to get anybody's attention.

At this point, he got up and went to his writing table. He pulled the chair out, placed it against the wall, and put his ear to it. He waited, holding his breath. When he heard breathing and more ruffling of sheets, his face reddened and he rubbed his ear over the wall to return the signal. Excited, he undressed, approximating the spot closest to Rudolph's head. When he heard a giant sigh, he sighed into the wall and initiated a few sounds himself, coaxing the monk to even bolder exclamations. Should he move the chair down a little this way? Was he too far up? There was no stopping him now, and right before he was about to explode, his knees knocked the wall and he made a grunting sound like a little animal burrowing itself into a hole.

Afterwards, he noticed how quiet everything was. He suddenly paled at the thought that maybe Rudolph was just a restless sleeper, and that all the sounds were made accidentally, the monk just having an awful time getting to sleep.

Dennis convinced himself of this and by morning he couldn't bring himself to look at Rudolph. In the showers only William was there, soaping down and turning his body around vigorously. William said hello and Dennis retuned the greeting, but as he soaped up he felt that Rudolph was in his room waiting for him to leave the showers. He had no way of proving this, but his suspicions were confirmed somewhat when William, a worried look on his face, kept peeking out of the showers whenever he heard a noise in the hallway. Rudolph was obviously getting a late start.

Through the shower room window, it was possible to see the sun over the ocean. There was a breeze blowing and it made the place seem like a tropical resort, or at least a place other than a monastery. Dennis stood on his toes to see if he could catch a glimpse of Kirkland Manor, but he could only see a jagged shoreline which looked very far off; it could even have been a jetty or a very long ship passing.

"Nice day outside, huh," William said, looking at him quickly, then bending over to soap his ankles, moving on up his legs and soaping his kneecaps. Dennis watched, saying, "Yes, really nice," but concentrated on William's buttocks – shapely and very white as compared with the rest of his body – which led him to think that the monks worked in the fields with their shirts off. "You have a nice tan,"" Dennis said, "Do you do lots of outdoor work?"

Watching William this way got him wondering if perhaps this is what Father Merton meant by the Theology of the Body.

"We do carpentry, cut down trees, work the gardens, and fish." The monk then smiled and seemed to laugh as if enjoying a secret joke. Dennis waited for William to ask him a question, but the monk kept soaping his arms and then opened his mouth to catch some water. For some reason, Dennis copied Rudolph, bending over and soaping his ankles and then moving on up his legs in the same hurried fashion, even turning around under the spray in time with the monk.

Later that morning, William was dressed in plain white vestments and standing by the altar in the chapel when Merton led Dennis and Rudolph in procession up the center aisle. As soon as they were seated, William started Mass. Outside, seagulls called, and the rhythm of the waves mingled with William's, "Let us pray…"

Two children from the island, a boy and a girl, did a liturgical dance, the girl breaking into a Hula before the next prayer.

The vestments hid the shape of William's body, but when he raised the Host, his tanned forearms under the white alb provided a striking photograph. Rudolph rang the set of hand bells and Dennis once again looked up into the face of the crucified Christ. The body had a pinkish glow and the eyes looked upward in a hideous combination of pain and ecstasy.

The boy and girl next made great swirling motions with a bowl of incense.

Later at breakfast, the four of them sat around the table used for Mass and ate their cereal, peaches, and toast. Dennis couldn't figure out how Merton got the Rice Krispies, but there the box was, right next to the cream pitcher. The meal was good and they ate slowly while Rudolph read from a couple of books.

"Jesus did not die into nothingness. In death he died into the incomprehensible and comprehensive absolutely final and absolutely first reality...God."

Dennis recognized it as a quote from Hans Kung, but he was not expecting what came next, a poem from Merton's Journals published some years after his death.

"Graceful girl looks up at train, turns away, throws a bar of

red soap in the grass, takes bucket and stands in stream, pours

water suddenly over her head once –then moves out and does

it again and again rapidly, vigorously. Her wet shift clings to

her body. She is very beautiful –in her gestures.... "

Rudolph continued to read as he alternated pouring coffee from an urn. When he read sections from a biography of St. Francis of Assisi that dealt with the appearance of the stigmata on the saint's hands he read with a great deal of expression. He even held up a hand so that it was easy to imagine the stigmata being planted there. Rudolph read with such conviction that Dennis looked at his own hands and remembered putting bolts in the center of his palms as a kid with the hope the stigmata would be sent to him through some miracle.

But if somebody was to have the stigmata, it would have to be William! Imagine deep grooves in those hands, Dennis said to himself. He snuck looks as William poured more cream into his Krispies, mixing them with his spoon and then sinking them into the milk. Father Merton deserved the stigmata, wet girl in the shift notwithstanding. But he could only see William wearing white gloves on the days of the bleeding, perhaps needing assistance in the form of someone to hand him cotton swabs dipped in alcohol.

Dennis was permitted to roam the monastery grounds all day if he wished, while the other monks went about their work routine. Rudolph and William were going up the shoreline to do some fishing while Merton was going hunting. Dennis wanted to go with Merton but this was a feast day or something and Merton was required to spend a certain number of hours alone. Merton, in fact, had set off into the morning haze with a string bow on his back, his Trappist robes pinned up above his knees. Rudolph and William, on the other hand, took off their robes and dressed in loincloth coverings like something out *of Lord of the Flies* or *Tarzan,* and very risqué. They asked Dennis if he wanted to go with them, but Dennis held back. "I should meditate, you know; I think I'd like to do that."

The monks looked at him a little strangely, for they must have known that he wasn't too spiritually advanced —not realizing that work in the fields was a form of meditation.

The monks looked striking without their shirts. William was a bit chunkier than Rudolph, while Rudolph was lean and well-muscled. William had hair on his chest, but Rudolph's was smooth and brown.

Dennis walked with them out to his rowboat. It was turned over and pulled way up on the beach. It was definitely a sea beach now and not just an extremely wide river or lakefront beach: there were high waves, dead jellyfish and starfish along the shore, and the top of Kirkland Manor could no longer be seen on the horizon. Dennis took off his shirt. He felt the sun burn his pale skin as he watched William and Rudolph walk off together, fishing rods strung over their shoulders.

He stood on the beach and wondered where he would land if he boarded his boat now and set to rowing. It would be some place other than the monastery, he was sure, but as it could be a less friendly place, he didn't want to take the risk. Besides, he was getting to like Father Merton and he was interested in exploring the Theology of the Body.

He went back to the buildings, upstairs to the cells, straight to Rudolph's room, and opened the door. Inside, he first examined the writing table, where he found a number of books with papers inside. There were works by Gregory Baum, Karl Rahner, Mary Daly, Hans Kung and Edward Schillebeeckx. There was also a large inkwell and fountain pen tucked in a neat groove on the side of the table, and above the desk was an abstract painting of a ballerina. On the floor there was a set of dumbbells, and a small book of essays by Bertrand Russell.

He examined Rudolph's bureau drawers and found sandals, leather straps, shoe polish, a small book of prayers by Matthew Fox; and under a clutter of watch bands and buttons, he found a package of prophylactics. He held them up and saw that the box had been opened and one had been taken out. When he put the box to his nose he smelled the familiar rubbery aroma.

Next he looked at Rudolph's dirty linen basket. He went through it, picked out a couple of soiled under drawers and brought them over to the desk to examine them under the light. The stains he saw made him wonder about the reality of asexuality in monastic life, and about the mystery surrounding the Theology of the Body. He wondered who did the monastery wash and then remembered that the monastery was out at sea and isolated from parishioners who might launder it otherwise. What he did next was something he never thought he'd ever do: he put his tongue to it and ran it along the frontal cup. He imagined Rudolph walking in on him as he did this; "It would be so awful," he thought, taking yet another pair and finding a curled pubic hair hanging like a thread.

He went into his own room and sat on the cot. He leaned his head against the wall, and in doing this noticed how thin the wall was. It shook. He leaned a second time and heard a crack. Indeed the walls seemed to be made of papier- mache. He turned around and felt it with his fingers. When he dug in with his fingernails, he was amazed to discover that it was a kind of Styrofoam. All four walls were made of this substance, and led him to believe that the rooms were once open space – and that the walls were, at best, only temporary.

There was a calendar on the wall right above his cot, and an idea came to him. It wasn't a new idea exactly, for he had had the same idea when he lived in Kirkland Manor and thought of executing it several times when handsome men in the room next to his. But Kirkland Manor's walls were made of plaster and wood –impossible to cut through without raising a ruckus and a lot of attention. Here, however, a hole could be made practically with one's hand if enough effort went into the digging and scraping, which is what he started to do as he lifted the calendar. First, he picked a circular area with his nails, while banishing from his mind any thoughts of repercussions. When he was tempted to stop, he told himself that this place –this monastery –was just a *dream* and that, theoretically, he could do *anything he wanted.* After all, the rowboat was right outside and if he got into too much trouble, he could leave and go to another place. It would be that easy. Yet the cutting became more difficult and the Styrofoam became thicker as he advanced farther into the wall. He went to his desk, got a ballpoint pen, and stabbed the Styrofoam several times as he pounded the end of the pen with his fist. Finally, he cut through to the other side and, once this was done, wound the pen around as one would a crank and more of the wall gave way, making for a hole the size of a quarter.

After this, he fell asleep, but was awakened by a sound in the room next to him. He turned on the reading lamp, lifted the calendar, and saw Rudolph on the other side, taking off his habit.

Dennis watched as Rudolph, in a pair of boxer shorts, went into the closet and took out a barbell. Flexing before a mirror he dragged out from behind his bureau drawers, he warmed up by extending his arms and twisting them around, then touching his toes. He went over to a CD player, found a disc, and played it. It was Tony Bennet and Amy Winehouse singing "Body and Soul," another cryptic reference to the Theology of the Body. As the two singers carried on, Rudolph got down on the floor and began lifting. For every lift there was a "clunk" as the barbell hit the floor behind his head. Dennis couldn't get a good view of him now because he was almost hidden behind the cot, so he strained his neck sideways and took in a different section of the room. He also made little "Psst" sounds through the hole, though he stopped periodically when he thought he saw something on Rudolph's crucifix move. The motion made him think of the Spirit or angry Angel who woke him after the previous incident with Rudolph, calling his name and saying quite clearly, "You don't do *that* in here!"

Dennis was a little reluctant to continue, but the swooshing sounds of Rudolph's up-and-down motions, and the vague smell of body sweat coming through the hole, prompted him on. The classic grunts that weightlifters make didn't help matters any, either.

His blowing sounds got progressively louder until Rudolph, aware that something was happening, put the weights down and sat up. Dennis' eye covered the hole, and in no time Rudolph spotlighted it with his desk lamp. Dennis kept from blinking, and stared at Rudolph, while Rudolph walked towards the hole.

In the middle of the night Dennis awoke, someone having shaken his cot. It was more of a thump or a kick, enough to make him bolt up in a panic as if an intruder had entered his room. Once again he heard the words, "You don't do that in here!" race through his head as if sent by an electronic device. What was this? He turned on his desk lamp but no one was there; since he didn't dream it, he knew it must have been the angry Angel.

15

He waited in terror for it to say something else, but he heard nothing. He also listened for sounds coming from Rudolph's room, but all was quiet there too, so he lay back and started to drift off to sleep again when another thump hit the foot of his bed. This time he lay very still and tense, and started a prayer, "Oh please Lord, I am sorry, I'm just a poor sinner. Please forgive me, Lord." He waited. He thought he felt a lessening of tension in the room, as if the Angel had disappeared. He looked up at his window and the light from the half moon was just enough for him to see something pass between its bars. He tuned on the desk lamp thinking that light would scare away the Angel in case it was still hanging around. He had borrowed Rudolph's "*Essays in Skepticism*" by Bertrand Russell and had placed it on his desk chair. He thought, "What nonsense!" and got up to see if the Angel had caused any disarray. He inhaled deeply for hints of sweet perfume or incense, as that was what saints with the stigmata gave off and sometimes personages from the other side, such as angels.

Dennis opened his door, went down the corridor past Merton's room, then downstairs to the chapel, and finally out the front door. There was quite a breeze blowing in from the sea and the sky over the water was very black, as if were really the falling off point way out there. He heard the waves coming in, the same sound they made during the day when it was beautiful out, and the same sound they have made for millions of years, but he listened with a different intensity now. He felt ashamed, an outcast. He didn't know how he could face Rudolph in the morning, or even ever gain. He looked at the nightlight atop the monastery where Merton said there used to be a dome and a cross, wished it good-bye, and set out to walk further down the beach to his rowboat. He considered the black ocean. He wouldn't go out tonight, he thought. He would sleep in the boat after he turned it right side up.

In the morning the monastery bells woke him. He pictured Rudolph all showered and shaved, ringing the bells as he did day in and day out without ever lessening the vitality of his ring. He waited until the ringing stopped so that Rudolph wouldn't see him from the bell tower, pushing his rowboat off the beach. Instead he waited until he thought Rudolph would be dressing for Mass. He then went behind his boat and gave it a shove, pushing it into the surf and jumping into it so that the front tilted upward a bit.

Soon, he was bobbing over the waves and getting the oars in gear, while inside the chapel Rudolph lit the candles on the table altar, which still bore crumbs from the meal the evening before.

"Dennis! Dennis! Dennis!" he heard Merton scream a little later, though it was only a feint echo as Dennis was a considerable way down the coast of the island, the morning tide having been with him.

He stretched out in the boat and let it drift after rowing for a short time. He was thinking of Rudolph and Merton talking about his disappearance before he dozed off. His face was directly in the sun and his delicate skin reddened by the minute, so that by the time he awoke his face felt as if it had been coated with plaster. He had only to yawn to feel the layers of sunburn on it. He felt his face and said aloud, "Oh no, I am going to burn!" Fortunately a land mass was to the right of him and he steered the boat in that direction. He rowed until he hit the rollers and then he glided, crashing over the breakers till he could get the boat to go on no further.

It was a flat land mass, mainly beach, with bits of green here and there. It looked tropical, for one palm tree graced the sands. Dennis pulled the boat ashore and walked a few steps toward the first patch of green. He could see that they were ferns, very low lying with white rocks gathered about their base. He walked among them, stepping over various plants and tiny pools as big around as buckets; looking up he saw a great expanse of ocean ahead of him. This meant that the island was not more than a quarter mile wide. As for length, he looked on both sides of him and saw that were he to run in either direction he would come to the ocean in three or four minutes. Certainly the island had looked larger from where he was in the rowboat, but now it had the circumference of a schoolyard. Nevertheless, he felt safe, and since he wanted to be alone after his experience with Rudolph, this suited him fine.

He went back to the palm tree, looked over the ocean, and thought a moment. "I'll make a new start here," he said to himself. It was this attitude that enabled him to think about building a small hut ands becoming a hermit like the early Church Desert Fathers, away from the temptations of the flesh in the form of William and Rudolph. Dennis knew he had a lot of praying to do on his past sins, and he had a hunch that his coming to the island was the will of God.

17

He thought of Saint Mary of Egypt, the sixth century saint who had such a love for sex that she became a prostitute at the tender age of twelve, and how her love of sex lasted until her visit to the city of Jerusalem when she attempted to visit the Church of the Holy Sepulchre. When she discovered that she could not enter that holy place, she promised God that she would forsake sex for a life of prayer if she was permitted to go inside. After her prayer was answered, she fled to Egypt where she lived she lived as a hermit in the desert.

Dennis decided that he would become the male version of Saint Mary of Egypt!

He checked the palm tree for pineapples but, realizing palm trees didn't give pineapples, he found coconuts. In the hot sun, he wondered how he would shimmy up the tree in order to pluck one off. He wished he had some sunscreen; wished that he had brought some with him before leaving Kirkland Manor, for his face pounded with heat and already the feel of impending burn was everywhere. Still, he took off his shirt – he knew he must get used to the sun if he was going to be a true native – and tucked it behind his trousers. Then he grabbed hold of the palm tree stem and wrapped his legs around it, pulling himself up. Luckily the tree grew on a slant so that the climb was easy and when he got to the coconut, he knocked it off with one chop of his hand.

He had roasted coconut meat for supper. He drank the milk and rubbed some on his sunburn. That first night he slept under the stars and felt the burn on his face. But just as he was getting used to the burn and just as the first haze of sleep rested his body, the sun shone again and he opened his eyes to the feel of facial blisters and more heat. "Your punishment is hard, Lord!," he thought, walking into the ocean in order to rub salt water over himself, thinking all the while of Rudolph, who seemed to be without sin – sans condoms, of course – and who was now perhaps sitting at the altar table having breakfast among the shadowed rafters while he spooned fresh fruit and cream. "I could be there doing that too," he thought, "if only I knew how to conduct myself."

He would have to get started on a hermitage of some sort if he didn't want to burn up completely. He spent the morning gathering ferns and fern stems and then climbed the palm tree again for palm leaves. By early afternoon, he had a shaky thatched hut about five feet high attached to the base of the palm tree and held together with the stems he used to lace the leaves.

In the meantime, he decided that he would start his own order of monks. He didn't know what he'd call the Order or how their habits would be designed or even if anybody else would join, but he made plans nevertheless. He didn't have any fabric or material at hand, so for the time being the habit would be ordinary clothes, a horrible yet necessary concession to modernity. The one exception would be a fern stem tied around the neck as a religious symbol.

He thought this would be okay as a temporary measure, and if anybody else came along, then he would elaborate it and also make copies (on *what* he didn't know) of the daily schedule, which would be mandatory for everyone to follow. The schedule would include rising at dawn and a rule against five minute catnaps or "dilly-dallying" once a monk opened his eyes. Next there would be ocean prayers, where everyone would face the ocean on their knees and pray until the surf gave them a good soaking. After that there would be the hunt: somebody would be assigned to pull down the next coconut and catch one of the little animals that scampered among the ferns. As big as mice, but of a different color, they'd always disappear before he got a chance to inspect them closely.

For now, he had to content himself with solitary praying before the ocean. He decided that his skin was so sensitive he would tie some of the fern leaves around his head so that the branches fell over his forehead and eyes. In this way he looked like an early Roman senator, but the branches provided adequate shade and he was able to keep from getting more sunburn. He attached some branches over his chest and back mostly for the same reasons but also because he thought the fern concoction would make a better religious habit than ordinary clothes.

# # # # #

Merton took the monastery boat out and began going up and down the coastline searching for Dennis. He told the monks that the visitor had disappeared, and Rudolph nodded with a knowing "I expected that to happen" look, running his fingers along the bridge of his nose and then disappearing into the confines of his room where he inspected the quarter-size hole. There he opened one of his favorite books, *The*

Modern Liturgical Movement Need Not Mean the Elimination of Faith and Morals, by Father Novus Wreckovation, a Dominican priest. With a pencil, he underlined passages he thought referred to Dennis or that somehow alluded to his sin, most notably, *"The scientific evidence of how same-sex attraction most likely may be created provides a credible basis for a spiritual explanation that indicts the devil."*

After marking other passages, he looked out his window at the edge of the blue sea, allowing himself a slight feeling of compassion for the boy who, as Father Merton put it the day he arrived, "Came to us from nowhere in a scruffy rowboat."

Merton wanted Rudolph to come with him and help look for the boy. Rudolph said he would but only if Merton issued a Monastic Order but otherwise he preferred to stay in his room. Merton knew Rudolph well enough to know that when he carried out orders he detested, he was very unpleasant to be around. He did not want Rudolph looking at him as if he were the incarnation of some biblical abomination.

In the end, Merton decided to search for Dennis himself, as this way he could have the leisure of rowing as fast or as slow as he pleased. It had been a long time since he had been out to sea, so he welcomed the opportunity to get out one of the boats and push it into the surf, hop on it, and bob over the waves.

"I want to show you something, Brother William," Rudolph said, touching the monk on the elbow. William followed Rudolph into the monastery, up the stairs to the corridor of rooms, and then into Dennis' room. William had not known the reason for Dennis' disappearance, but when he saw Rudolph lead the way into Dennis' room, he knew that it was something serious. "Look in here," Rudolph said. "It should be right about..." Here the young monk instinctively went for the calendar on the wall and lifted it. William saw the hole. He couldn't place its meaning so he waited in silence while Rudolph held the calendar up, as if waiting for a reaction.

"What is it?" William asked. Rudolph repeated William's question, as if not believing what he heard.

"It is penile," Rudolph said directly. "It is penile, a peep hole for the eye. It is the Styrofoam Cyclops of Sodom and Gomorrah. For, as the Master said, "If they right eye offend three, pluck it out, and cast it from thee: for it is profitable for thee that one of they members should perish, and not that they whole body should be cast into hell..."

William looked at the hole even as Rudolph's words seemed to extract the thing and put it in a museum with the descriptions he just gave it engraved as anthropological titles. But then something clicked in William's mind. He remembered being in a men's room a long time ago and he saw a hole much like it; and there certainly was no question of its meaning then. "Dennis made this?" he asked.

"Dennis," said Rudolph flatly, staring at William as if waiting for an editorial comment that would jive with his own. William started to laugh and sat down on Dennis' bed and began touching the thing.

"Has it been used?" he asked, giving Rudolph a smile and a wink.

"Used?" Rudolph repeated, as if he couldn't quite believe what he was hearing. Surely what he heard William say was the result of a loose screw or bolt, unhinged because he had too much sun. But William stood up, put a hand on the monk's shoulder, and squeezed it.

Rudolph would have none of this. He quickly brushed William's hand away and looked at him angrily. "You accuse me, even jokingly, of being a part of this?"

"Brother Rudolph, where is Dennis?" William asked.

"He's left. Last night he eyed me and egged me on..."

"You don't have to go into detail, Rudy..."

"...Last night he wanted me to do something. He propositioned me. He put his fingers into the hole and beckoned me. Today he's left the island for shame; as he should have, and is somewhere out at sea."

William was curious. "Are you sure you didn't do anything to make him run away?"

"I ignored him, William. What else was I to do? I couldn't do anything else."

"You could have talked to him through the hole," William said. "The sea is murder. You know what goes on out there, the sharks and killer Sting Rays. He could be ditched on another island many miles out, all alone, and then we'd have to answer to God for that."

"Answer to God? Seems to me the one who poked out the Styrofoam wanting penile play is the one who should answer. Go read your catechism, Brother William!"

"Not the Dutch catechism, certainly," William said.

"What you say has a Baltimore ring!"

In a huff, Rudolph left the room and walked to his own room and shut his door. The slam reverberated in William's ears.

# # # # #

Merton knew where Pinpoint Island was (so named because of its smallness) and he was well on his way there as Dennis lay on the beach weeping. He was saying "Oh strike me dead! Strike me dead!" as his sunburn rolled him over imaginary coals, and as his two days of semi-excited planning rumbled into despair and depression. Lying there, he no longer wanted to start a new Order of monks. He just worried about how to live. Must he stay there all his life, sunburnt, eating coconuts? He had read *Robinson Crusoe* but Crusoe's island was big and lush, with human beings on it to befriend —or fight; but at least there was adventure. As a boy, Dennis thought he would never get tired of the sea and he often dreamt of living next to it. When they turned Robinson Crusoe into a movie he watched excitedly as Crusoe chased the loin-clothed native up the beach, Friday finally falling on his stomach and Crusoe falling on top of him.

But piles of dead jellyfish kept being washed ashore and sand crabs, too, and it was impossible to catch one of those mouse-like animals that scampered around the ferns. He tried fishing with a stem and trouser thread, but the waves kept throwing around the line until the bait floated away.

He cried because, despite the problems he once had with facial acne, he nevertheless wished he was back at Kirkland Manor boiling his little pans of water on the hot plate and then applying the boric acid compresses to his skin. He wished he was still being ignored by Ames, too, the cruel Ames who said that he knew better than Dennis and that's why he was kicking him out of bed. Ames, who would never be

Dennis' boyfriend – just a Beacon Hill buddy who asked for no special privileges and just to be left alone.

"Oh Ames!" he cried out, languishing in the sand, the pain he felt causing him to imagine himself in a movie, clawing the beach, dying, or about to be put in a hole in the sand so that his head would be exposed when the tide came in. "Why is gay life so hard? Will I ever find love?"

Pinpoint Island had been an island of Pagan Ritual. Missionaries from the East and West traveled here a long time ago to convert the inhabitants (all fair skinned savages with blue eyes), but instead were converted themselves, abandoning their Roman cassocks or Byzantine-style onion domes for fern skirts and shirtless orgies. This lost island caused both Catholic and Orthodox authorities great embarrassment; never had there been a case of priests converting en masse to a pagan religion.

Some said the mass conversions happened because of the angle of the sun on the island; that somehow the combination of the white beaches and the hot sun brought about a brain change among the priests so that they soon began to see Christianity as irrelevant. The coconut milk rubdowns and nighttime beach fires of the savages were just as trance-inducing as morning Mass or Divine Liturgy. The priests soon felt a claming peace (much like the peace of Holy Communion) hearing the bones the savages beat out on copper discs after sundown. The Churches sent additional missionaries when there was no word that the savages had been converted, although one Latin bishop ordered his missionaries to take a potion which deadened the senses and made them indifferent to exotic influences. Nevertheless, the savages refused both the Roman cross and the Byzantine dome and the missionaries refused the discs. Both sides got to beating and banging to such a degree that an earthquake, caused by the vibrational force of the clangs and the in-house war between Rome and the East, sunk the island and drowned everybody. Only a small portion of the original island managed to survive, a land mass so small it had but one palm tree.

When Dennis spotted Merton rowing ashore, he stood up and waved. Merton was waving an oar, a sign that told Dennis he had by no means been excluded from anything. Dennis helped Merton drag the boat out of the water and then they just stood there looking at one another.

"You've decided to leave for good?" Merton tried not to look at the sun blisters on Dennis' face.

"I don't know," Dennis said. "Rudolph will never forgive me for what I've done. Probably nothing like that has ever happened in a monastery before."

"Oh?" Merton said, adjusting his black leather belt. "One can never be sure of that, can they? Besides, what were you thinking of when you drilled that hole? Did you think that Rudolph would oblige you? Dennis, you must be aware that Rudolph comes from a traditionalist Midwestern family. He knows little about the Theology of the Body. Some discernment is in order."

"I got carried away, Father, I thought he was sending me signals, I thought…"

"In my younger days, before I entered the Order, I had some wild times in Greenwich Village, and sometimes even today I want to slip back. God knows, I've prayed about it. I thank the saints I've been able to maintain control in most things I do. Yet there…has been a change: Since the Council a window has been opened; moral issues are not as black and white as they used to be; there is room for expansion. God, you see, sometimes sanctions the gray areas. When I fell in love with that nurse in Louisville that I wrote about in my diaries, I sensed all along that I had the default blessing of God. "

"Is that what you would call The Theology of the Body?"

"More or less; love as a sacrament but only if raw sex is transformed by love so that it becomes a kind of sacrament."

"So loving Rudolph might be okay if Rudolph loved me?"

"That would be one of the gray areas."

"Well, Father, suppose Rudolph had to sleep in a cell that was beside the cell of a beautiful young nun. Would he be perfect then? Is he made of armor?"

"He may be made of armor, though I've seen him weaken in the fields. He was cutting down beach weed one day and I witnessed it. I

24

was embarrassed for him it seemed so pathetic. Like the gasps of a dying man. Anyway, perhaps Rudolph will have a chance to be tested, for if the Abbott General in Rome approves the admittance of women, he will be put to the test."

"Good," Dennis said, imagining Rudolph standing at the lectern back at the monastery and reading the meditations. "Then maybe he will be humanized a bit. He will understand maybe."

"Won't you come back with me, Dennis?" Merton looked as a father might look at his son after a tender reconciliation. Dennis pondered the surf, then met Merton's gaze and offered, "I was getting used to the idea of staying here by myself where there's no temptation, even though my sunburn is killing me and I'll probably get skin cancer. You might think this is crazy, Father, but I was even thinking of starting a new order of monks here on this island, an order made up of people like myself, men with same sex attraction, so we'd understand one another and not go haywire when something like a hole-in-the-wall happened. At least there would be no walls around here –though you can never tell what will be."

"A new order would be a hard thing to establish. Elaborate preparations would have to be made. I mean, what kind of screening process would you have? The only people who come here are tourists from the mainland, and they aren't of the monastic garden variety. They leave their yachts out at sea and paddle in here for beach parties. I think you would be greatly disturbed. I once saw a gang of surfers who got lost at sea end up here and set up camp. A bronzed and handsome group they were, but from my boat I could see that they acted like gorillas –fighting and kicking sand in one another's eyes. They wouldn't take too kindly to holes. Then again, desperate situations often lead to desperate solutions. Besides, this is no place for a sane person to live. There's nothing here. Unless you wanted complete mortification…and were absolutely sure…I could give you some robes and some crosses, and I'd write the Archbishop and tell him your plans. It will be a hard road, however. Already you look like you're about to suffer sunstroke…"

Dennis tied his rowboat to Merton's and together they rowed back to the home island. William met them, walking into the surf up to his knees and getting his robe wet. Dennis kept looking for signs of

Rudolph as the two embraced. He was hoping that Rudolph was watching and picking up signals that he was on the verge of a new commitment. "But he probably thinks I'm just hugging William because I want to drill a hole in his wall," he said to himself.

At dinner that night, the four of them ate in silence. Although he faced Dennis on the other side of the altar table, Rudolph kept his eyes fixed on his plate and would only periodically look at a spot above Dennis' head. After the half hour meal, it was obvious to Dennis that under no circumstances would Rudolph allow their eyes to meet.

"He thinks if he looks at me, I'll drill another hole. Well, now, maybe I might, just to show him something..."

When he got to his room, he found that the hole had been plastered up. It had been dry for a long time. Dennis could see that this was so because when he turned on the desk lamp he felt the hard patch with his fingers.

That night he was afraid to move in his cot for fear Rudolph would think he was up to something. He lay flat on his back and tried to sleep, but pretty soon the stillness got to him and he turned over. A crink in the cot machinery sounded loud and clear, sounding almost as if it had been banged with a wrench or a small hammer. Hearing this, Dennis muttered an "Oh, no!" and waited to see if Rudolph would respond. He did —a bang, perhaps caused by a fist, came from the other side of the wall.

He froze...he also felt angry. With his fist he pounded the wall right about where he thought Rudolph's head to be. He knew then that he was suffering the logical consequences of having tried to seduce a holy man of God, small box of condoms notwithstanding. "I shall be hounded like this for a long time; O Lord, teach me to bear it with a smile!" he said to himself.

Chapter Two

As time went on, Dennis became more involved in the monastery's affairs. He was regarded as a postulant by Merton and William and was even accepted somewhat the same way by Rudolph. To do this, he had to prove himself capable of near-perfect behavior, especially when Rudolph was around. He had to promise himself not to look at Rudolph while they ate or while at prayer. And when Rudolph assisted Merton in distributing communion, he made a point of tilting his head backwards when the chalice was held under his chin so as not to tempt Rudolph into thinking he was receiving just to get close to his fingers. In fact, William felt free to open his eyes when he received – but he shut his tightly. Merton was gracious enough not to assign conflicting work schedules either. He kept Dennis and Rudolph apart, or if they had to work together, he put William with them.

When Merton asked Dennis if he was sufficiently adjusted to monastic life and wanted to enter the novitiate, Dennis said he was, and that he felt most of the tension between himself and Rudolph had all but disappeared. "It has died a natural death," he told Merton.

"Yes, Brother Rudolph feels that if you don't bother him, he won't bother you. He is willing to surround you with Christian love provided you don't, as they saw, waver. It's Rudolph's way if saying 'hate the sin, not the sinner.'"

"Doesn't he think I have any self-control,?" Dennis said, putting on a face of strong self-determination.

"It's not that, it's just that Rudolph's been duped before. A long time ago, a novice fell in love with him and wanted to run off with him to Pinpoint Island. But he did it under the guise of a week long retreat…just the two of them. He kept telling Rudolph that they should try the Carthusian Rule on an isolated island somewhere."

"Now that's deception!" Dennis said.

"It certainly was," Merton reflected. "And it tore Rudolph apart. Not literally, but spiritually, for he returned to the monastery in the rowboat late at night. He came straight to me, shaking me by the shoulders and pleading with me to listen to what he had to tell."

"Nothing violent happened…he wasn't raped, was he?"

"No, no, no. This brother proposed love to him and mentioned the love that St. Serge had for his friend, St. Bacchus. He wanted Rudolph to participate in the Order of Uniting Two Men, an Eastern document from the 11th and 12th centuries. He called it a marriage ceremony from the early Church and insisted that love between two monks can be solemnized. What he failed to realize was that Rudolph didn't love him in that way at all, not to mention that Vatican II never said anything about same sex marriage. Your hole-in-the-wall, however, exposed his nerves to the crude."

Dennis was hurt by this, though he could see that Merton was trying to make a point. Merton had been *around;* he knew all about this stuff, and outside of his vow of celibacy, which he saw as a movable feast thanks to the spirit of the Council, he probably didn't think that same sex relations were wrong. Because he was spiritually advanced, he was able to view Rudolph with cautious amusement, but he was also able to see Dennis' actions as purely animalistic. "Did you really think that Rudolph would stand up and bring his penis close to that thing?" he asked Dennis one day, while the two of them combed the beach for crabs.

"Aside from this, are you ready, really ready to become a novice?" Merton crossed his arms as Dennis insisted that he was ready. He said that as long as he had been at the monastery he'd wanted to join.

"I thought about it," he said. "I have no life at Kirkland Manor. If I went back, I'd fall into the same old traps: Dermatologists; one-night stands with the local boys; vanity; the hypnotizing power of French existentialist writers. You know, Father, I'd be wasting my life. Here I can really be somebody, do things."

The short novice-installation ceremony was held early on the day following this conversation. Kneeling before the altar table where there was still a jar of mayonnaise from a previous lunch, Dennis accepted the folded white robe handed him by Merton. Behind him, Brothers Rudolph and William chanted some prayers, Rudolph answering the loudest when they had responses to make. After this there was a stirring rendition of 'On Eagles Wings,' during which the boy and girl liturgical dancers reappeared with their incense-swirling cereal bowls. "Behold, how good and how pleasant it is for brethren to dwell together in unity," the monks prayed. "Yes, we accept this man into the Order; keep him holy Lord, keep him constant." Rudolph seemed to be emphasizing the word 'constant.' It annoyed Dennis at first, but then he told himself it was probably only for his own good. He put the robe on with some help by Merton and when he had it on he stood up and felt like a new creature. Soon he would have his black belt and rosary, and the outer black tunic, and he would be a monk. He genuflected, received a blessing from Merton, and followed him out of the chapel. William and Rudolph filed in after him and began a hymn from one of Merton's journals.

Five breaths pray in me: sun moon

Rain wind and fire

Five seated Buddhas reign in the breaths

Five illusions

One universe:

The white breath, yellow breath,

Green breath, blue breath,

Red fire breath...

Amen! Amen! Thought Dennis, a new day! Outside, he breathed in the salt air, his sixth breath, and would have run down the beach had not Merton directed them to assemble under a spread of palm trees for a community meeting.

William ran back into the chapel and brought out some rubber kneeling pads. He arranged them in a circle and Merton was the first to sit. After reviewing the rules of the Order for Dennis' benefit, Merton opened the meeting for general discussion. Dennis let his eyes wander over the beach. Should he ask them now? Going over it countless times he envisioned several reactions. Charges of insanity. Laughter. He decided to cut to the chase and speak up as he had heard the others do on numerous occasions.

"Father and Brothers," he began as if ringing a hand bell. Rudolph and William fell silent and looked at him with genuine interest. Merton encouraged Dennis with his eyes, even nodding his head as if to say, "Come on boy, that's it!"

"Father and Brothers," he repeated, looking briefly at Rudolph who seemed to be eyeing him with a tiny glimmer of love, "as a new member maybe I have no right saying this, but it's been on my mind for some time. I've been thinking that since we're here on this island, maybe we should think about changing the habit. I know you may consider this a foolish preoccupation, and I know what many Council experts say about the unimportance of outward appearances, but I believe that we ought to consider adapting our habit to the island sun..."

Merton seemed interested and sat forward, exchanging a glance with William that seemed to say, "What could he possibly have in mind?"

"In the hot weather, something should be put over the head, and I think that we should wear the epanokamelavkion, or veils, like the Eastern Church Hieromonks and bishops, only in our case I think we should wear white because of the sun." Dennis was blushing; he lowered his eyes and for a moment he was afraid to look up. When he did, he saw Rudolph eyeing him sharply. It was so hard a glance that he had to look away. "They could be veils like the Armenian and Russian bishops wear, that kind of white..." He wished somebody would answer him, but the three of them seemed quite taken aback.

"White is white," Merton said finally.

"Do you think this is a silly idea, Father?" Dennis asked, picking up a twig and drawing a line in the sand.

"No," Merton said, a little too unconvincingly for Dennis. "It may be though, that veils in the Eastern style will be too cumbersome. How would we fish in them, and comb the beaches and work the gardens? If you mean the two-story box veils of some Ethiopian patriarchs, then you must know how easily they slip off..."

"We would wear them only inside the monastery, and during prayer. When we worked, it would be optional."

Rudolph, who had been shifting nervously during Dennis' presentation, spoke up.

"We are Western monks and we adhere to the Roman rite. Nowhere in the liturgical functions of our rite does it call for such a headdress. On this island, it would be short of ridiculous. It would serve no purpose." Rudolph took a quick look at William as he finished his sentence then folded his hands on his lap. He seemed especially adamant in his dissent, really annoyed, but Dennis somehow found the bravado to answer him.

"What good are robes then, or crucifixes? Why don't we all just wear Levi's? What good is anything? Just because we're the Roman rite doesn't mean we can't be flexible and adopt Eastern ways. Father does it with Zen, and that's a further stretch than this is. Why do we have to be so narrow? We are one Church, aren't we? The veils would keep the sun off our heads too!" Dennis said all of this in one breath and it was quite a struggle for him to get it all out, excited as he was at the prospect of challenging Rudolph.

"Dennis may have a point," William said, turning to Rudolph. "The only thing I'm worried about is what will happen when the box structure weighs too heavily on the forehead. It could hurt the circulation. And I really don't think that any of us has the time to make veils. Still, I think your vision is beautiful. The white veils would be most impressive in the chapel at night." William smiled at Dennis and he was comforted somewhat, but Rudolph got up in a huff.

"Excuse me, Father, but I cannot take any more of this absurdity. Vatican II called for the simplification of religious habits, not an elaboration. Even our nuns are ditching their veils and robes for skirts and mini-dresses, perfume and luxurious hair-dos. We are in the springtime of the Church, the great modern beginning. Am I excused?"

"I will let you go, Brother Rudolph," Merton said. "So you want veils?" he asked Dennis after Rudolph had gone.

"Maybe not," Dennis answered softly.

"Maybe not? Then what was all that talk about?" "Brother Rudolph thinks I'm crazy," he said.

"No, he doesn't. If Rudolph had his way, the Order would be fitted in Brooks Brother suits; we'd all be walking around like Hans Kung necktie clones. Rudolph hates frills of any kind. Have you noticed that his habit is shorter than ours? It's more masculine, he says. This all started when Rudolph was on the mainland and went with some other monks to an orchard in the country. A sports car filled with young

31

women sped by and they shouted, 'Hey, you cutie in the skirt!' Rudolph never forgot it. I've told him several times that he is a monk, not a player in the world, but he continues to have issues. He's so serious about this that he has a campaign underway with our Superior in Rome to modify the habit. He wants the new habit to reflect the spirit of the Council. In fact, he just got through circulating petitions regarding this issue before you came."

William laughed at this, but Dennis heard nothing that was laughable. "Change the habit to what –a suit?"

"No, I believe just a simple white shirt tunic and a black cloth belt, much like a karate uniform with pants."

"How macho," Dennis thought. "Do you think he will be successful?"

"If he continues to put as much steam into the project as he's been putting into it for the past two years, he may win. But that doesn't mean you can't go on with your veils. Lately, more and more freedom is being granted the monastic orders regarding habit modifications. As quite aside from Rudolph's project, very soon it may be up to the individual monks as to whether or not they want to wear the habit. Rudolph was already successful in the matter of church design. He convinced me to dismantle the high altar in the chapel and put in an IKEA table so that it would reflect the new philosophy."

"What's happening to the Church?" Dennis asked. "The Eastern Orthodox would never do a thing like this. You'd never see an Orthodox priest or bishop walking around in Hans Kung neckties. I always thought the Catholic Church was the original Church of the apostles, and the Church that most valued tradition. I wonder about that now."

"Dennis," Merton said calmly, "you're confusing habits and the cosmetic vanities of worship with spirituality. The basic foundations and teachings of the Church never change, although it may be possible to interpret these things in a new light. The Holy Spirit guides the Church and gives it new revelations, much like the Theology of the Body. Religious habits and high altars are like wisps of air or pretty calendar pictures, here today and gone tomorrow."

"I am confused, Father, but mostly I was thinking of aesthetics and style."

"Gosh, Dennis, you're really into this. You're serious, aren't you?" William offered. "Personally, I can't see why you can't make a veil for yourself and wear it. If it will make you a better monk and if it will make you happy, I think Father Merton would give his consent."

He was beginning to feel cheated as a new novice to discover that the Order may give up the habit. He didn't want to be the male equivalent of modern nuns who looked more like lesbian feminists than committed religious. He was relieved when Merton said that he could make a veil if he wanted and wear it anytime he wished. Merton said he could start now if he wanted, and told him where there was a clean supply of linen and a sewing kit.

"You can make what you want," Merton said, "as long as you don't cover your face like an Iraqi Muslim woman."

Dennis went to get the linens and the sewing kit. He measured a piece of sheet after cutting a strip of cardboard from some old poster board. After stapling the cardboard so that it fit as a circular band around his head, he sewed a veil over it, leaving enough material so that the sheet flowed down to his waist when he placed the structure on his head. He knew that Russian bishops and some hieromonks pinned some kind of icon to the front of their veils, so he got a Miraculous medal and stuck that on. Standing in front of the mirror he knew he looked like a professional. He turned around very fast to test the veil and to see if it would fall off. It held and when he stooped down, it didn't fall off either. From a distance, walking towards the mirror, he was an impressive sight with his robe and veil flowing all at once. He couldn't wait to get out in the wind or walk along the beach in it, especially if a tourist or a supply boat came by so he could be seen and admired.

But he was afraid to go out among his brother-monks in it. He knew that Rudolph really couldn't laugh at him, because then he'd be laughing at the Eastern Church. Still, he wasn't an Eastern bishop and possibly a laugh could be had out of that. "I'll tell them that it makes no difference whether a western monk tries to look like an eastern bishop or a karate-chopper!" he thought as he made his way out the door to test the box's staying power outside.

A slight wind seemed to caress the veil in a loving fashion as he made his way into the chapel where the monks were assembling for evening prayer. He took some holy water when he entered; as he did so, he felt a presence behind him. He didn't want to turn around, so instead he studied Merton and Rudolph kneeling before the table, where the box of Rice Krispies had finally been removed.

"Dennis," William called out, "Let me see you." Dennis turned around.

"Holy Cow! Beautiful! Let me touch." William fingered the box structure, flicking the medal with a finger. He took hold of both ends of the veil and studied Dennis' face. "You look fantastic. You know, Dennis, you're really quite striking."

Dennis felt good. William put a hand on his shoulder and gave it an affectionate squeeze. Together the two of them made their way up the chapel's center aisle. They genuflected and went into the row of chairs in front of Merton and Rudolph, Dennis listening for sounds of disapproval from Rudolph –a whisper to Merton, or even a chuckle. He heard nothing, and when it came time for him to read the prayer responses aloud, he did so proudly. Rudolph kept staring at Dennis' veil, which fell below his waist.

Life at the monastery was calm for a time. The box veil also seemed to transform Dennis, at least that's what Rudolph said to Merton one afternoon as the two of them were weeding the little garden by the white chapel.

"He's really improved. He hasn't looked at me, how shall I say, lustfully, since he put that thing on...." Because Rudolph had never read Merton's journals, he never knew about the Abbot's own sexual indiscretions as a religious but naively assumed that they both shared a similar moral and philosophic outlook. Merton was Rudolph's idea of a "confidant," even though Rudolph never bothered to inquire about Merton's real feelings.

One evening a few weeks later, Dennis left the palm tree grove where the monks had been debating birth control and abortion. As he got up, he saw a ship close to shore and two rowboats heading towards the beach. "Hey look!" he called out. Merton looked up.

"Thank God!" he said, straightening his robe before running down the dunes to meet them.

The supply ship came once a month just after sundown; its coal blackness gave it a sinister appearance on the darkening waters. A freighter with what seemed like tentacles and multiple poles crisscrossing one another along the entire length of the desk, it was an ugly monstrosity. By sunrise the rust and corrosion of the freighter's hull had a shocking look.

Rudolph and William raced off after Merton. They could run freely but Dennis was hampered by having to hold onto his box veil.

Two fat men landed first. Their faces were greasy and shadowed with grime. They had knit hats pulled low over their heads and their hands were covered in soot.

When the men were able to walk in the surf, they jumped the boat and pulled it ashore. The monks met them with raised arms and cheery hellos and the men waved back. On the beach, one of the men stepped back and let Merton peek under the supply canvass. The man pointed and muttered something under his breath. Dennis watched as Merton cupped his ear as if he was having a hard time understanding him. Just then a wind kicked up and Dennis' veil blew up over his face. The fat men seemed intrigued by the veil.

They unloaded coffee, sugar, health food cereal and sacks of potatoes onto little red wagons. Everybody left but Dennis; he was told to stand and wait for the second boat which would be arriving momentarily.

He heard the swish of oars in the water. Pretty soon he saw the outline of a man tugging at a rope, the rowboat he was pulling getting nearer the beach. A wave knocked him over but he was up in a flash, taking hold of the boat with a resiliency that was Olympian. Was this some charmer from Atlantis, come back to present time to a life of sheer drudgery? He squinted to make him out more clearly. He had on a knit hat but he had taken it off after his plunge and now, as he came to the beach, Dennis could see that his hair was a mass of tangled black curls.

He wasn't handsome; he had a sort of rough face with a wide nose, but there was a kind of beauty in his eyes. From his wide open shirt,

Dennis could see that he was solidly built, his muscles of the angular variety capable of twisting and turning with snake-like flexibility. Looking at Dennis, he pulled his rowboat ashore and immediately they both knew that something bound them together, for had their eye contact been x-rayed, sparks would have shown up above their heads.

Dennis watched him for a moment. Then he said, "May I help you?" The man continued to work and did not answer, hauling off supplies and setting them down on the beach. For the first time, Dennis felt ridiculous in his box veil. He wanted to take it off but there seemed no way of doing it without being questioned by the brothers when they returned. The man then looked at his veil but in a way that implied no judgment. Dennis began to formulate a question, walking towards the worker as the latter paused to read the lettering on a box. "He wants me to say something; there's nothing wrong with that box," he thought. He knew he must do it quickly if he was to do it at all.

"What's your name?"

"Mike," the man said, not turning around. A panicky feeling came over Dennis. The new spiritual reserve he had built up was about to be knocked over; already he felt it draining from him and a general weakening beginning at about his ankles. He fought the temptation for a moment and remained where he was, silent, not moving but staring at the ground. He would do something if the man turned and pulled him into his arms. He would let him do that, but he couldn't encourage it. He knew the man was waiting for a response of some sort because his fidgeting had turned into a complex operation. He was now on the hull of the rowboat, bracing each side with his legs and doing something with a rope. Dennis rationalized his behavior by reminding himself that monks have a duty to get to know the "face" of God in other people. Silence, of course, would have been the appropriate spiritual response, especially when it came to sins of the flesh.

"My name is Brother Dennis. How often do you come here?"

"Twice a month," Mike said, moving more boxes ashore.

"Do you ever take a coffee break? Do you ever come up to the monastery for a beer or something after work?"

"Nah," the man said, looking up at Dennis briefly, amazed at the mention of a coffee break. Dennis thought that the man had somehow figured out his secret.

"Do you know how long it takes them to arrange the stuff in the kitchen?" Dennis asked. Now he was really going. He felt the spiritual reserve crackle like tin foil and flush out the other side of him. What kind of monk was he?

"Depends. Sometimes twenty minutes, sometimes more."

A voice urged him on: say it, say it.

"We can take a sort of coffee break and go over by the rocks." Dennis pointed to a group of rather large boulders, among which were caves and small salt water pools. His whole body shook and he could hardly speak.

"Where?" Mile asked, putting his knit cap on.

"Over there," Dennis said, his voice cracking.

Mike didn't answer but continued to move the boxes. There were only a few left and as Dennis watched, he imagined that he had been rejected, that Mike was thinking he was some sort of crazy person or fag monk for wanting a ten minute coffee break in the rocks, at night, with no coffee –this, plus a box veil! He felt embarrassed and guilty; the spiritual reserve he had discarded came back in the form of remorse and shame. He'll tell the others on me, he thought. He was also afraid of a sudden punch to the face. Yet just as he was about to apologize to Mike for his lopsided suggestion, Mike stepped off the boat, hitched up his trousers and said, "You lead the way, brother!"

Dennis noticed the erection in the man's trousers right away, going down his right leg a considerable distance. In the boulders! The idea was insane. Merton and the brothers would be back at any time, and how would he explain his absence? Rudolph would catch on immediately, and then what? Nevertheless, he led Mike towards the boulders, realizing he just might be walking to his own destruction. At the coral reef, they went over to the taller rocks and behind the largest, they stopped.

Dennis heard voices. They came from a distance but they were clearly heading his way. He said to Mike, "Why don't you come over here." There was a small space next to where Dennis was sitting. Mike came over. It was hard to see in the reef but he could see enough to move his right leg against Mike while sliding his hands outward toward his new friend. The voices grew louder as Dennis put a hand on Mike's leg and slid it along, resting it finally on the lump beneath the trousers. As Rudolph's voice became distinguishable, Dennis unzipped the zipper and reached inside for the long coil, taking it out after some fumbling. Quickly he put his mouth to it and moved in even-paced up-and-down strokes, while Merton called for him.

When he had finished, Mile zippered up and announced, "Don't come back with me!" He swaggered out of the coral reef with his hands in his pockets and headed for the others as if his intention was to ask for a cigarette. Dennis rearranged his soiled robe and straightened his veil; it had flipped to the side and all but fallen off his head during the man's orgasm.

To say that Dennis felt like throwing himself into the sea would be an understatement, for he not only felt surrounded by darkness but like a huge bong was banging inside him. He even began to hurt physically. He lingered in the reef while imagining what Mike might be telling the others before sitting down on the rock where it had taken place. "Oh my God!" he whispered, lowering his head into his hands. "What have I done?" He began an act of contrition, wishing God would take away the banging feeling as quickly as possible. He sat there for several minutes and didn't move until he heard the horn of the freighter.

He wandered around in the dark for an hour or so before returning. When he did return, he saw William and Rudolph in the corridor of rooms. He attempted to duck away and wait till they left, but Rudolph saw him.

"There he is!"

"Hey," William said. "Where have you been?"

"Walking," Dennis said, trying to look sincere, but feeling the old bong eating out his insides. "I took a walk down by the coral reef and just kept walking…"

"Will you read for me at Mass tomorrow?" Rudolph wanted to know.

"I can," he said, thinking of the sight he'd make at Mass with guilt written all over his face.

"Good night then. Bless you," Rudolph said, retreating down the hall.

"You know," William added after Rudolph had gone, "He's taken another view of you. Isn't that wonderful! There's been a change. He had a talk with Abbot Merton and now he says he fully understands your predicament. I think that's beautiful Dennis, don't you?"

Chapter Three

There was another community discussion on religious habits when permission arrived from the Abbot-General in Rome to modify the robe and tunic. With the permission came approval of Rudolph's karate-style uniform for those monks wishing to change to more modern dress. When Merton read the Abbot-General's permission, Rudolph could hardly contain his glee. He bolted from his chair and said, "Thank God we'll be rid of these skirts!" He sat down again, folded his hands and took a long look at Dennis, who had changed the Miraculous medal on the front of the veil to a small Byzantine icon. But Dennis looked away; he was not, he told himself, going to become involved in any more heated discussions with Rudolph.

Merton told the monks that the modified habits would be sent on request, and he asked William if he was interested. Dennis waited for William's response but the monk vacillated between a nervous chuckle and serious consideration. He obviously had Rudolph on his mind because the latter looked at him with an expression that seemed to say, "Well, you all but promised." William delayed saying anything but instead ran his hands over his habit as if wiping off crumbs. "I...I really don't think it's suitable for me right now and I've given it a lot of thought. I would rather not."

Rudolph turned away. He felt betrayed. Dennis, meanwhile, beamed in his box veil and managed to avoid shouting "Praise the Lord," as that would have surely aggravated the situation. Merton excused himself by saying that he had been in the Order for a long time and that for now, at least, the new habit was not for him. These "for now's" seemed a half-hearted attempt to compromise Rudolph; this compromise worked further when, as they got up to take their evening stroll, Merton and William both went over to comfort Rudolph.

"Congratulations," Merton told him, putting a hand on his shoulder.

"You'll go down in history for this," William concurred, "especially with photographs of the new habit in the *Cistercian Apostolic Yearbook.*"

Rudolph thanked both monks but quickly left for another part of the monastery. William attempted to call after him but Merton told him to be quiet. The two monks then turned their attention to Dennis.

"It's going to look like there are three different Orders here," Merton said. "Sometimes it's hard to keep up with these changes. Vatican II is really socking it to us."

Dennis thought, "You coward, you could have snuck into Rudolph's room and destroyed the modified habit pattern, or at least ordered him to stop designing."

Not more than an hour later, while the monks assembled under the palms for their nightly talk and recreation period, Rudolph showed up in the karate habit he presented to the Abbot-General in Rome three months before. Since he was the designer, it was only natural that he model an advance copy. Indeed, he looked like a movie star on the set of some Hawaiian melodrama. The white trousers came down midway between his knees and ankles and his muscular calves were given ample airing. His feet looked golden in the sandals and the V-neck of the shirt plunged lower than anything Dennis had seen in Calvin Klein underwear catalogues. He looked remarkably handsome, especially with the black sash around his waist, as it accented his build.

Merton was forthright. "You do not, Rudolph, look like a monk!"

"That is the whole problem, Father. Monks don't have to look like anything, My vows are in here." Rudolph pointed to his heart.

He sat down, more or less pleased with himself, and he held his head with the air of someone who is way ahead of their time and who has to contend with slugs who keep the communal tread wheel stuck in wet cement. Dennis was horrified because when Rudolph sat and spread his legs, his crotch area was lumped far larger than any male ballet dancer's groin. The full outline of his penis was so visible it could have been traced with a pencil. It was very big and, with his legs spread and his trousers riding way above his ankles, he looked like an Adonis in the Turkish baths Dennis used to visit. "You can even see his nipples!" Dennis thought, eyeing Rudolph's chest and the wide space between the muscular male bosom. "How am I going to live with this?"

William asked to feel the material and reached for Rudolph's sleeve. At his touch, Rudolph spread his legs even further apart and the

42

thing in the middle seemed to fall down from a more upright position into a bigger, collected lump. Dennis folded his hands under his chin and considered his religious vocation. "This jerk doesn't understand that there are men who love men and who can't take things like this. What's he trying to do?" He looked at Merton, who seemed to be detached from it all.

"Yes, and you see how flexible it is," Rudolph said, standing up. "I can twist and turn any way I want, which I couldn't do in my old habit...you see?" And he proceeded to do what looked to Dennis like floor exercises, turning around and bending at the waist where the expected but not really anticipated shock of two buttock halves –white flesh through the thin material! –revealed the anal Crack of Doom.

"I see how this might relate," Merton seemed to whisper, "to the Theology of the Body. The Spirit moves in mysterious ways."

The next morning, Rudolph's karate trousers could be seen under the surplice he wore to assist at Mass. He wanted to wear only the new habit, but Merton thought this too radical and ordered him to put on a surplice. Theirs was a heated argument, with Rudolph insisting that he had the Council on his side, and that Merton in fact was a liturgical reactionary. Merton, as if to prove his progressive spirit, surprised the monks when he allowed the use of pita bread or large oatmeal cookies for the consecration, the most sacred part of the Mass. Rudolph, however, was not happy that he was forced to wear a surplice and conducted himself at the altar table as if he had a chip on his shoulder.

The tension between Merton and Rudolph manifested itself at breakfast in Rudolph's hurried reading of scripture. Although he knew that Merton liked the readings to be conducted slowly and with dramatic feeling, Rudolph raced through the text as one would read a shopping list. It was most definitely behavior unbecoming a monk, and Merton was not pleased.

Dennis felt that a certain emotional balance had been corrected, that finally God had allowed Rudolph – because of his uncharitable attitude – to become tangled in a personal crisis of his own. He was careful however, not to let this feeling get to his head for fear that it would ignite another karmic problem for him down the line.

A couple of nights later as he prepared for bed, he heard the horn of the freighter. It had been a month since the ship last passed and, at the horn, he stopped ruffling his pillow and waited for the second blow. With it came the monastery hand bell and the sound of Merton walking the corridor calling for "supply work." This simply meant that the four of them had to go to the beach and help cart the supplies to the refectory. Naturally a severe feeling of discomfort came over Dennis. He thought of playing sick –he could have, Merton would have understood. As he gazed at his crucifix, he almost summoned up the courage to tell Merton that he was ill. At the last minute he found himself walking down to the beach with his brother monks.

Rudolph walked way out in front while Merton walked behind Dennis; William lagged far behind. Altogether it was a lopsided stroll, the mood of the monks at supper was one of extreme lethargy, as if they all secretly entertained thoughts of relinquishing their vows.

When the first rowboat came in Dennis looked for the other boats, but he could see nothing but water. The two burly men got out, waved a hello, and began unpacking boxes while William and Rudolph dutifully lent a hand. Merton took out his keys and prepared to lead them back to the monastery and told Dennis to stay behind and wait for the last shipment.

Dennis wasn't sure why he was selected for this job, unless it was the novice's role to greet a corresponding member of the freighter crew who had the least seniority. Monastic rules were full of details like this. He had also hoped to avoid another encounter with the source of his temptation, but now he felt all of that disappear when he spotted Mike. It was as if his spiritual reserve was escaping through an invisible Contemplative Funnel.

"Hi," said Mike, getting ready to drop some boxes onto the beach. But seeing that the monk in the dark was Dennis, he let go of the boxes and stepped out of the boat. "Are you ready?" he asked, hitching up his belt. Dennis was aghast. He watched Mike and saw that he was leading him in the direction of the reef, walking confidently ahead as if the arrangement was the most natural thing in the world. Dennis felt more of his resolve slip and began to advance ahead while deep in his subconscious, a voice pleaded with him to turn back. Nevertheless he found himself in the cove where they had done it the first time. Mike wasted on time lying on his back on one of the flatter rocks, his trousers down and his genitals exposed. Dennis crept up to him.

"What's the matter, man?" There were swordfish and squid in Mike's eyes; he looked at Dennis before turning his head away. Dennis sat down beside him. "Nothing," he said.

Mike reached for Dennis' hand and placed it on his scrotum. He did it swiftly, as if he was used to taking many a monk's hand. Soon, Dennis needed no encouragement and was avidly at work.

When they finished, Dennis wanted Mike to stay with him. Mike would have none of that. "I have to go now, man, the other monks will be comin' back." He said 'monks' as one might say boss or king; Dennis pictured three wooden figures moving at a snail's pace along the beach. "I suppose so," Dennis said, annoyed because he was just beginning to feel the workings of passion and wanted to sail on that for a couple more minutes at least.

The monks weren't really coming back and, as he watched Mike buckle up, resentment built up in him and pulsated like the scampering of the mysterious little animals on Pinpoint Island. "He's had his orgasm and now he wants to go." When Mike did leave, he heard the movement of boxes, and noticed that he felt nothing. He was waiting for the feeling of encircling darkness, but instead he felt only joy.

This was to be short-lived, however. Later that night, unable to sleep because he feared the approach of the Angel, he turned on his nightlight and sat up in his cot. Huddled against the wall, he began to perspire. He knew what he had to do, yet the decision seemed so enormous, so final. To take the rowboat out at this time of night seemed like flirting with death. The chances were great that he wouldn't come upon Pinpoint Island. It was as if the dark and the wind were omens of something new and strange about to happen to him. He could die out there, drown, get eaten by sharks. Would it be better to try and live a life here? Was he crazy to think he could live a life of celibacy? For days after he first had sex with Mike, he was either suspended in guilt or fighting to get the feeling of purity back. This led to the crisis he was now experiencing. Only this time, he could see that the crisis had peaked: it demanded a resolution and fast. He could not temper it with next-day Holy Communion or fervent prayer.

He took a few essentials – a toothbrush, a found bottle of Dior Homme cologne, a change of underwear –and left his room a couple hours before dawn. Down at the dock, he turned his boat right-side up and lifted it into the water. He got in, arranged the oars, and set off. He paddled as hard as he could and without let-up; he purposely rowed in the direction opposite where he had previously gone.

Rowing wasn't necessary after a short while. There were strong currents that pulled the boat and a restless ocean that kept him holding onto the sides. He had lost sight of the lights of the monastery a long time ago and he knew that he was a long way off. Was he moving out of the tropics? It did seem colder here and the ocean more threatening. A chill came over him and he wrapped the ends of his veil around himself like a scarf, hoping to sight land. But that was not to be until at least twelve hours later.

In the midst over the water he thought he saw a light, a human form hovering over the waves, a beacon or an angel that seemed to be guiding the boat. He could only guess the time of day based on the position of the sun in the sky. He began to have some regrets about his decision to leave the monastery although he was careful to cut these thoughts short. He knew it was no use dwelling on it because he couldn't get back to Father Merton if he tried.

After the sun had gone down, he saw lights on the horizon. At first thinking it an airship or star, he later concluded that it was land and the lights the neon haze of skyscrapers. He lost no time in redirecting his boat and rowing hard while he ran down the list of possibilities: was it New York, Paris, San Francisco, Honolulu?

With his rowing ability and the current, it took him an hour to get into the harbor. Luckily he came in where the small boats docked and where it was possible to leave the boat safely. Leaving the boat to drift out to sea, he made his way off the docks and onto a side street. He passed restaurants and bars with exotic outdoor lights; banks as large as cathedrals and gleaming structures that looked as though they had been designed by Frank Gehry or Zaha Hadid. He kept walking, though he was beginning to feel a little panicky. He had no money and knew no one in this city.

A large armored silver car passed him. He turned to look and saw a group of people inside with their noses pressed to the windows. They were looking at him. A little girl waved. When he waved back, the car stopped.

"Can we take you somewhere, Father?" It was a matronly woman who seemed to be smiling and sneering at him at the same time. The children had a similar look of benign contempt. "No, thank you," he said, stepping back, eager to get away from the car.

"Fucking weirdo!" the woman screamed. The car went on ahead, disappearing in the distance. He spotted a church. He could see its cross from a block away and walked towards it. He found when he got there that it was an Orthodox church, so he walked up the steps thinking he could go in and ask for a loaf of bread. He stood behind one of the tall pillars framing the door and closed his eyes to drum up courage. But the car that had stopped earlier now passed in front of the church and came to a halt. Dennis turned to hide but it was too late. He felt a series of rubber bullets hit the church door, and then he saw clouds of what he thought was pepper spray come at him. The family in the car stared at him with such hatred he felt they would attack him had he not held up his right hand and performed an intricate gesture he imagined duplicated an Orthodox blessing. The blessing might as well have been shots from an AK47 because the car then lunged forward in a jet propulsion blast of burning rubber, making a sudden U-turn down a small side street.

He walked into the street again and passed a number of people in wheelchairs. There were also kids along the curb in various stages of nodding out or aimless walking. A blonde with the face of a skeleton was busy scanning debris on the sidewalk. A number of boys, their faces hidden in hoodies, worked laboriously to reconnect broken needles to syringes. Other groups of people held out panhandling cups.

On that desolate street there was no way of getting money unless he panhandled. Some addicts paced back and forth in front of an ATM machine and Dennis considered asking them for some change. He finally gave up and followed one of the addicts to a glass-enclosed subway entrance. The entrance also served as the lobby of an office building decorated with large artificial trees in big white tubs. An elegant staircase led into the lobby area from the street and it was in this that the addict sat down to join another community of outsiders. There were men and women and child vagabond types, all of them deeply haggard looking and sitting or lying down on cardboard or old coats. A long line of tents with adhesive tape patches seemed to stretch on forever. Many of the people had blackened faces as if they'd fallen victim to a bombing blitz.

He walked up to the man he had been following. "Excuse me," he said, "but can you tell me what city I'm in?" The man's face was the color of rusted steel and the wrinkles on his face were so deep they looked as if they had been carved there with a pairing knife. His breath might as well have come from a container holding rotten tongue specimens.

"You want spare change? Spare change ain't a problem. Who are you anyway, Snow White?"

He was referring to the box veil. It must look odd, Dennis was sure of that. The man kept looking at him as if he was a male nun. Indeed, the question seemed to be forming on his lips. He wanted to ask but could only come out with, "I knew the women gave up the habits, but…"

Somebody sitting on a ledge that overlooked the staircase –a three hundred foot drop –shouted that it was late for a priest to be out.

"I want to know what city I'm in," Dennis asked again, but nobody answered him.

Chapter Four

Rudolph was very concerned at Dennis' disappearance. Although he tried to conceal his worry, he eventually admitted it to the community. "Where could he have gone?" he kept saying. "Just when I thought there was real hope for him; just when I thought we were reaching him, you disappears!" Together the monks discussed the disappearance and debated going over to Pinpoint Island one more time. They had gone to the island only hours before and combed it thoroughly, even scanning the bushes with wicker brooms in case Dennis was laying low. The situation frightened them because they really weren't sure Dennis took the rowboat; he could have ditched it to sidetrack them in their search and then left for the other side of the island.

The island of St. Basil was a mammoth land mass extending far beyond the monastery, a virtual wilderness none of the monks had ever bothered to explore. It was left unexplored because there were no adequate paths through its forests and glens, and no way to pass through the fifteen foot high bramble and thorn bushes that surrounded the monastery on three sides. The bramble bushes had the look of an impenetrable wall, almost as if God had willed the monks to be geographically cut off.

But when Rudolph had his mind set on saving a soul, he wasn't easily discouraged. He told William that Dennis had passed through the bramble bushes and was "somewhere in the low-lying region where we've never gone." William thought his idea plausible, while Merton dismissed it. Merton told them that he thought Dennis had passed through to another dimension and had not run away in the ordinary sense at all.

"Swami Yogamougananda Jr. writes of reaching other dimensions by actual physical routes. He says that these dimensions exist somewhere in reality and can be reached by certain meditation practices."

Rudolph, although skeptical of the Abbot's fascination with Hinduism, suggested that they begin chopping down some of the bramble bushes and start clearing a path. He was convinced that this would lead them to Dennis.

Merton, however, remained unconvinced. "Clearing acres of land is a gamble, and big one. Dennis will come back; there is no need to search him out. Believe me, the dimension he is in will send him back to us just as it propelled him outward."

An agreement was reached not to tamper with any dimensions, but simply to wait for Dennis. Nevertheless Rudolph got to fooling around with a shovel and pick one day and the temptation to chop through the bushes was just too much for him. He stuck his shovel into a mass of thorns and branches and swished it around. Thousands of small prickly things broke off; with an added thrust, large branches fell and it wasn't long before he had a ten foot path cleared. He was amazed at how quickly the bushes gave way. In fact, the longer he worked, the more he realized they were not real bushes at all but more like paper imitations. He calculated too that the more he developed this method of chopping, the faster the bushes fell. At the rate of ten feet in five minutes, he could go a mile in an afternoon. Rudolph, of course, was not only thinking of finding Dennis. The relative "softness" of the bushes and the dust from the prickly things produced visions in his head of a large monastery expansion; the utilization of land once thought inhabitable.

Rudolph broke the news to the monks that evening. He came out and said it wasn't so much the whereabouts of Dennis that concerned him now, it was the possibility of farming new soil and expanding, perhaps constructing a meditation path in honor of Swami Yogamouganada Jr. This new path, he said, could be created "in the spirit of Vatican II." "Besides," he said to Merton, who sat under a palm sipping papaya juice, "we might come upon the dimension, and when it happens it will happen just like that. With no warning. "

# # # # #

Dennis' main problem was finding a job and a place to live. For a while he stood outside a fast food convenience store holding an empty coffee cup. Passersby would give him small change but kept confusing him with a band of local heroin addicts. He then went to a couple of shelters, one Catholic and one Salvation Army, and he slept and ate there. The brothers at the Catholic place didn't believe him when he said he was a Trappist novice. "He's an imposter. There is no such thing as a Trappist monk in a veil," he heard a brother whisper to the priest in charge. The staff thought him crazy, a poor unfortunate and, while they gave him more help than they gave the others, they were convinced that he had gotten hold of his religious habit through devious means.

"Just where is this Trappist monastery?" asked the head priest. "On the island of St. Basil," Dennis said, "not far from another little island called Pinpoint, and very near Harvard Square in Cambridge, Massachusetts."

"Don't you mean Cape Cod? Cambridge is not a peninsula."

"I can't be sure, Father. At least we get our supplies from an American freighter."

The priest and his assistant looked at one another. Dennis knew he was not making a good impression and kept his eyes lowered.

"You can come back here and work," the priest said. "You can stay with us and help out, but first you must take off that silly veil. We dress in jeans and flannel shirts around here – even our nuns look like the hearty lesbian feminist activists uptown – so there's no need to dress like that. We never employ the homeless, but you since you seem interested in serving God, I can make an exception. Would you like that? You can have long term room and board if you wouldn't mind sleeping in the dormitory."

The priest showed him to a corner bed away from the others and next to a window. Beside the bed was a small cabinet with a drawer for personal belongings. The priest told him he could wash and fold his habit and then take it with him when he left. Dennis was glad to hear this. The priest's assistant nodded in approval; he was a bland looking young man about Dennis' age with hair of yellow and a complexion so pale he seemed to fade into the cream colored walls. He watched as Dennis took off his habit and put on a denim work suit, never suspecting Dennis' intention to put the habit on once it had been cleaned.

In his new clothes, he surveyed the room. Old men here and there played cards or chewed tobacco. One lay in bed with his mouth open;

he had no teeth and was a still as a corpse. A mild smell of disinfectant was everywhere.

"Get out!" said one old man, who had been staring at Dennis from across the room and who jerked his head violently. Dennis looked away. "Get out!" the man said again, this time walking towards him until he collapsed on the floor.

He wondered whether he would end up like this old man, maybe in this very room, many years from now. It didn't seem fair to him that people like the priest and brothers seemed to lead lives of quiet un-interruption while others bounced over stormy seas in kayaks or canoes.

He could see that the nights in this city were long. After leaving the shelter he had passed what seemed like forty-eight hours on a park bench and it was still very dark. He also didn't think the people he met very friendly; most of them were of the street-crazy variety who scowled at him or who, so he thought, whispered things about him as he passed. He didn't know why they should be doing this other than to taunt him on account of his religious habit. So the idea came to him to take it off for good and wear the denim work suit be brought with him from the shelter. "Damn that shelter anyway," he said, "I am tired of sleeping with religion and loonies."

The first thing he did was remove his veil. With a solemn apology to Saint John Chrysostom, he tossed it in the river. "Better to toss than to leave intact on a park bench where it may be molested," he mused. He then removed his cross and folded up his rosary. These he buried, marking the spot with a pile of stones. But he thought he should keep the robe. That at least distinguished him somewhat. Passing a middle-aged couple on a fashionable side street, however, he heard them agree that he must be Hare Krishna.

# # # # #

Rudolph and William had completed a two mile path into the bramble bush jungle and discovered the remains of a cobblestone pathway directly underneath it.

"Living relics! I think this must have been an actual road a long time ago." William was on his hands and knees inspecting the thing.

"Going to Saint Augustine's City of God," quipped Rudolph. "I don't see how we can stop now. I've never been this excited since that time we saw the UFO take a dive into the ocean."

"That was not a UFO, but a demon," William insisted, laughing suddenly as he recalled the visit of a Russian monk to the monastery who insisted that the message of UFOs is to prepare humankind for the antichrist or the savior of the apostate world.

"Oh yes, old Seraphim Rose – he and the Abbot really got into it," William added, shaking his head. "He called us heretics, didn't he?"

"He said we were iconoclasts when Abbot had Mike dismantle the old high altar and put in the table. What an old fossil. The Orthodox Church is an old fossil."

They continued to chop through the jungle bushes and more of the cobblestone pathway was revealed to them. The lifting away of the bushes became easier and, in a short time, it wasn't necessary to use even a shovel or pick to rid the path of sediment. They had merely to swish the shovels into the bushes and they fell to the side like tumbleweed. William kept saying how it was like a miracle. Rudolph agreed, laughing as he plowed ahead of William, increasing the pathway about a foot every second.

Merton, preparing for Vespers, was about to ring the chapel bells when he saw several of the bushes rolling along the ground. The bushes came slowly at first, then in rapid succession like machine-gun fire. He went out and looked at them piling up.

The monks found all sorts of strange instruments in the earth as the uprooted bushes blew away. Some of the objects resembled bones, others trinkets; they even found a tiny pyramid on a chain. Most unusual of all, they uncovered a bronze statuette of Priapus with an oversized permanent erection. At the base of the figure, in Latin, was the following epigram:

I warn you boy, you will be screwed; girl, you

will be fucked;

a third penalty awaits the bearded thief.

If a woman steals from me, or a man, or a boy

Let the first give me her cunt, the second his

Head, the third his buttocks...

"The sins of antiquity," Rudolph offered, pocketing the artifact. "Perhaps Dennis can use this as a pectoral cross. I'm sorry, William, I did not mean that..."

They both examined the findings carefully but were interrupted by a gust of wind, a typhoon-like blast. "I think we'd better head back now, don't you?" one said to the other. Yet just as they agreed to do this, the wind began lifting the bushes and the path behind as well as in front of them began to clear on its own. They got down on their bellies and put their arms over their heads as the prickly balls passed over them. Sensing trouble, Merton was already running towards the pair. In the distance, he saw the tip of a white Dome rising above the trees as he made his way to them.

The wind calmed down and all was quiet, though haziness crept over everything like fog. William uncovered his head and, seeing Merton, he yelped like a puppy and ran towards him.

Merton didn't mention the Dome until the next day when the three of them took their morning walk along the beach. Naturally the monks were excited and wanted to go there right away. They were so carried away by the discoveries they were neglecting their monastic routine. They had already forgotten morning prayers. This frolic along the beach now took the place of that.

"Do you think the articles are from Atlantis?" William asked, kicking sand in front of him. "And what about that epigram; it's more like a curse really. The words point to us as the thieves or transgressors because we found the piece. 'The second his head...' what does that mean?"

"Ask Dennis," Rudolph replied. "But no, not Atlantis, are you crazy? Greece or Rome..."

Merton was uneasy. For years, the cloistered order of his life and the virtual isolation of the islands enabled him to lead a life of serenity and peace. Although he experienced and knew well enough the *Dark Night of the Soul*, he was better able to come to grips with it when he compared the remoteness of the monastery with the solitude of every soul. But the sight of the Dome bothered him. What was it? It wasn't anything modern, that he knew. He had an idea that it was something carried over from pagan days, perhaps something demonic although the Spirit of the Council would certainly advise against such conjectures.

For Merton, the Dome felt familiar somehow. He felt he could almost grasp its meaning. It was much like trying to remember a dream. Was it a sign pointing to heaven on earth? Was it antichrist?

"What do you say, father, can we work on the path today?" William asked.

"We had better stick to our schedule. Remember, we are still a religious order, not a bunch of archaeologists." How sour Merton seemed. But the fact was he knew he wouldn't be able to rest or work in peace until he knew where the path led. "Maybe after lunch," he said by way of compromise.

# # # # #

Dennis was able to get a room at the "Y" after accumulating fifty dollars in panhandling money, his robe eliciting sympathy and a quick response from people. "At least you're not a heroin addict," many people said as they handed him dollar bills. He knew he could never have done as good in ordinary street clothes, and so he promised himself if he ever saw Rudolph again, he would use this experience as one reason for retaining the habit. He was sure that standing outside in a karate uniform would not have had the same effect.

Exhausted, he fell into the small cot and went to sleep, but woke up in the middle of the night. There was a dry taste in his mouth from the Syrian bread and Swiss cheese a stranger had given him earlier. He left his room for the lavatory where he brushed his teeth with his fingers while listening to the talk of the men in the lounge watching a late show movie.

"Got some change?" It was a disheveled looking hipster with an ashen face, tattoos, and dirty hair, though with very good looks buried beneath it all.

"I think so," Dennis said, noticing the buried good looks and also thinking of his own panhandling.

"You new here? How'd you ever get to this fuckin' place?"

"I just walked into it; it happened fast." Dennis handed him a dollar.

"Got to buy me a hot dog and coffee... can't sleep; can't do nothing.'"

Dennis asked where he was from.

"Not from here, man. I used to have my own apartment, a girlfriend, job, and lots of cash. Now I'm stuck here till I get money to go back to Florida. Hate this place, man."

"People have been mean to you?"

"Everyone's mean. There are wheelchair gangs here. They kill you if you have the wrong tattoo or piercing. Walk anywhere, man, and you get these glass barriers. It's like, you bump into them and they crash down, big shards of glass that cut up your body. Not good."

"I'll say," Dennis said. There was something about the guy that touched him. He felt some sexual attraction, especially since he was out of the monastery and no longer had to struggle with celibacy. For the moment, anyway, he felt he could control his desire, perhaps because he was tired from walking around the city in search of money and shelter.

What's the name of this city?" Dennis asked.

The boy stuttered the beginning of a name but then stopped himself and began to look confused.

"It seems like I've been walking in this place forever. When does the sun come up?"

"The sun?" The boy looked at Dennis as if he had said 'the Yellow Peril.' "The sun never comes up here. Do you know what they told me when I got here? They said that I'd never get out and that I'd have to get used to the dark, and that —get this Jack —the sun is DEAD. Dead! No sun here!"

"How can it be that there's no sun?"

"...Only place you're liable to find to find sun is over near the Dome, but just try getting' there. Lotta people try but most of 'em just see the Dome and can never get to it. Folks here are blocked."

"The Dome, where's that?"

"Somewhere along the edge of the city; like along the freeway, I think. Some say the waterfront. Anyway, you can see the top of it shinin' sometimes but that's the only sun we got."

"And this is really a special place?"

"Yeah, like a temple from olden days. Those gladiator movies, you know? I never saw it but I seen pictures. It's awesome, like a capitol building somewheres and its got all these lawns and gardens around it. It was in the newspaper here about a week ago. A reporter says he saw it. He walked into it, took a picture, and then he started to investigate, he was somewhere else. Lotta people don't believe it. But I talked to one guy who got right up inside the Dome and he says he felt like air, man, and he couldn't even see his body."

Dennis started to tell him about his own exodus from Kirkland Manor but changed the subject after a few words. "Do you believe it?" he said.

"Yeah, it's true. My name's Rudolph, what's yours?"

"Rudolph?" For a second Dennis thought he was meeting a body double.

"Don't hear it too often, do you? Lotta people say like you did. I go 'Rudolph' and they go 'Rudolph?'"

"Do you sleep here?" Dennis noticed the boy's duffle bag.

:Na, I snuck in. I was wonderin' where to sleep when I came in here. Usually I ball up in the stalls back there but they got this mean-ass security guard who comes around with a club and beats ass. Nearly cracked my head open one night. But nobody can crack my head open cause it's hard as cement. Wanna see?" Rudolph knocked his head against the wall and the sound emitted was like two cement blocks smacking against each other.

"More of that and you'll get brain damage. Listen, if you don't have a place to sleep, you can stay with me."

Rudolph's eyes widened, "Cool – then there's the fags," he added by way of postscript. "They're always comin' up tryin' to get a leg on, gropin' and reachin' and tryin' to unzip till you have to show them no way. Some don't take 'no' for an answer."

Dennis was disappointed to hear the boy's tirade but he had heard similar rants and in the end it often meant little or nothing.

Dennis went to his room when Rudolph said he'd catch up to him after jumping in the shower. In a few minutes Dennis heard a knock at his door. Rudolph, smelling of soap and toothpaste, entered fully dressed. Dennis flipped on the bedside lamp.

"Like I was sayin', this Dome is really big. They say that standin' inside it you can't even see the top of it because it's like sky inside…with clouds. It's some place! Maybe you and me could go huntin' for it someday. That would be cool."

Dennis was perturbed because Rudolph had put his clothes back on. Who showers and then dresses with dirty clothes? He expected him to walk in naked or at least with a towel around his waist. "We can do that."

"Man, if you wanted we could start off soon. I know abouts where it is. We could bum our way. Got a knapsack?"

Dennis was sorry he didn't watch him take a shower. Now there was a slight chance he might never see him naked. "Look Rudolph, are you really going to sleep in your clothes?"

He got down on the floor and spread out a blanket. "Clothes is my animal hide."

"You really going to sleep on the floor?"

"Yeah."

"Well you might as well come up here with me. No sense in making yourself uncomfortable. Come on, I'll roll over."

"I don't want no man to roll over. I'll sleep here. Everything's cool this way."

"What can you lose by coming up here? Aren't you liberated?"

"My thing is the ladies.... Can't do it with anybody but the ladies." He scratched his left nipple. "You a Krishna monk anyway, right? You're not supposed to care. Read your Bagahahara or whatever they call that book."

"You can pretend. Don't be so rigid!"

"Maybe if I was drunk or stonned, or if you put some lipstick on and dressed up and all. Even then, man, it would bum me out."

"Krishna monks do it. You can see them in Boston along the Charles River late at night pulling their robes up. And even Catholic monks are loosening up. Ever hear of the Theology of the Body? Well, it's this philosophy that says sex can be like a sacrament. You know, if there's feeling and some love involved, it's all good."

"I'm going to sleep, dude. And don't fiddle about either because then I'll have to do somethin.'

When the little alarm went off, Rudolph turned on the overhead light and went to the window.

"Is that a dirigible in your pocket or did you bring me liverwurst?" Dennis asked, still hoping that things would go his way.

"Man, I thought I just saw part of the Dome. Sometimes it shines off and on like a flash and I thought I saw a glimmer of it way over to the east. Yeah."

"Do you know of any cheap restaurants? I'm hungry," was all Dennis could manage.

They gathered their things and went downstairs to the lobby. Rudolph said he knew there was a McDonald's, but then Dennis realized he didn't have enough panhandling money. Rudolph said they could sell their blood for ten dollars a pint after which they would get breakfast. So they went to the blood clinic but it wasn't open; they'd have to wait an hour or so. They hung around, their stomachs growling and Dennis thinking of breakfast being served in the monastery. It was at this time that he resented losing his proper slot in Life. He thought that being confined to such a horrid city was a punishment of some sort and this led him to periodically glance at Rudolph as if he was Satan

A sharp blast of loud whistles and horns took him by surprise but no sooner had the blast sounded then Rudolph was lying face down on the ground with his hands over his head. "Get down! Get down!" he screamed. In an instant Dennis saw people on the street – junkies, the homeless, and a large assortment of shrouded figures who did nothing but walk in circles – follow Rudolph's example. They dove into prone positions, flat on their stomachs, arms over their heads. At the sound of the blast those in the middle of the street ran to the curb so that they could also assume this position. Dennis felt a trembling of the earth and saw something massive on the horizon. It was smaller and more contained than a tornado, and was traveling rapidly at street level. He could not make out what it was but he knew it was something terrible and that the people were afraid of it. He assumed the prone position himself when he noticed a great light emerging from the coming force.

"Don't look at it!" Rudolph said. "Close your eyes."

A swishing sound and then the roar of a diesel train enveloped them. He felt the warmth from the light pass over his body and he thought he detected a human voice, laughter and a series of shrieks, as he lay there trembling on the sidewalk. He knew it to be an adverse energy, but what?

In a moment it was over, and without fanfare or conversation the people got up and resumed what they had been doing, the shrouded ones walking in circles, the homeless with their hands out, the addicts injecting their syringes or nodding off next to overflowing dumpsters. In a far off corner he thought he saw people attempting to copulate but they would only get so far and then they would scream in anguish.

"Five times a day," he passes," Rudolph said. "Five times we get down and cover up."

"Who is he?" Dennis asked. "What do you mean?"

"The mayor," Rudolph offered. "Don't look at him, dude, that's all I can tell you. When you hear whistles, lat flat on your stomach no matter where you are and cover your head and stay like that till he passes. If you don't, he will take you away."

"Take you where?"

"…To the lower level where ya don't wanna go."

In the blood back, a nurse took their names and they were checked for a variety of diseases. Then they were sent to a back room where a pint was drawn from each of them. They emerged, holding cotton swabs to their arms and walked to McDonald's.

"Looks like everyone's got somethin' ugly on their minds, don't it?" Rudolph said, surveying the restaurant. "Some of these people are here every day, mopin' over their coffee and hamburger like it was their last meal. Why, some even fall asleep and I saw one old guy drop his face right inside his hot coffee. Wasn't funny cause he screamed, and then the same fat security guard I told you about came over with a gun. Fuck, this dark is awful. Looks like them long winter mornings when you were a kid and had to get up early for school."

Dennis saw several men with a growth of hair up the sides of their cheeks and foreheads. He had never seen anything like it before. He was trying to figure out whether they had low hairlines or whether they combed down their bangs on purpose for the special effect. But he could see bald men with the same thing and dit made him uneasy.

"These guys with the hair on their forehead...I only saw one guy like that when I first got here. They look like apes. How come they look like that?"

"Jus don't talk to 'em. They ain't friendly, in fact they're real mean and I see 'em kill old ladies when they looked at 'em wrong. So keep your eyes to yourself if you know what's good for you."

"What kid of human being would act like that?"

"Who says they're human, man. Jus do like I say and don't mess with those guys. If you ever see one comin' don't look 'em in the eye cause they might do anything. They're the most dangerous thing here aside from the Prince, but they only started going through the motions of killin' when the sun went down..."

"So the sun did shine here once," Dennis mused. "What happened?"

"One day the news here said SUN BLACKS OUT and everybody was out here talkin' about it and runnin' around. The sun will come on again but nobody knows when. Look at that −" Rudolph pointed to a scowling man in a tattered coat coming through the swivel doors. Hair covered his forehead, cheeks and chin and, once in McDonald's, he turned to someone behind him and cursed, a grunty sound coming from his voice box, a mix between a baby's rattle and a coffee grinder. Dennis was amazed to see the few people who hadn't facial hair lower their heads and keep their eyes on their food, as if terrified of being singled out by these monsters.

"What did I tell ya?" Rudolph said, lowering his head too.

"My God, what's in this hamburger?!" Dennis pushed his platter on the floor and stood up in a panic. He put his hands to his mouth and spit out remnants of the burger. "It's blood! Blood!" He gulped his coffee in a panic and looked around to find a men's room. Rudolph told him to relax and said that the hamburgers and all the sandwiches in the town were sometimes laced with blood, and that that was a good thing. "You won't die," he said. "You're protected. The blood can't hurt you. It's to help you remember. Take a deep breath, dude; the sandwiches is what keeps us going. They are your friends."

"They are not my friends," Dennis said. "I'm sorry I came here. I don't want to be here. I want to go back. My God, why can't I go back?"

"You had your chance. Love the place you're in, dude."

Dennis looked around and saw that most of the customers in fact were heartily devouring platters of blood hamburgers. Many used napkins to wipe excess blood from the corners of their mouth while others seemed to slobber, the red juices running down their chins and onto their clothing. He then had a terrifying thought: what if the blood bank next door supplied McDonald's with the blood they freely took from residents.

"Eat," Rudolph urged. "The hairy men are vegans and they get mad when they can't find tofu."

"They have a right to get mad about that," Dennis said, hunger driving him to bite into the remainder of his burger. "There's no law that says you can't be mean and scowl at people. But I know there's a burger law somewhere. Look, maybe somebody should start a shelter for the hairy ones."

"Man, you start a shelter but there ain't no way you're gonna round any of them up. Maybe one or two, but as soon as you turn your back, they're gonna be up to somethin'."

When they were outside, they passed one hairy man who wouldn't take his eyes off Dennis. The streets were crowded with people walking in circles or trying to get into one of the many massive tattoo parlors lining the streets. Many of the residents had large tattoos on their foreheads, arms and necks. A popular tattoo among men seemed to be the word "Pain" spelled out on their foreheads. Other people walked dogs of various sizes who, if they weren't squatting and shitting, were shitting as they were being walked. Some hairy men stood on street corners yelling for tofu. When they passed a newsstand Dennis noticed that the daily paper had an enormous headline: DOME SIGHTED AGAIN. Underneath the headline there was a full page photo of a ball of light looking much like the rising sun on some distant plain.

"Has our savior come at last?" the sub-headline read.

"I don't lie," Rudolph said, referring to the headline. "Now there's gonna be hordes of people clamorin' to find this thing. People with knapsacks, cops, hairy men. But the hairy people really don't want anybody to find it/"

"Look Rudolph, if walking around in the dark is always going to be dangerous, I think we better just panhandle close to the "Y" for a while, you in your room and me in mine."

"Fuck, you think you're safe there? You think those hairy men don't come sneakin'in there and hidin' in the restrooms or walkin' the halls waitin' for you to come outside before the cleanin' maids come? To survive here, man, you need blood burgers, so we gotta go outside or we'll wind up someplace worse. There's no rest here, dude. People climb up buildings and get in your windows or hide under the bed or walk through doors when you're asleep. Don't you get it that this is no picnic in the grass? You don't know where you are, do you? How long you gonna take realizing that this is it, man? You're cooked. You better get used to it or things will be worse for you. That's why some of us is tryin' to get to the Dome. We're tired of this crap. Police, guards, hairy men, blood. It sucks. So if it takes some work to find the Dome, I'm in. I ain't spending eternity here. Every mornin' I tell myself there's a way out and always right when I get to feeling down, like maybe when I think there ain't a way out, I picture the Dome in my mind."

The city's whistles and horns sounded at that moment, causing everyone on the streets to lie face down on the sidewalk.

Chapter Five

A cat scampered by from underneath a parked car.

"Man, I gotta get me some of that," Rudolph said,

Dennis sensed what was coming and looked away. Rudolph followed the cat to a clump of bushes. "Fifteen days ago I was in Chinatown, man, and this chick, I mean, wow, she was in a paper jump suit. I started followin' her you know, thinkin' I was goin' to have a good time in a hotel but when I looked at her closely, she was half wolf person, all hairy with big teeth. I took off fast!"

Dennis was indifferent. "Why would you be surprised in a city like this?"

"But I gotta find me a lady all right. Look at the one comin' this way. Oh la la. Holy damn. Think I'll ask her for a smoke." Dennis got as far away from Rudolph as he could as Rudolph stopped in front of the woman and held out his arms like a traffic cop. "Hey, miss, you got a cigarette?" The woman smiled, searched through her bag as if looking for one but instead produced a gun which she shot in the air.

"The male is obsessed with screwing;' she shouted, quoting Valerie Solanas, "he'll swim through a river of snot, wade nostril-deep through a mile of vomit, if he thinks there'll be a friendly pussy awaiting him. He'll screw a woman he despises, any snaggle-toothed hag, and furthermore, pay for the opportunity…"

She walked away quickly, adding, "The shit you have to go through in this world just to survive."

"Hey miss," Rudolph said, trotting along after her, "Let me explain."

While this was going on, Dennis thought he heard church bells and at each ring his mind wandered back to life at the monastery and to another Rudolph. In fact, that Rudolph looked much like the Rudolph on the sidewalk recovering from the blow he'd just received from the stranger after offering her his telephone number.

Psychic phenomena was everywhere in the city so Dennis decided to give an idea of his a go when they were in another part of town.

"Have you ever had dreams about being in a monastery or about monks or anything like that?" If this Rudolph was a time-warp version of the monastery Rudolph, then he was sure to have dreamed like that.

"Jus dreams that I was in the Dome. Monastery?"

"You sure you never walked around in a white karate uniform in your dreams – ever?"

"Karate? Yea, I know karate. Got an orange belt. Can chop a guy's hand off. One time I was defendin' myself against this dude and I cracked his knee bone. Don't know if I did permanent damage but I heard a crack like somethin' was splittin'. I never do touch a woman though."

The more Dennis studied Rudolph's face, the more he was convinced this Rudolph was the monastery Rudolph produced in miniature.

"You feel like walking into a church with me, just for kicks?"

"I thought we was huntin' for the Dome. There ain't no churches here!"

"Why don't we go try to find one."

# # # # #

Merton and the monks were collecting so many interesting things that they spent nearly everyday clearing a path they hoped would take them to the Dome. By now, they had bottles filled with fossils and all manner of jewelry, plus a number of vases and oins. It was now a sure thing that they had stumbled upon artifacts from the lost continent of Atlantis. Some of the coins read: *United People of Atlantis* and *Atlantis, Atlantis.*

When William brought back the mummified remains of a baby, Merton was sure these people had an unusual way of dealing with death. A series of silver pins covered the mummy. They eventually put it in the church along with the other artifacts.

The monks began to spend their nights on the path in sleeping bags, with only one of them going back to the monastery each morning to deposit new things. They could no longer see the tip of the Dome since they were on ground level and the remaining bramble bushes blocked their view. Still, a rich form of vegetation seemed to be behind the bushes and birds of every imaginable color flew in strange patterns and sang what seemed to Merton like tidbits from Mozart and Stravinsky. A sweet incense was also beginning to penetrate the atmosphere. The first time the monks smelled it, they stopped their work and exclaimed, "Paradise!" Then as they cleared more of a path, the incense became so potent they had to stop working and rest –not so much rest as just stand still and stare into space.

Once, William dropped to the ground. It wasn't a violent drop, but a gradual one. Once on the ground, William rolled over on his side and assumed what Rudolph thought was a most sensual pose.

Sometimes, the incense became so strong at night that they'd groan happily in their sleep.

Clearing away the bushes became such a delectable task that there were arguments as to who should cart the artifacts back to the monastery. Once out of the range of the incense, Life had a firm base in reality. Coming back from the work area at the monastery was especially hard because the reinvasion of incense into the body was a shock that sometimes put one to sleep. Other reactions included hallucinatory convulsions, auditory confusion, and an overwhelming desire to fly. At one point Monk William even shouted at the sky: "I want a woman!"

# # # # #

Dennis still roamed the city hour after hour, asking for money and expecting, at odd moments, to be received back into his old Time Warp. When he and Rudolph finally found a church, he saw that it was a church without a tabernacle or images. He began a prayer nevertheless. "Please let me be received into my former time, O Lord! Let me just walk into it, for I have ditched my rowboat." He looked in vein for a statue or something sacred to focus on but found only cold cement and vast, empty white walls.

"Look, man, there's a hairy guy come into the church!" One of the hairy monsters had indeed walked up the center aisle and was looking around. Several women in the pews, butch Sisters of Saint Joseph in military haircuts, froze. A custodian in a Knights of Columbus helmet and armed with a semi-automatic, seemed to be taking aim. But the hairy man who was now walking to where Dennis and Rudolph stood was really a much more subdued version of his aggressive cousins in the street.

"Where have they taken Him?! Fuckin' mess!"

The nuns recoiled in horror. A horrible smell emanated from the hairy one and, as he came closer, the odor became more potent.

"Who'd they take?" Rudolph asked.

The man knelt at the kneeler that faced an empty grotto that did contain, to Dennis' surprise, a tall, slim twisted silver crucifix with an elongated praying mantace figure on it. Hair on the man's knuckles and fingers made them seem more like paws, and his breathing was more of an oozing, as if he were pumping heat out of an old radiator. For a moment there was quiet but then Rudolph stood up as if someone had come up behind him and stuck him with a syringe. His "Ohh!" echoed throughout the church, and it took a while before Dennis knew what had shaken him. A black lizard and snake crawled in and out of the rocks below the twisted crucifix as a thin stream of smoke seemed to rise above it all.

"Smoke of Satan, I'm getting' the hell out," Rudolph said,

# # # # #

The trek back to the monastery became longer as the monks worked harder at clearing the path. And going back and forth was exhausting, so Merton decided that these trips would cease until further notice.

When the freighter men came to the monastery with a fresh batch of supplies they looked in vein for the monks. They pounded on all the double doors and rang the huge courtyard bell. Mike, his hormones raging, climbed over the inner monastery wall and checked every niche and crevice. Realizing the place was deserted, the men went back to the ship and contacted their supervisor, who in turn got in touch with the

Cardinal on the mainland. The Cardinal was not amused. He imagined at first some island horror, but then secret suspicions began to eat out his soul: something told him Merton was knee-deep in sacrilegious mischief.

He called Merton's cell but kept getting voice mail. Finally he buzzed for the Archdiocesan Superintendent, a red haired celebrity priest known throughout the Archdiocese for his various campaigns to stamp out prophylactics, Allen Ginsberg's poetry, blatant teenage couplings at drive-ins, and the Traditional Latin Mass.

He was a much feared man because his passion was so intense. On his television show, seen throughout the mainland and on several islands, he celebrated a charismatic Mass every Sunday. Despite an outwardly calm and happy demeanor, there was a slight downward turn of his lips indicating the hidden person beneath the smiley face. He took great liberties with the television liturgy, such as having young women with exposed cleavage hand out communion and servers who did a sort of Hokey Pokey dance around the altar. Afterwards he would take special delight in reading the sensational accounts in Leviticus and Deuteronomy for he was then able to do what he did best: condemn various forms of sexual immorality.

"Homosexuals," he often said, "are the worst sinners. They are at the top of the heap."

The Cardinal assigned Father Felix Cronicon to take a ship to the monastery. The Cardinal knew the voyage would be like a vacation to Cronicon, for the sea passage was beautiful in summer. The Cardinal often went to the monastery for his yearly retreat; he and Merton were good friends, even though he disagreed with Merton on a number of issues. Cronicon, on the other hand, did not like Merton. He hated Merton because his celebrity was greater than his own. At a symposium once, he lashed out at him when Merton rose to defend a group of aboriginal nomads who sought refuge at the monastery after weeks of wandering at sea. The nomads wore a costume in which their buttocks were exposed and Cronicon wanted the Cardinal to force Merton to get the nomads to cover up. Cronicon's message was that they would be welcomed in "full Christian charity" only if they accepted decent norms.

Merton was forced to get the natives to stitch a piece of cloth over their buttocks.

Cronicon left for the ship *Conciliar* two days after receiving the Cardinal's order. He drove to the pier, parked his car and then walked with his suitcase up the ship's planks. He was greeted by a seaman, Querelle, who wore a cocked white hat and an open short that revealed a considerable amount of chest. Cronicon saw a tiny silver cross around the sailor's neck and managed a smile as he handed him his ticket. In his cabin, the priest unpacked and stretched out on his bunk. For a moment he forgot everything and closed his eyes. He awoke when the ship was at sea.

# # # # #

Rumor had it that the passageway from the city to the Dome was on the waterfront. A plaque reaching just above the surface of the water had the word *Dome* etched on it; underneath this there followed instructions to trace the letters of the word *Dome* if the person wished to be transported.

The First Level, or Toll House, was crowded, especially at the entrance where a series of invisible doors let people in after they traced the last letter in *Dome* with their fingers. In this area, there was mass confusion. Babies were lost or stepped on. People panicked and soon developed dark circles under their eyes. They went around looking into the eyes of strangers until a monitor directed them to the Sliding Board Exit. But while waiting to pass through the Level and gain admittance to the Dome, some people didn't last. There were cardiac arrests; people too lazy to climb the five-hundred steps to the Sliding Board Exit found a corner niche, sat and vegetated. They grew fat or thin, depending on how they breathed, and some collected moss like underwater statuary.

Dennis and Rudolph came upon the plague quite by accident. They had wandered down to the waterfront to sit on the docks when Rudolph saw the plague he had heard so much about. It was submerged in the bay most of the time, not often visible to the eye.

"See that sign. All we have to do is rub it. Get our fingers down there and rub it."

"Rub it for what?"

"We don't have time, man. The plague can disappear in a second. If you want to go to the Dome, just do what I do and don't freak when I disappear. You'll disappear too."

"Disappear? Rudolph…" Before Dennis could finish, Rudolph had already traced most of the inscription and was about to trace the letter *e* on *Dome* when he blurted out, "here goes." As quickly as he said it, he disappeared. Dennis decided he must act quickly so he got on his belly and started tracing. He heard a grunting sound behind him and turned around. It was a wolf man.

The wolf people had developed a peculiar medicine that, when injected into a healthy person's veins, turned them into wolves. People who were not wolves struggled daily to keep themselves free from contact, because once injected with serum, all was lost. Some wolf people camouflaged their faces so they appeared as normal human beings, making it easier to inject strangers.

"Oh la la – I got you baby, stick, stick!" This wolf man was obviously a lowly one (there were some who spoke eloquently). The lowly ones were grungier than the rest and famous for blatant street injections. They grabbed you from behind, gagged you, then stuck you. They were careless, often jabbing the needle in sideways so that a lot of people got away with only half the serum in them, evolving into half-wolves. These poor souls wavered between good and evil and walked around as if someone had just spun them around very fast three dozen times then hit them over the head before shoving them into a dark room. Sometimes the wolves would stick these people again. After another injection they developed until they were down on all fours, with just a remnant of a human face. These creatures were the real horror of the city.

Dennis tried speeding up his tracing as the wolf man ran onto the dock. Holding out a syringe he came sliding down to where Dennis was just as he began the 'm' in *Dome*. Dennis froze. He had heard about wolf-transformations during his walks throughout the city and he had always feared for his safety. He was able to kick the wolf man in the head, but did this at the expense of his tracing and the wold man had enough time to get hold of his pants and pull at them until something

71

snapped. With an unsteady finger, Dennis managed to trace the 'e', but not before the point of the needle grazed his skin.

Dennis disappeared.

# # # # #

Late one night, as Cronicon relaxed in his cabin and read the Diocesan newspaper, he heard voices outside his door. It was the deck boy, whispering something to one of the kitchen chefs. The chef was very upset. "You must stop doing this to yourself, Justin, you must pull yourself up! Now come to my cabin where I will fix you some coffee." Cronicon heard someone groaning, "I'm sick!" then came the sound of tables and chairs moving as if someone had stumbled.

"I need my medication."

"Get up."

"Knock it off!"

Cronicon went to the door and looked through a small peephole, where he saw two heads interlocking, the chef's arms around the deck boy. "Hang onto my neck, Justin, there!" Cronicon watched as the chef hugged the boy tighter. He guessed at the meaning of the gesture; surely this was no fraternity-brother squeeze.

"No, no, you're not gonna drink again. And no more using. You are bombed and stoned all the time. Do you want your face turning red like that Father what's-his-name?"

Cronicon looked into the mirror, then at his glass of port. He imagined the deck boy lying face up on the chef's cot, legs in the air and toes curling.

"I cannot tell you what to do. I cannot follow you around. But you are useless to me as a lover. Nothing works! Booze and heroin have ruined you. Your beautiful body is worthless. What's more, you've stolen from me the last time! I am going to wash you. I am going to clean your system. How's that? With this olive oil and lubricant, I will purify your pores. Take off your clothes, Justin, now!"

In a few minutes Cronicon heard a series of light slappings, the chef obviously using his hands to go over the boy's back and buttocks. The slappings increased until they were so loud Cronicon left the cabin.

He slammed the door but that had no effect on the sailor's body massage. "Lift your leg, spread your toes, say…"

Cronicon fled to the upper deck.

"Saint Basil's monastery! Saint Basil's!" the chef shouted two days later while running down the cabin corridor. "Father, you may have bacon and eggs upstairs before embarking, if you wish."

Cronicon put all his things into a straw bag. He didn't answer the chef but looked under his pillow and in the drawers and closets for anything he might have forgotten. After a second call and knock, the chef went away and, a few minutes later, Cronicon opened his cabin door. He walked down the corridor and up the stairs past the dining room. He wanted to be the first one to disembark.

Climbing over the rocks on the coral reef, he made his way to the beach. He walked close to the surf, but the little waves that came in and wet his shoes only increased his annoyance. He fought a certain tingling in his loins, caused by memories of the chef and the deck boy. He had to resist temptation at any cost. Increasing his pace, he went up the sea-grass path to the monastery. When he got to the entrance, he saw the doors wedged open and expected to see one of the monks in the courtyard, but there was no one, not even a token bird at the birdbath. He did spot, in large block letters scrawled over the main wall, a graffiti like message, *Brother Dennis, I need you, call Mike,* with a cell phone number written underneath. He walked up to the second set of doors that opened into the chapel. They were tied back with rope. As he approached, he knew that something was wrong. He wished the Cardinal were here with him, for he had a feeling that he was about to uncover a major church scandal.

He went up to the kitchen table altar then walked down a side aisle that came around to the front door again. On the floor in front of a side altar table, he saw an object that immediately struck him as being out of place. Coming closer to it, he could make it out but didn't want to believe what he saw. The stone-like face of a child stared up at him like some primitive god from the mud piles along the Yucatan, Its eyebrows looked fake for they had been blown up out of proportion. He dismissed the find, however, as a tropical liturgical innovation done in the spirit of Vatican II.

He left the chapel in great haste, not even stopping to examine the other artifacts arranged around the mummy. He went straight to the monastery proper where, again, more doors had been left open. Inside, he called for Merton. He picked up the hand bell on the small table next to the door and rang it as he went down the corridor past the refectory. Going upstairs, he noticed little, though the patch job over the small glory-hole in Rudolph's cell struck him as a curious oddity. He rang the bell while checking Merton's cell. On the writing table he found some notes.

"...We are determined that our love must stay spiritual and chaste – I think there is no other way!! But the longing for her is frightful – and of course so is the conflict that goes with it. I know how much she wants me too, , and I also know that a crude botched-up affair in the woods would be worse than nothing...."

Cronicon looked out the window but didn't notice the path the monks had cleared, despite the fact that it was a good six-and-a-half feet across.

He called the Cardinal. "Eminence," he said, "there is no sign of them. They aren't anywhere. Perhaps they are away working or fishing, but the condition of this monastery is terrible. I found a mummy in the chapel; it may not be liturgical."

After speaking with the Cardinal, Cronicon went downstairs and out through the courtyard. In a distance he saw the ship moving down the coastline. He also saw several people onboard who seemed to be bobbing their heads to music. He went back to the courtyard, bolted the doors from the inside, and locked the church. He went into the monastery, where he locked more doors before heading into the refectory to make some tea.

When he heard noises coming from the bushes outside, he went to the small refectory window and looked outside. He saw a man, naked except for his underpants, run into the chapel. Cronicon went outside and followed the man into the chapel.

The nearly naked man looked at Cronicon just as he was about to lay more artifacts on the side altar. Cronicon immediately recognized him as one of the monks he had seen on retreat here with the Cardinal.

"Brother!" Cronicon said politely, but with steel girders ready to break in and scream.

While he knew who Cronicon was, William nervously looked him over. He could not restrain a chuckle as he continued to place the artifacts on the side altar. When he was finished, he walked up to the priest and looked him in the eye. Cronicon could see that the monk wasn't quite right; his eyes looked glazed and he seemed jumpy.

"What's wrong with you? Where are the others? Why are you half-nude?" Cronicon then told him that the Cardinal had sent him to the island. For some reason he thought of the chef telling off the deck boy; the scene of the deck boy being slapped came to him and it was only through self-restraint that he avoided doing the same to William. "Where is Abbot Merton?"

A look of recollection came over William. "The Abbot is with us," he said, looking down at Cronicon since he was small in stature. "But do you know that we have discovered an easy route to a Pleasure Dome! The Dome, think of it...William Blake! Coleridge! Everyone up to now has only written about it."

"You're drunk," said the priest, though his voice faded considerably when he said the word *drunk,* because he wasn't sure.

With this William ran off, climbing the courtyard wall and taking to the path. Cronicon chased him, amazed at his own physical dexterity when it came to climbing walls.

On the path, Cronicon imagined himself walking across the Red Sea after Moses had parted the waters. That was his impression of the pile up of bramble bushes on both sides of him. Although the route was mostly clear, there were small twigs and roots that remained uncut. They stuck up and had to be walked around. It wasn't easy walking for the priest. Twice he stumbled and when he had walked what seemed like several miles, he sat down, leaned his head against some bramble bush roots, and closed his eyes. He imagined what it would be like to fall asleep forever. No sooner had he gotten up than he saw something coming toward him on the path. It was far enough ahead of him that he was able to see that it covered the entire width of the path. In his imagination, Cronicon compared it to a speeding subway train and saw himself trapped in front of it. He said a silent prayer but even that didn't stop it, though it may have given him the incentive to scramble down between the thorny stems of bushes. His instincts told him to lie on his stomach with his eyes to the ground; he knew he could not look at the passing force. When he was firmly positioned the roar passed over him like an express train.

When he came to he breathed in clouds of dust and sand.

And what were these little animals, no bigger than rats, right on the heels of the force and wearing little Egyptian headdresses, all gold in color? It was an absolutely creepy sight, making Cronicon feel as if he had been transported to a mythological land.

He continued walking, but after a time began to get thirsty; this didn't help his mental and physical state and, in his imagination, he began to wish for a miracle. He wet his lips and rolled his tongue around inside his mouth to work up some saliva, but everything was dry. He sat down again. He thought of Christ fasting in the desert, and of Moses tapping the rock with a stick. He looked around for a stick and, picking one up, he nonchalantly twirled it like a baton and meditated on Moses, then spied a small rock. He whispered: "Perform a miracle for me O Lord, and let this rock drip," not thinking for one minute that anything would happen, but out of the rock came four or five steady squirts of water as if he had stabbed a water balloon with a sewing needle. Cronicon quickly got down on his knees and clasped his hands together in thanks. "O Moses!" he said. He opened his mouth and let the rock shoot its spray over his lips. He remained this way for some time, until the ground around him became soggy. He then stood and went on his way, throwing the stick aside.

A little further along, he began smelling the incense. It came to him in small whiffs at first, then as a great mist. He tried unsuccessfully to fight off the effects: giddiness, a desire to skip rather than walk. He also noticed the scenery around him beginning to change. Where once there had been bramble bushes, now rich lawns with goldfish ponds and magnolia trees dripped thick nectars into silver vase containers placed underneath them. There were also miniature pagodas as big as closets, with elaborate roofs and a bubble enclosure equipped with an incense-pumping device.

In a clearing ahead of him he saw a columned structure as high as a skyscraper with a white-dome roof. It looked more like a well-preserved ruin than anything contemporary. Ivy covered the columns and the sound of running water and people splashing was everywhere. Cronicon recognized Abbot Merton right away: he was wading in a waist-deep fountain along with the other monks, their naked torsos gleaming in the sun.

Merton waved. "Praise Priapus! Praise Helios! Praise the Lord!"

"Hello, father. Take off your clothes!"

Cronicon stepped up into the columned interior and walked to the edge of the fountain. In the center was a cluster of statues from which the water come –human forms with streams of water coming from nostrils, ears, navels, penises, breasts and buttock cracks. The water sparkled like vintage champagne. Cronicon watched as Rudolph floated on his back. He looked over to William, who was lodged between two statues on the multi-layered cluster, his mouth open underneath the sprays of water coming from the breasts of a young girl.

"What has happened to your monastic vows!" bellowed the priest. But as much as he tried to sound official, he was distracted and his eyes wandered to the water. Merton got out of the pool and sat beside him. "Nothing has happened, father, not really; we have just found the mainspring of Heaven. Just look at this place! Now, if it would only be possible to use it intelligently, we could all come here to relax. The Cardinal could come too. Of course we couldn't abuse this loveliness. For instance, I have instructed the monks that we must leave in an hour."

Cronicon studied the spurting nymphs and satyrs with distaste. "No, there's danger here. I am not fooled by any so-called loveliness. It's a trick. It will ruin the religious life at Saint Basil's. Who will want to leave? Look at the fruit trees, the figs, the trays of bananas all over? Does some pagan miracle cause this food to exist? Why leave, Abbot? How could you go back to a life of simple austerity after an experience such as this?"

"Father, you just pick up and leave, that's all. Just close your eyes to it."

"The fountain is immoral," Cronicon said, looking out over the lawns and miniature pagodas and over the other side of the Dome where there were more fields and ponds. Cronicon was beginning to yawn; he was feeling soft. He had little inside himself to drive home his argument anymore. "What's happening?" he half mumbled, experiencing a desire to lay down somewhere. Finally he turned around and stretched out on the grass, his eyes scanning the sky. "Dear Helios" he said to himself. "Why am I here?" He heard the monks splashing. Somebody was being dunked.

Merton clapped his hands, but nobody noticed until he did it a second time. "Okay," he said, sounding like a high school wrestling coach, "we must leave. Take some figs and fruit and let's be on our way." But Cronicon lay sleeping. "You may come along or you may stay here," he said. Cronicon opened his eyes for a second and then shut them. "You do what you want," Merton said.

With that, Merton led the monks to the pathway while Cronicon slept until sunset, at which time two full moons shone on either side of him, and large white birds perched on the trees and flew criss-cross over the Dome.

When Cronicon awoke, he rolled onto his side, reached out to a tiny fig tree, and snapped off a fig. Though he was not hungry, the taste and feel of the fig in his mouth felt good and he found he was able to chew on it for a long time, as if by his own will deciding how long the fig should remain intact. He tested his suspicion and ordered it to melt and it did immediately. Next he saw the white birds and his first thought was "How beautiful," and before he knew it one was standing beside him looking him in the eye. He had merely to extend a finger and the bird perched on it, and when he was tired of looking at it, it flew away. Pressing his face into the grass he noticed the smell of incense. "Oh!" he said aloud, and the two moons seemed to dance for him, one moving around the other in a virtual cha-cha. Cronicon found he could arrange the moons any way he wished simply by looking at one and moving it with his eyes across the sky. He scrambled them this way and that, plunging one down to earth while keeping the other in the sky. Then he put them together in order to make a bigger moon, but when he wanted them disconnected he merely had to wish it and they fell apart. Soon he was asleep and dreaming that he was on a raft with silk sails, a cool breeze cuddling him.

He awoke to a violet sun and the chatter of little red and yellow birds. One climbed on his leg and tickled him, injecting him with a feeling of vigor and excitement. He no longer felt like laying down but wanted only to go into the pool. He ran. He ran down to the lawns on the other side of the Dome and as he ran, birds flew alongside him. He felt so good he wanted to leap into the air. And looking at the burds, he envied them their ability to fly. No sooner had he thought this than one bird turned towards him and seemed to nod. Before he knew it, he was in the air on his belly, flapping his arms. In a minute, he was soaring upward over the golden roofs of the miniature pagodas. He merely had to think that he was going too fast or flying too high to be immediately lowered, and had only to think 'slow' or 'fest' to adjust his speed. He always wanted to know what it felt like to fly through clouds, so he did just that, twirling upward like a top as his body went through one and out the other side. Could he sit on a cloud? All at once he was lounging on the fluff and looking down at the top of the Pleasure Dome.

But then, out of nowhere, came something like the sound of thunder. He was on the ground and felt the earth shake. A wind or a great force seemed to be speeding towards him, a darkness speckled with light racing close to the ground, an unstoppable train of death and fear that caused him to leap on the ground and cover his head and eyes until the great mystery had passed over him.

# # # # #

In the Underground Dome labyrinth, Dennis could feel the still aching syringe prick on his buttocks and looked over at Rudolph, who was huddled in a corner talking with a group of people who appeared to be on a cigarette break. People of all ages walked in circles and chain smoked. They didn't know where to walk, although a nearby attendant in a white coat kept watch over them. A young man Dennis' age who had been in the Labyrinth for years because he refused to go through the Rite of Passage, sat in a chair in a new pair of shoes and a suit that looked way too big for him.

Rudolph started talking to him first, and when Dennis saw them he sat down between them.

"I never robbed a grave in my life. Imagine robbin' a grave? What did you get out of it? A smelly corpse? Ugh, man, that is really sick."

"You robbed a grave?" Dennis asked.

The boy nodded. He said he knew it was an act of desecration but that he couldn't help himself at the time. The attendant looked his way about this time and seemed to be uneasy about his talking to Dennis and Rudolph.

In the interim, Dennis and Rudolph were having their "Deeds in Life" checked on a large flat screen computer. The scanner revealed every misdeed, untoward thought and evil act, violent or otherwise, as well as sexual fantasies and experiences, alone or with others, since age 7 or the age of reason. Several attendants dressed like crossing guards or toll booth agents stood around monitoring the screens and taking notes. The information on a person also printed out through a slit in the wall. The attendants took great delight in horrendous reports because that meant an easier job when it came to rendering a judgment. The grave robbing boy looked on with particular interest while Dennis' information was being assessed.

"We see that you have committed several offenses. These will have to be atoned for. Do you know anything about our method of atonement?" The attendant gave Dennis a hard look that had perhaps only known tenderness in a mother's lap.

"No."

"Well, you may leave the First Entry Level if you wish and go back to the city. That's up to you. But if you want to stay, you have to take your punishment before you pass to the Second Level. You must atone."

"What does the scanner say I did?" Dennis assumed the attendant was bluffing him.

"It says you dug a hole through a wall near a monastery garden, and that you had an affair, while a monk, with an oil rig man employed by Goldman-Sachs. It says that when you lived in Harvard Square you canvassed the streets for men, many of them heterosexual, and that you used devious means to get them to have sex with you. It says you hung outside a wine and spirits store and agreed to buy pints of rum for eighteen year olds in exchange for oral sex back in your rooming house."

"But I prayed to God about that. I thought all had been forgiven. I went to Pinpoint Island and suffered awful things. And then, you know, I got lost in this crowded city and then met Rudolph."

"And then you promptly tried to seduce Rudolph by offering to roll over like a girl." The attendant read from the scanner sheet. "It says here you must be thrown into the Snow Room to freeze and to be chased by wolves. It is one of the lesser punishments, but if the wolves get you before we retrieve you, you may conk out."

"Hey man," Dennis said, "I told you sex would get you in trouble."

"Your scanner sheet," the attendant interrupted, "is two pages long. It says you objectified women, used them as masturbation receptacles, and murdered your cat, Leo. You will have to be fried."

"What?" Rudolph said. The attendant had said *fried* as one might say *boiled to a crisp* or *smothered in onions.*

"Fried means just that. It means stripping naked and being greased by attendants and placed in a room-size frying pan. You will burn on all sides, being turned so as not to sizzle too long in one place, and so you won't…conk out. When we take you out, you will have completed your atonement. Thank you. Step this way, Dennis."

"What's he gonna get?" Rudolph pointed to the boy who ribbed the grave.

"You will please not concern yourself with that unfortunate boy's punishment. Believe me he will not go out of here skipping rope."

"Oh geese," Rudolph cried, "this is crazy."

"Do you want," the attendant asked, "a never- ending life of pleasure ro do you want to go back to the city and suffer unemployment, homelessness, and the twenty-four hour night? You see, you can go back, but you can never return, not even as an old man, to do this over."

"It's cruel, Man, you people are hard mother fuckers," Rudolph said.

"Careful, vulgar displays are taken care of by Sister Kaneff." Rudolph turned and saw a nun holding an aluminum pointer. She slapped it once in the palm of her hand.

"Dennis, you have fifteen minutes to prepare yourself." With that, the attendant left, and Rudolph and Dennis huddled together and lamented their fate.

Fifteen minutes later, the attendant returned and unlocked a door inside another door. Out came steam and cold air. "In side," he said to Dennis. He threw him a sweater with a hood on the back. The attendant took him by the arms and gave him a gentle shove into the Snow Room. The Snow Room was at arctic temperature. There was manufactured snow everywhere and snow even fell from the ceiling. Light that resembled stars in the sky also came from the ceiling. Artificial scenery gave the impression of a city in the distance. A machine pumped in icy wind. He began to shiver.

Rudolph was taken by the scruff of the neck into a side room, undressed, and greased down with a block of lard. He screamed and ranted the whole time. His stringy black hair got caught in the attendant's hand and, for a moment, they had to stop buttering him. But Rudolph was no match for the attendants, all of whom kept him in place without so much as grimacing. Finally, when they had him buttered, they took him to the fry-pan room where a sizzling frying pan large enough to seat thirty lay waiting. Someone had just thrown in some cakes of lard and there was about an inch of liquid on its surface. Rudolph was thrown in on his back. He screamed so much he was turned over later than he was supposed to be, and he was rolled over like a small weenie. His atonement lasted ten minutes, during which time he didn't die, but merely felt the pains of the death agony. Though the cruel spatula pressed down on his back and kept his face flat to the pan, he was taken out and given a cold towel after his time was up. He was then placed in a container of Noxema and ice. When this was finished, the attendants were all smiles.

"Would you like some dinner, Rudy? Rudy, sit here, it is more comfortable."

A luscious dinner was served him: Prime Rib, a spinach quiche, pita bread and champagne. A beautiful woman gave him a neck massage. The attendants even asked him friendly personal questions.

"Where did you go to school? Where do you live?" and so forth. A mat with a picture of the Dome on it had been placed under his plate.

"This ain't fair; you two-sided bastards. You treat me like a yo-yo," he said. Rudolph wasn't one to mince his words. However, the attendant holding the ice packs to his cheeks withdrew them and it was evident that much of the blackness had disappeared. Rudolph would look as good as new in another day or so.

"Where's Dennis?"

"In the snow," said two attendants at once.

True, Dennis was in the snow, and he found that the more he jumped around to keep warm, the colder it got. Pretty soon he was on his back on the floor, waiting to freeze. He knew the rules: he was supposed to feel the sting of freezing and the 'letting go,' so he let go and discovered that it wasn't painful – after the initial hurt. Then a thought shook him: where was he and why was he here? He became angry and stood up.

"Heavenly saints, let me live," he shouted. He closed his eyes and prayed, mumbling the words as he felt something hairy and horrid touch his body. He could feel a cold tongue run across his cheek.

"Well now, how's our boy?" Dennis felt someone squeeze his ear lobes. "How about a warm bath and a heating blanket?"

In the other room, Rudolph thought the attendants were feeding him in order to throw him into the Snow Room and give Dennis a turn in the frying pan.

Dennis, still shivering, was brought into the room with Rudolph.

"Don't worry about this place, Rudy," he said. I have it figured out. We're in Hell but most likely Purgatory –thought I didn't believe in it, but Holy Moses, this is it. But it'll end, Rudolph. Purgatory has an end."

"Jus' get me out of this place, man, jus' get me out."

Chapter Six

On the ship *Conciliar*, the chef recoiled rope, then paced the ship in his sleeveless undershirt. The deck boy was below napping wearing just a pair of jeans; in his tiny cabin the sounds of David Bowie washing out the call of the gulls. There were no passengers onboard. All were at the monastery and the ship was docked until their return.

At the monastery gate, Merton shook the hands of the retreatants as they walked ashore. Most of the men wore white, a few with aloha shirts and cameras. The women were tidy and respectable. Merton's gaze rested on *Conciliar's* white sails, thinking they provided good contrast against the blue sky.

Merton thought of Cronicon back at the Dome. He had let him stay too long and he was worried that the Cardinal would phone and ask to speak to the priest. He didn't want that. He knew that Cardinal Taj Mahoney was a determined man, a pleasure-loathing cleric if there ever was one. And he'd be sure to send a squadron of his own aides to the Dome, first to inspect it, then back to the mainland to seek the governor's aid in closing it. The man's unpredictability was legendary. Once, during a Young Adult Liturgy in the cathedral, the congregation of youths started dancing at the Kiss of Peace. The Cardinal, who began dancing around the tabernacle himself, objected when several people genuflected rather than join in the dance. In his pamphlet, *A Stark, Spartan Liturgy Makes for Good Morals*, Mahoney advocated a return to Plymouth Rock morality. "The use of incense and traditional liturgical customs opens the door to sins of the flesh," he wrote. "Eliminate liturgical fuss, and what you get is a straight utilitarian Mass without effeminate contamination."

Merton called for Rudolph. When Rudolph appeared, Merton could see that the Dome had completely refreshed him.

"We must get Cronicon back here. It is late."

"Oh, Abbot, must I walk that path? I'm exhausted after last night."

"Then see if William will do it. Tell him he can run naked, if that will cool him off. But we must get Cronicon out of the Dome."

"The guy is probably swollen with song and ecstasy." William changed into short running pants and rubbed his legs with a substance called Red Hot. It was used to tone his muscles and give his legs a sheen, and after a rubdown, the monk smelled of exotic spices. "I'll be back soon," he said, running down to the start of the pathway.

A little later, Merton and Rudolph cleared the chapel of the baby mummy and other archeological finds to make it suitable for Mass. It was important not to confuse the visitors, for many had come to view the monastery as a center for radical liturgical innovations. Carefully then, the visitors filed in, talking and laughing amongst themselves while nodding casually towards the crucifix that had so enthralled Dennis.

An hour or two later when William was well along the pathway, he began to notice a body of water ahead of him. As he got closer he saw that it was virtually a swamp. It seemed to confine itself to the path and not the bramble bush jungle on either side of it. In the middle of the swamp he could see a cluster of bubbles, as if someone were swamp-diving or exhaling under water. He walked alongside it and waded through, the water coming up to his knees. In twenty minutes he had reached the other side, considerably muddied and tired. He lay down next to the swamp for a snooze and, when he awoke a half hour later, the edge of the swamp was just over his feet. It occurred to him that the water was growing. Urged on by this knowledge, he ran as fast as he could to the Dome.

# # # # #

But if William was frightened, Dennis had really accepted the inevitable and was now fully adjusted to life within the First Level. After the torture he found that the attendants tried to make life as pleasant as possible. The establishment of volleyball, swimming, and finger painting made the days pass rapidly. At poolside, he met a young man who he liked immediately. Seeing him in a bathing suit spurred him to start a conversation, but the young man only liked women and said as much. "Oh well," Dennis sighed, watching the guy stand on his head underwater. It was a good thing for Dennis that the tranquilizers dispensed by the Management had induced a lessening of erotic interest. He felt completely free of the need for sex and was able to move without being hindered by desire.

86

# # # # #

When William reached Cronicon, he found him stark naked and sitting in the lap of a boy statue, one finger over a spouting nipple.

"Father! You must rearrange yourself. There's plenty of time for this later on. Right now we must get back to the monastery."

"Ah sweet boy," Cronicon said. "Look at this work of art. Look at this chest! Do you know what I have been doing? I have been playing with the moons, and flying, and just now, turning the water that comes from this young man's breast into honey. Honey, real honey! If I ever go back to the parishes, I will seek out boys such as this. I will make them do unspeakable things! I will! I will! And there will be no scandal because these boys must be shown the way – the unspeakable pleasure!"

"The Abbot ran some experiments here earlier. Everything is possible. Everything we are taught is false! But we must work to save it and get back to the monastery before the Cardinal gets wind of it."

"Deep-fry the Cardinal. I want to live like the ancient Greeks," Cronicon was delirious.

"Just come back long enough to phone the Cardinal and tell him everything is okay. Will you do that? It will help preserve this holy place."

"Oh!" Cronicon said with a long groan, placing his head on the statue's shoulder. "When I get back, I will march through the parishes like Attila the Hun!"

"Come on now, you can walk with me. Hold my hand."

"Zeus," Cronicon called, scanning the skies, "send something to transport me. A little car or bus, a chariot maybe. I should like to fly again. Have you flown, dear fellow?"

"It won't work, Father. You can only fly in the area of the Dome. Once you pass over into the land of the Other, you will fall to the ground. I've seen birds…"

"Nonsense," Cronicon said, standing up rather lazily and flapping his arms while shouting "Fly!" until he rose, zooming over the statue.

"Come down anyway, please." William sat on the edge of the fountain and hung his head in defeat.

When William finally managed to convince Cronicon to return with him, he found that the pool of water was considerably higher. Both men waded through it even though it was up to their necks. Cronicon knew what had happened, but he was too embarrassed to say anything about it. He did, however, look over the top of the bubbling pool for the wooden stick he used to strike the rock. He hoped he could rework the magic or whatever it was that was causing the flood, but no stick could be found. He was very exhausted, and now that they passed out of Dome country and entered the Monastic Reality, his muscles began to ache from his strenuous flight.

He kept wanting to sleep but William kept pulling him along. Cronicon was on the lookout for the rats in Egyptian headdresses, but what they found instead was a grille, much like a subway grating, exposed beneath the soil.

William got down on all fours and peered through the bars. It was very dark but he could hear human cries. "Who are you? Say it again!" The answer was more of a wail than actual words.

Cronicon knelt down with William. "There are real people down there. They're in pain or something."

"Whoever they are, their lives may be in danger. Look at the water, it's rising and quickly coming towards us. Father, I don't think there is any way we can return to the monastery and forget about this. We have a mission here."

William called into the grate. "Come to the subway grating where you see sunlight." He shouted again and again until both of them could see a cellar some distance below.

Dennis, wandering the corridors in a remote section of the First Level, heard William's cries and teamed up with the group of people shouting back. They now said, "Where are you? Tell us!" About ten in number, some broke into tears, sensing liberation was at hand. Since they were in a corridor where there was no light, they had to keep lighting matches until they found the source of William's call.

# # # # #

At St. Basil's, Merton had just finished conducting a tour of the monastery, and now the visitors were left by themselves. Some split up, going over to admire the Grotto of St. Happanious of Crete. Some went back into the chapel to gaze at the crucifix and shake hands. A few noticed the path and could see that it went through an otherwise high-growth area. The hundreds of bramble bushes piled up near the monastery wall were a curiosity item too.

Three or four visitors decided to follow the path, certain it was a meditation lane cleared by the monks for long walks. Although they helped each other over the stubbles and rocks, at a certain point they began to get an eerie feeling, realizing perhaps that they were deep in the interior of a jungle. But still they hurried along as if late for Sunday Mass, their hearts racing and a light-headed feeling making them all a little giddy.

"I would really like to mow this. Then again, maybe not. Gee, I feel as if someone had taken out my stomach, put a little ice in there in its place, and then thrown me in the air. Quite a queer sensation!" one woman exclaimed.

"You think those sexy monks run and jump along here," another woman said, feeling like she wanted to fling off her blouse as she jogged ahead of the others.

They continued to hurry along when they saw two figures on the path before them.

"Monks!" said the woman who wanted to strip. The group stopped and waited for the monks, and when the monks drew close, it became obvious that there had been some trouble. Cronicon could hardly stand up, and William was holding him up like one would support a drunk.

# # # # #

A day later, Cronicon phoned the Cardinal from his recuperation bed and said that he had been to a Pleasure Dome. "Obscene beyond word or description," was how he described it. He said that if the mainland people ever got wind of its whereabouts, it would be a disaster – and the end of the Church. He said the population would waste themselves and make themselves sick, experiencing that 'Heaven-in-life' or the Allen Ginsberg-Henry Miller syndrome (a term

Cronicon used during one of his anti-pornography campaigns). The Cardinal wanted to jump on the case right away, but first he wanted to see the place – privately. He asked Cronicon when the ship *Conciliar* would return, but since Cronicon had no way of knowing, it was agreed that the Cardinal would take a helicopter for an unannounced date. "Anyway," Cronicon said, *"Conciliar* is manned by two flaming homosexuals, one nearly an underage boy and a runaway from one of our institutions!"

Pleased with himself he hung up, feeling better now that he thought the Dome might be shut down –as long as it was there to go back to, he felt uncomfortable. Better to have it closed altogether, then there would be no choice.

Merton walked into Cronicon's room with a tray of cold pears and sour cream.

"Abbot," Cronicon said, splitting a pear in half. "You should know that I cannot sit idly by while that Dome of yours is so accessible. I must make a full report to Cardinal Mahoney and in order to do that I must see the place again and take notes. I hope you understand why the Dome must be closed."

"You are free to do as you wish."

"Then you don't care whether I go back? You would, in fact, like to see me lose myself again?"

"I didn't say that. You know what you are able to handle better than I do."

"Who says?"

"Well, I should think you do, now that you've had time to recover. Perhaps there is something in your system that needs to be worked out. Maybe it's important that you get this out, bring it to air…a theology of the body kind of thing. So, we will wait for you."

"Theology of the body is for married people only," Cronicon said.

"Depends on the theologian you quote," Merton added.

"But you and your monks –don't tell me you don't lie awake at night dreaming of the place. Why do you not wish to always stay there? How can you rise at dawn, pray, work in the fields, knowing all the time that only a few miles away lies the Eden of our time...an incredible find which may change the course of history!"

"It is my philosophy that you can rot in either place. I could tell you what manner of psychological deception we've had at St. Basil's before discovering the Dome: Petty jealousies magnified a hundred times and pent-up frustrations conjuring up all kinds of monsters in the name of righteousness. It was horrid. We had a monk who wanted to murder another monk because of unwanted sexual advances. Now the killer monk wakes up in the morning, sees the sun, and cries 'Hosanna in the highest!' And he means it. But really, I have told you something very personal and in confidence." Merton bit his tongue. He'd gone too far.

"Sexual advances? God, Abbot, what will happen next, especially with the influence of the Dome? What perversions, daydreams, intoxications? This is not the Theology of the Body! I am confused. Where is the monk who made sexual advances? Is it the brother who flaunts himself in his underwear? I should have guessed."

Merton, deep in thought, didn't answer.

"Tell me now. It will be kept a secret."

"He is on a metaphysical journey. He disappeared some time ago and left no word."

"Is that all? Well, leave it to that type to disappear. I'm not surprised. If he comes back, you should send him to the Cardinal. The Cardinal has a program for people of his kind. We cannot have religious homos evoking all kinds of feelings among the others, you know. Vatican II did not go that far." Cronicon then whispered in Merton's ear, "What kind of sexual advances? I'm interested as a normal man. Anal? Did anything actually happen? Spillage? I've heard about these things but I'm not that familiar. Only on the *Conciliar* as I said..."

"Let's go into the chapel and meditate." Merton gave Cronicon's sleeve a tug.

Before they could leave the room, there was a knock at the door. Merton opened it and before him stood Rudolph and Mike, the

Goldman-Sachs freighter man. Rudolph said Mike was here to fix a lock. Merton quickly ushered Mike outside.

"How do you feel, father?" Rudolph asked, bowing Asian-style.

"Brother Rudolph, is it? I was just telling the Abbot that the Dome should be closed. I would have fallen into total depravity there had it not been for your Brother William." Cronicon drew in a long breath. "Tell me, Brother Rudolph – and you can refuse to answer this question if you wish – but was there a homosexual monk here who made sexual advances? It's fine to tell me because Abbot Merton says the monk in question has deserted."

"Homosexual?" Brother Rudolph repeated. "Oh, well, I don't know what you mean."

"I mean," Cronicon began in a whisper, "were there any monks here who put a hand on anyone? You know, a hand in the wrong place, on the buttocks, you know…"

"We wash each other's backs in the shower," Rudolph said, "and I've rubbed soap all over William's knee, and leg too."

"I'm not talking about that. I'm talking about kissing, and –well, you've been out in the world – sloshing off; sloshing each other off, you know. Things like that." There was a pause. "Brother Rudolph, you're obviously an innocent creature. I have forgotten that there are innocent boys around such as you. Forgive me. But will you please show me the room of the monk who deserted?"

They went upstairs and down the dormitory corridor. When they came to Dennis' cell, Rudolph opened the door and stepped inside. Cronicon inspected the desk, Dennis' books, and went over to the bed. He pressed down on the mattress, lifted the pillow, and checked the sheets.

"What are you looking for?"

"Evidence," Cronicon said, who then noticed the patch job on the hole-in-the-wall. "What's this?" he asked, rubbing his hands over the rough surface. "Somebody knocked a part of the wall out. Um, very strange." He sat down on the edge of the cot and inspected the plaster, running his fingers back and forth over it so that particles of it fell off. He did this until the outline of the hole was visible. "Look at this, a real home of some sort. Looks like someone took their hand and dug it out. A spying device or...who sleeps over there?"

Rudolph didn't like the possibility of Cronicon inspecting his room. "I do."

"You do!" Cronicon waited a minute before continuing. "And when was the hole filled? Was it here when Dennis came, or did Dennis do it?"

"Dennis, probably."

"You mean he cupped it out with his hand?"

"Yes."

"Why did he do it? Why would anyone want to drill a hole in the wall at about waist level? Is your bed on the other side of the hole, directly under it? If it is, I'd like to see it."

Cronicon inspected Rudolph's room. He noticed the weights and the bottles of vitamins, but especially the other side of the hole. On Rudolph's side, the patchwork wasn't quite as well done, and ragged edges showed. Cronicon examined the hole closely. "I know what this is," he said. "I saw a number of these in the Army. We were stationed in Hawaii near the Honolulu YMCA, and in several of the bathrooms there were holes. I slept next to the john as a matter of fact. It was horrible. I kept waking up thinking I heard the walls shake. The presence of this thing in a monastery is a true abomination, spirit of Vatican II notwithstanding. I wish I had met this Brother Dennis."

Outside in the courtyard, the visitors sat under trees. A scream sounded from the path, coming from where the grate was.

Upset, Merton rang the monastery bells. After the tenth bong, the visitors gathered around him and waited for instructions.

Merton told the visitors that the people in the Underground must be saved. He told them that a great reward awaited the world if those trapped in the Underground were set free.

The visitors took picks and shovels and started along the footpath. When they got to the grate, Merton told them to dig around the grate so that they could lift it off. Everybody pitched in, even Cronicon, who helped two elderly women who offered handshakes while shouting, "Peace be to you!"

In the dark corridors beneath the grille, Dennis and his group heard the shovels and picks. They tried very hard to get at the source of the pounding. Different ones at different times said "Over here!" and the group was constantly being led this way and that. Finally, a newfound lover of Dennis' named Domino discovered the grate on the ceiling of an alcove. The group could see stones and dirt fall alongside them as the visitors above began to cut through. "Here, here, here!" many screamed. As Dennis peered up into the sunlight, he thought he saw the folds of monk's robes. Then he heard Rudolph's voice.

When the grate was lifted off, the First Level people got a good view of the people above them.

"They want us to shimmy up!" one of them said,

Since Dennis knew his brother-monks were nearby, he strayed from the crowd a bit, afraid to be too much in view. He knew he wasn't ready to reenter the Order, and he was in no mood for either a reunion or confrontation. His two-week stay in the First Level had given him some insight: he now knew he didn't want to be a monk.

Dennis heard Merton's deep and resonant voice. It seemed to echo throughout the cellar-corridors. "We're here to liberate you. It hasn't been easy. We have found a new Heaven and new Earth. Please come to the end corridor. You will see a monk standing with a candle – that's me – waiting to give you a boost up out of that place. Come quickly!"

Applause broke out among the visitors as the First Levelers were hoisted out of the hole. The monks didn't recognize Dennis. His beard camouflaged him as did the dull gray uniform he was forced to wear. It was only when they were walking back to the monastery that Dennis went up to Merton.

"Abbot?"

The voice gave him away. "Dennis, my boy, I had a feeling you were here!: He gave Dennis a hug, after which he held him at arm's length and studied him. "You must have a lot to tell us. NO doubt you experienced many things down there. Am I right?"

Cronicon lingered about as if debating when to strike. He kept a steady eye on Dennis and watched as Rudolph came up to him and slapped him on the back.

"All your people are talking about the Dome. How did they know? It's true, you know. We're near it, up that way a bit. You can visit it with us, box veil and all."

At these words, Cronicon, who was in the middle of listening to a discourse on living conditions in the so-called First Level, stopped to see if what he really heard come out of Rudolph's mouth was true. When he heard Dennis remark, "I would like to come, but I've thrown away the veil," he bit his lip and walked forward. He positioned himself next to Merton as if to say, "Here I am, now introduce me." But at this intrusion, Dennis seemed to lose his balance. He stumbled and leaned on Rudolph as one would against a lamppost. Then he ran off entirely. Indeed, everyone who saw him run compared it to the running of a fawn or a delicately limbed animal.

Rudolph chased Dennis but his energy was lax. He was tired after only a half mile of side-stepping burrs and twigs. Cronicon was left quite speechless. He was prepared to shame Dennis right in front of the visitors when he ran off.

Dennis was headed for the Dome. When he arrived, he climbed to the top of the columned structure and positioned himself in its center so that, from a distance, he looked like a statue. He sat with one leg drawn under his buttocks and the other straight out in front of him. When Rudolph got there, he couldn't tell Dennis from the gargoyles.

The pool had been growing steadily since Cronicon's tapping of the rock and was now of considerable size, so much that when Dennis went to cross it, he would have sunk had he not readjusted his running style and skimmed over it, just touching the surface with his heels. Rudolph had to swim it when the water was above his waist. It was both muddy and treacherous and he slipped once and was sure there was quicksand on the bottom. But the exotic perfumes coming from the Dome gave him added strength and he managed to slip out.

The water was starting to pour into the grate hole and it was slowly mingling with the sea surf on various parts of the island. It was lapping up the island bit by bit.

Cronicon mentioned to Merton: "That water is the craziest shape. If I weren't with you all, I'd think I was dreaming."

The water was shaped like a pyramid, a moving mountain of surf that had a middle section considerably higher than its sides. It moved towards the monastery in fast, jerky movements as if it were pulled along mechanically. To get across it, one had to swim or wade up to the apex and then slide down the other side.

"If I didn't know better, I'd think the water had legs," Cronicon said. "I'd say we better leave or we'll be in a heap of trouble. It rather looks like a tidal wave is forming."

At Cronicon's words, most of the crowd moved away, not wanting a disaster after such a heroic rescue effort. William led them all in the direction of St. Basil's, while Merton called into the grate one more time.

"The rest will die," Cronicon said. "I think our job should be to find the source of this vile thing. Who runs it, why they run it, and all that."

Merton joked. "At first it had me fooled. I thought it was a big Heavenly design. Like Purgatory. But now I can't see that at all. In the real Purgatory the body is not supposed to be purged, only the spirit. But look at these people! No, I can't believe the Lord would do this, not to these people, not to our Dennis."

"Dennis?" Cronicon asked. "Why, I don't know why you find it especially hard to see him paying for the things he did at St. Basil's, even if he burned down there for his sins. That's logical. Our catechism teaches that, Abbot. Perhaps I was mistaken: yes, I am. It is God's plan. Yes, I see it now. It was Purgatory. And you've set them free, Abbot, the whole screwy lot of them. Did you see them? Sloppily dressed, warts on their fingers, rotten teeth, people with AIDS, and pregnant girls giving themselves abortions – did you see that? That big woman with her buttocks in a sling and a dog collar around her neck; did you think her saintly, worthy of emulation? She obviously wanted to arouse temptation down there – or perhaps it was the women she was after, for there is no distinction of gender in that place."

"She ripped her shorts accidentally on the way up the rope ladder. I saw it. The rope moved into position and assumed the form of a sling."

"Don't believe that, Abbot, she's a slut. I saw the way she was looking at the young men. She walked in front of them all, wiggle disgracefully. The young men snickered and grabbed their crotches."

The pyramid of water seemed to be making its way towards them and the clergy backed off, running towards the others who were well along the path. The water lost its shape, spread out and filled more of the area, then gathered itself up into a pyramid again. In a couple of swoops, it poured into the grate and the echo of sloshing sounds could be heard throughout the Underground Corridors. It happened very quickly, and the monks looked on in horror. In the Corridors, the attendants switched on the alarms. It was a siren-like wail that could be heard up on the path. Everyone looked in the air for signs of an aircraft or aerial spirits.

When Dennis went into the fountain, he was so taken by the smell of incense that he started at the water and followed the zig zag patterns of the goldfish. Rudolph saw him and came up behind him.

"Why did you run away?"

"I had to," Dennis said, glancing towards the lawns and inhaling deeply as he considered the miniature pagodas.

In the distance they noticed the water spreading and entering the green land of the pagodas. The edges of it covered the outer border of Dome country and whiffs of steam rose in the air as the incense-producing plants were submerged. It seemed as if disaster was about to strike. Steam rose from the coming flood as the entire bramble-bush jungle came to resemble a swamp.

Rudolph was beside himself. "We're doomed. Everything is becoming like the open sea. We might be able to wish for a wall of some sort, a wall with a bottomless moat around it so that the water would fall off."

A mammoth shaking of the earth seemed to indicate an earthquake. Cronicon equated the quake with all the sodomy that had occurred on the island. The new wall could be seen by everyone in the monastery, and though they marveled at its appearance, their only concern now was the water. It had built up considerable momentum as it rushed towards them like a tidal wave.

"This is the Last Judgment!" cried as he watched the first crush of waves hit the distant fields. The sudden appearance of the wall had caused the water to rage in this manner and the reaction was fear and panic.

"Where is the young man from the freighter?" Merton wanted to know. William, who was spoon-feeding someone Cronicon said had HIV-AIDS, got up and searched the monastery to see if he could find Mike. When he returned with Mike a little later, Merton told him that the land was in danger and that they would have to use his boat. Would he go back to the ship and send back some lifeboats to transport everyone?

"William," Merton said, "go into the chapel and get the mummy-baby and the coins. Also, see if you can dislodge the..." He was going to say 'crucifix' but he changed his mind. He really didn't even want the mummy-baby.

"Perhaps the ground shook during an act of sodomy," Cronicon said. "Dennis is at it again! So perhaps, perhaps, this old freighter is to be the Ark. Bless this fine man Mike, who so readily comes to our aid...Bless you, Mike!" Cronicon whistled as Mike hauled one of the lifeboats ashore.

Soon they had everyone is one boat and rowed out towards the freighter. Merton didn't like leaving without Rudolph and Dennis; he considered this a bad sign, but Cronicon was hard-pressed for an immediate exodus. Merton thought about asking Mike to let the lifeboat drift a couple yards out from the shore and wait until the water submerged the island. This way they could row to the Dome and persuade Dennis and Rudolph to return.

The scene in the lifeboat reminded Merton of the lifeboat scene in the movie *Titanic*. Rowing out to the freighter, he tried to imagine his meeting with the Cardinal. Now he would be in the Cardinal's hands and could be assigned to any Midwestern monastery. Merton was also fearful that Cronicon would tell the Cardinal about Dennis and the patched-up hole. That would no doubt convince the Cardinal that Merton had run a house of moral laxity.

On the freighter, the lifeboat people could see the Dome wall in the distance. For many the wall resembled the Tower of Babel or a very small Great Wall of China in the form of a Styrofoam cup. The freighter crew said they could see sailboats and other goings-on on top of it. The idea to travel there once the water reached a considerable depth occurred to several passengers; some people even forgot the dangerous aspects of the event and laughed as if everything was a dream.

Since there was very little food onboard, the crew had no time to wait around until the water on the north end of the island met the front shore. They had no interest in the Dome wall other than to say that it must have been constructed by General Electric when they weren't looking. Most of the crew were tired and horny and wanted to get back to their regular lives as quickly as possible. Some of them even displayed their impatience by telling passengers to step back from the ship railing because it was weak and people had been known to fall overboard. They did this by going around snapping people's hands as they clutched the railing. Some passengers balked and called the men brutes, but this only inflamed the crew so that when someone asked if there were toilets onboard a crew member said, "You'll have to lay it here and throw it to the shrimp."

It was agreed that the freighter wouldn't move out for a day or two in case Dennis or Rudolph floated up to the freighter on a raft. The delay was a precaution Merton was able to obtain from the captain after some pressure. Merton paced the deck and avoided the other passengers but Cronicon's constant scribbling in a notebook aggravated him. Merton's only source of comfort was William, who did his best to cheer him up.

"We cannot worry about the future of the Trappists. Everything is in God's hands. I say we round up the people and play charades."

"I have no spirit for that, I'm afraid," Merton said. "But I'll try if you insist. Call the passengers round."

Cronicon, however, would not play. He sat alone with a pair of binoculars spying on the ship *Conciliar* which was decked out in flamboyant sails. Through the lenses he was able to see the deck boy and the chef spread out a map. Cronicon watched for signs of erections and close physical contact like interlocking hands, a quivering knee, or a sudden-as-lightning posture from the *Karma Sutra.* Much later, it may have been several hours, the freighter passed through a thick fog. It had been going along full speed all this time, and Cronicon had fallen asleep in a deck chair. He awoke to find the fog coming at him in drifts; it was as if some machine were pumping it and he was an actor in a play. Were these supposed to be clouds, this fog? Cronicon called for the captain, and then for a sailor when the captain didn't answer. When there still wasn't an answer, he sensed something wrong. Standing up, he could barely see to walk and had to stretch his arms out in front of him like a blind man. The clouds kept blowing down over the ship, so he was able to reach starboard only by holding onto the deck rail. He stumbled on a plank on the floor, which turned out to be the ship's ramp, and he headed down as if drawn by some mysterious force.

Coming off, he found himself on a dock and he lingered around the ramp calling for help and trying to separate the fog with his arms. He thought perhaps he had died. He expected at any moment to meet the Master yet, instead, he saw the side of a house and an open door. He walked inside. Sudden;y there was no fog, the room was in focus. There was a bed, a desk, and on the radiator he saw a large container of boric acid, a fireplace to his left, and a mirror above it with pictures of motorcycle men around it. The door slammed shut behind him. Everything became instantly clear to him. It was like the Full Magnitude realization that must come after death. Right away he looked out the window for rowboats. He thought he heard a voice – it may or may not have been a recording. It said:

"Okay, now. You row out again until you get it right."

The End

Part II. After All This

<u>Chapter One</u>

We have far to go. I shouldn't have faith, but I do. Julius has told me several things about the terrain. He is – or was – a scientist, and so he should know about such things. The prospect of traveling out over the country, of sleeping under trees and in parking lots and God knows what else, scares me. Part of me wishes I were dead. The rest died so swiftly.

I remember a lightning flash blinking in the sky after three days of darkness. After that things dropped over after something fell from the sky. There was a great noise and screams and then crumbling buildings but at the same time it was clean.

While I experienced only slightly more than a sunburn Julius suffered third degree burns and had to rob an abandoned drugstore for medication. Soon I joined him going into places. At first we ate ourselves silly in empty restaurants. Naturally there was a chance the food was contaminated, but we had to live. I won't describe the horror that greeted us all around. In many ways, however, it wasn't really horror. There were no tortured looks on the faces of the dead. People seemed to be sleeping. As we stepped over the bodies, I said to Julius, "I don't feel anything. The lightning flash must have done something to me – taken away a deep part of my soul."

Julius wept as he turned on the soda spout in a store where we'd gone to get supplies. The soda was cold, and I put my mouth to the spout and drank heavily, a part of me feeling like a rat because I wasn't mourning the dead who were all around me on the floor.

In my apartment, we ate what we could from the things we brought back with us. We had to eat fast because there was no refrigeration and everything good would soon spoil. Then there'd be nothing except the canned goods and the cereals in the supermarkets, so we filled up on submarines, cold Swiss cheese and beer.

We looked out over the city. There was not much movement and we could see ruins everywhere. I told him how quiet everything was, and how we were lucky to have each other. "I wonder how many others are alive," I said.

Julius said there had to be other survivors.

"We will find them in time," I said. After all, while it seemed that the worst was over, I still felt scared, especially at night when we could hear strange sounds in the city. Perhaps some parked cars or a home gas range suddenly and for no apparent reason exploded. But more than anything, I feared a return of the lightning flash. I knew I was lucky to be alive, even if it appeared that only Julius and I had survived. We weren't Adam and Eve, or even Adam and Steve, but at least we were company for each other. And who, after all, would want to bring children into a world such as this?

Often I went around to television appliance shops and searched to see if I could find a live signal. I never even got static. With all communication snuffed out, I felt the severity of the situation even more.

The entire country may be like this," I told Julius. "Even the world....What are we going to do, live in New York until we die?"

# # # # #

One night Julius was weeping again into his pillow. I didn't say anything but sat at the kitchen table and buried my own head in my arms. I said a prayer to Saint Mark – I had an icon of him on my desk. Looking at the icon now, in light of the setting sun, I could feel it trying to speak to me. But attempting to discern the message of the saint was confusing and unclear. It seemed only to communicate a general faith that things would be okay – different, but okay. Julius wanted to leave New York in order to find other survivors; he was convinced there were none here, otherwise someone would have answered our daily round of whistle blowing. Julius wanted to go into an Old Navy store, get two knapsacks, fill them up with necessities then take off to see the rest of the country. We argued about this every night. My arguments were the same. We are safe here, so why move out? God knows what awaited us out there. "Since the towers fell, I vowed I would never leave New York like a scared rabbit," I told him. But Julius said he'd been having this recurring dream about another lightning flash.

"If there's another one, I know we won't be so lucky," he said. I finally listened to him.

So Julius and I went into a store and found two knapsacks, sleeping bags, and other equipment we felt we might need. Then we found two bicycles. It wasn't possible to take an automobile from the street. Something about the flash had rendered them inoperable. The bicycles seemed the best bet.

We rode back to the apartment through midtown Manhattan. We had to swerve our bicycles around the cadavers. We were both shocked when we saw the corpses of Anderson Cooper, Madonna and Lady Gaga all within a block of one another. Mayor Bloomberg was slumped down inside a NYPD patrol car. Cardinal Timothy Dolan was laying face down on the steps of Saint Patrick's cathedral.

It was all I could do to keep pedaling. I no sooner thought "Who's next?" when we saw all the employees of Goldman-Sachs melded together like a Jacques Lipchitz sculpture; something apparently had struck them in a such a way that their bodies joined and formed a twisted, discombobulated blob that seemed to reach for the stars.

Sometimes we got off our bikes and stooped down to examine their faces. A couple of times I had to fight a compulsion to touch them about the forehead and smooth their hair back with my hand. Julius had no such reservation, however. He would touch a cheek or stroke a chin and say, "Look at this beautiful person!"

It was truly sad and, on the night we packed, we didn't say much to one another. I placed the icon of Saint Mark inside my knapsack. Tomorrow we would be off.

#

We rode across midtown Manhattan and then came to the freeway. I hadn't expected to see a line of stopped automobiles and trucks stretching into the horizon. Most of the vehicles were on top of one another and many were scattered over embankments and whatnot as a result of the flash.

An overturned Greyhound bus really got to Julius. I thanked my lucky stars I wasn't in a car when it happened. My hope is that everybody died instantly.

It was difficult to steer a course through the sea of automobiles. In some areas they blocked the highway and Julius and I had to walk our bikes way around them.

We both stopped dead in our tracks when we saw what looked to be Sarah Jessica Parker atop a flagpole. Perhaps Ms. Parker was thrown from one of the thousands of cars trying to leave the city. We then saw a just a face on an embankment with hair that looked like Donald Trump's.

We had gone only about a mile out of New York when Julius turned to me and said, "We're going to die if we go on like this. I say we go back and forget the whole thing."

Once I'm on the road going somewhere, I cannot turn back. I said, "Julius, that wouldn't be sensible. You said yourself another flash was imminent."

I stood beside my bike and surveyed the landscape. Not far ahead of us was a family-style restaurant next to a farm. Behind it were fields that looked like they might house cattle or horses.

"Come on, Julius, we might be lucky and find a wagon and then we can hitch up a horse."

Julius looked at me like I was mad. "Next you'll be saying we'll find saddlebags."

We walked our bicycles over a field and, as we approached the restaurant, I said how amazing it was that a place like this was so close to the city. It was startling because you could still see the skyline and here we were in what looked like open country. By the time we walked on the property, we saw that there was one horse left alive, an old thing with pink spots, walking backwards over the trough. It looked kind of crazed. All the other horses were dead; there was no sign of people although they had probably died inside the buildings.

Julius studied the horse. "I think we should pull it!"

"I'll just look in the shed to see if there's a wagon or something, and you can lasso that horse for us."

I found a flat wagon in the back of the shed, the kind farmers use to transport bales of hay. With a little work we could have fashioned it into a Conestoga wagon.

Julius was having trouble with the horse. It was kicking something fierce. The flash had driven it crazy. But he kept at it, shouting at it and using his arm to drive it toward the flat car. We finally got it hitched. "I don't like this one bit. We don't know where we're going, and this horse is half dead," Julius said.

All I could think of was the great covered wagon Mormon pioneer trek to Salt Lake City. "Haven't you ever wanted to be a pioneer? There's destruction all around so we really have no choice. It's up to us to explore, settle, and pick up people, whatever. Life must go on at any cost."

"Why? Life is futile and without meaning. The dead are the lucky ones." Julius was very unhappy although I knew he really didn't want to go back to New York. He was sick of Manhattan every bit as much as I was.

"You know," I said, "it won't be so bad. We have each other, and we have this horse. We don't need other people. Everybody else is dead anyway. Our love is all we need. "

I really didn't feel that exuberant. I was trying to sound more positive so Julius would get a move on. He was starting to bite his nails and take on that faraway look that meant he would soon hang his head and sink into a complete depression. If past behavior was an accurate barometer, he'd stop eating, keep insisting that life was futile and useless, and mention suicide as a possible out. Then he would suffer an anger streak that would inevitably draw us into ugly arguments.

Finally we were ready to see if the horse could pull the wagon. I was doing the driving. I moved the reins and shouted to the horse. It started moving, not very fast, but it did move. When we were a little way off from the farm, I asked Julius what he wanted to call the horse, and he said "The End."

"Now that," I said to him, "is a perfect example of your pessimism; why not The Beginning?"

We ended up calling the horse Flash.

That night, we were sitting around a campfire next to a housing development. Flash was tied to a telephone pole while we cooked some eggs. Julius was pretty upset because he had to step over this pretty girl lying nude on the floor in order to go into the kitchen. He was really depressed, thinking he had fallen in love with her and wishing he could bring her back to life.

When Julius was drinking his coffee, I went into the house to take a look at her. She looked like she was taking a nap. "I see what you mean," I told him, "but she's dead."

Julius looked away. As much as we loved each other, he needed a woman.

When I got up in the middle of the night, I saw that Julius wasn't in his sleeping bag. I called out his name, and then thought of that poor girl lying in the kitchen. I thought, oh no, not necrophilia!

# # # # #

The next morning the air was filled with smog. It smelled like rusted aluminum and you were forced to take little breaths so as not to take in too much of it.

Julius came out of the house and walked to the wagon. I didn't say anything but sat there staring at the sky. I knew that any other earth changes would happen from the sky. The sky was the key. A voice I had heard while meditating told me to look in the sky for signs and symbols. As far as Julius is concerned, he has got to realize that he's not the only one with sexual feelings....

"Look, why don't we scramble some more eggs," he said, looking satisfied but worn out. There were rings around his eyes and his face sagged downward in a sad sort of way.

"I've already eaten." That was a lie. I had eggs last night and I was sick of them. I was sick of plunging through kitchens and stepping over dead people to get food. I was also angry because I had hoped that Julius would call me to be his lover, given the world's dire circumstances. Am I not better than a corpse? "Why don't we just hop on the wagon, slap Flash in the ass, and be off," I said. "I need some new surroundings."

"Me too," he said, squatting next to the sleeping bag. "You know, this could be exciting. I mean, as you say, we're the only ones alive, and there must be a reason for that. Maybe we have a mission to fulfill!"

Chapter Two

We started out again over the field. Julius was driving. I sat in the back sulking and looked at the countryside as we drove parallel to the freeway to Philadelphia.

For a long while we didn't say anything. It was peaceful. I had draped a sheet over the back of the wagon for a covered wagon effect. In this space, I set up our sleeping bags.

I was sound asleep when Julius brought the wagon to a stop. I heard him talking to someone. I shot up and looked through the sheet.

A boy and a girl couple in their twenties stood talking to Julius. The girl had short dark bobbed hair, dark eyes, and tattoos. The boy wore a knit hat and had a rather sparse goatee. They were holding hands.

Julius wanted to know how long the two of them had been walking around. The girl told him six days. They were shopping when the flash happened. They both fainted and when they came to everyone around them was dead. "Do you want to ride with us?" Julius asked.

They said yes, so we helped them into the back of the wagon. Julius took the reins again. We were near a complex of four different freeway entrances and automobiles were piled high all around us. It was a very depressing sight.

The girl's name was Melissa. She had a habit of pushing her hair away from her forehead whenever she spoke. The boy seemed disturbed about something. I noticed she kept holding his hand and rubbing his knuckles while he answered my questions. They said they were from suburban, New York. They were sure that everyone they knew was dead.

"Everyone I know is probably dead too," I offered. They wanted to know what I did, and I told them that I used to be a monk. They laughed rather nervously and then grew quiet. The girl fell asleep with her head on the boy's shoulder, and I admit I felt very lonely, watching that. A couple of times at night I'd wake up finding that I had unconsciously thrown my arm around Julius. He had done the same thing to me.

That night after we finished eating, Melissa and Brian just stared into the campfire. Their silence made me nervous.

At last Julius said, "Well, I'm turning in," and went inside the wagon.

"You know, you two," I whispered, "You can do whatever you want – as long as you're quiet."

"We intend to do whatever we want, with or without your permission," Melissa said, smiling. When the three of us went into the wagon later on, Julius was lying face down, naked, and the sight of his muscular buttocks drew an exasperated "Oh!" from all of us. He was in a deep sleep. It was hard to imagine how he could have fallen asleep so quickly, unless of course it was a plan to arouse some sort of group dynamic. I put a cover over him but, before I did, I caught Brian looking at him in a most peculiar way. The gleam in his eye lasted maybe a quarter of a second but when I covered Julius with a blanket, I knew that something important had transpired.

That night, not a sound from Melissa and Brian; there was only an occasional rustling of the bed gear. I had a rough time going to sleep. I found myself wanting them to make noises, just like I had done when I was in the monastery so long ago.

The next morning I was up collecting wood for the fire. I heard a stirring in the wagon and in a few minutes Melissa came out, brushing her hair and smoking. She told me she was originally from Rhode Island, and then added that she hailed from a wealthy family in the fishing business. I asked her why she left, and she said she left to try her hand at modeling in New York City.

I asked her where Brian was from and she said Altoona, Pennsylvania, a coal mining district where he was kicked out of his house because of a substance abuse problem.

"Was it heroin?"

She said yes, plus Oxy and Perkoset though he managed to kick heroin after hitchhiking first to Pittsburgh, then Philadelphia, and finally to New York. She said he took a variety of odd jobs along the way but that mostly he begged for money outside of convenience stores when he was not hustling men for sex. I admired the nonchalant way she said this. She seemed to accept the fact and made no bones about it one way or another.

"He'd go to this store in Philly's Fishtown section and ask customers if they had any jobs for him to do; jobs meaning anything from heavy lifting to sex."

I told her that I had met many hustlers and that I understood some of the troubles they encountered.

"Well," she said, "Brian is really sexual and free and so the sex with men angle didn't bother him. When I first met him he was really strung out. I talked my parents into letting him stay and work in the family fishing business. So we became friends.

"But it was too restrictive or peaceful for him because one Friday night he slipped away to New York City without telling me. He came back the following Monday. I cornered him but he just acted like he could do anything and there were no rules to follow. We kind of forgot this escapade for a while, but then he wanted to go back to the city. I asked him, "What's going on?" and he lashed out and said, "it's no woman," and that's when I knew there was a secret in his life. So I followed him one weekend into the city, and where does he go? He goes to this porno movie house near the bus terminal. I'm thinking, 'What the hell?' and don't know whether to follow him in there, but I do. It was very dark with all these men standing around, and then I see Brian...."

Melissa paused because she thought she heard a noise coming from the wagon. I thought I heard something also but dismissed it as someone turning over in their sleep.

"Any who," she says, "he goes up to the balcony, strutting like he's been there before, and do you know what? Three men go up after him. When I went up there myself, I couldn't believe what I saw. All these half dressed men and Brian sitting in a seat way off in a dark corner with two men on either side of him, with Brian telling them what he liked as more and more men came over. He didn't care who the men were. Some were huge with enormous bellies; some were so old they were bumping into things and one guy was even taking out his teeth. It was a mob scene with men grabbing and pulling and groaning. I was never so disgusted. I mean, here were men whispering into his ear…the same era I whisper into! Finally I had to leave, and I went to a coffee shop across the street and waited until I saw Brian leave with this little fellow in bifocals and a Bowler hat. They were walking fast like they had plans big enough to fill the universe.

"Well, I went home really pissed and tried to forget about it, and when he came back Sunday night I pretended nothing had happened. In fact, what I did was tell him that I had had my first lesbian experience with my best friend, Opal Bean, just to see how he would react. I said that Opal Bean and I were out on Daddy's boat when Opal reached over and grabbed hold of my legs and pulled me towards her. I told him that the motion nearly turned the boat over and that before I could say 'Oh no!' half my clothes were off and Opal was down there claming, causing me to have the biggest orgasm ever. Brian looked real worried and wanted to know if it was better than when we did it, and I told him, 'Honey, it was Apolycoptic!' Well, he cracked up totally. He called me a faggot – get that – and said that what I did was unnatural and that I should only do these things when he is there."

Just then Brian jumped off the wagon and came over to where we were sitting. He had on one of Julius' shirts and the ends of it were tied over his navel. He was smoking a cigarette when he sat down by the fire. He didn't say a word but hung his head as if in deep contemplation.

Melissa asked him if he wanted some French toast.

"Yeah." He shook his head, and looked over at me as I whipped up another bowl of batter. He took a long drag from his cigarette, and then ground it into the dirt with his left foot before lying back with his arms behind his head.

"We don't even know where the fuck this lightning came from."

"From China, silly," Melissa said, shaking a bottle of syrup.

"Where do you think, Dennis?" Brian said.

"It's a chastisement of some sort. God has had it with this sorry world. It needed a good cleansing and got it. We survived the impossible."

"You don't really believe that crap, do you?"

"All I know is this sort of thing has been predicted for years – the Mayan calendar, Nostradumus, the Bible, and the Fatima lady. The list goes on and on. Was all that crap?"

"Yeah well, I put my faith in science." After that Brian didn't have anything to say. In the wagon I heard Julius bumping into things. He cursed; parts of his body could be seen protruding through the wagon sheet as he fidgeted about.

"Does your friend have a mental problem?" Melissa asked, handing Brian his French toast.

"Who took my Albanian V-neck sweater?" Julius shouted, sticking his head out of the back of the wagon.

"They make sweaters in Albania? Hey, I think you have bigger things to worry about. We may be the only people in the world left standing, not to mention that our job now is to repopulate the planet," I said.

Melissa laughed as Julius, upset, walked over to Brian and gently nudged him with his right foot. "You," he said. "You have my sweater on. It's not nice to help yourself to other people's clothes."

"Take the sweater off and give it to him," Melissa said.

"He knows why I had to wear it," Brian said, pointing to Julius. "Remember, the soiled Y-shirt?"

"Stop!" Julius blurted out, quickly retreating to the wagon, but it was too late. Brian removed the sweater and went in after him.

A little later, as we sat around the fire eating, Melissa threw down her fork. "Do you see that?"

We looked up and saw a bird; it looked like a hawk as it made a wide circle over our camp. It was the first live animal of any kind we had seen since finding Flash. Where there were birds, there were live squirrels, possums, rodents, feral cats, and possibly people who were not dead.

As we pondered the bird, Brian was rubbing his stomach and yawning. He looked so beautiful lying there; I wanted to go over and sit next to him, but couldn't move. Melissa seemed to have me under some kind of spell. I found that I was able to view Brian's beauty without becoming unduly excited. There didn't seem to be enough magnetism in the attraction to draw me toward him just then. I was more than content to discuss things with Melissa.

We decided to spend as much time as possible in Philadelphia. We agreed to abandon the wagon for a while after we found an available house or apartment to inhabit.

Together, the four of us walked into the city and headed down Walnut Street towards Rittenhouse Square. Of course, as in Manhattan, dead bodies, buses and automobiles littered the streets.

In the Square, we sat on a bench with our eyes fixed on the piles of dead pigeons. A fountain was still running and Brian took off his pants and stepped into the pool. Had he done this only two weeks before, he would have been arrested and dragged off to jail. Now we could join him if we wished, but watching Brian dip his buttocks into the fountain seemed to satisfy us. Julius, however, took a dim view of it. Again, I don't know what I would have done without Melissa. She seemed to take the edge off what I would normally have felt for Brian, and so I sat there with her and laughed at him as if I really wasn't sexually attracted. I even wanted to put my head on Melissa's shoulder. Julius became more than displeased, noticing my involvement with Melissa. He came back with what I can only call an attack when Melissa got up and went over to the edge of the fountain and sat down.

"I don't understand women. How the hell are you able to make headway with her? You don't even like her."

"It's because I don't like her the way you do that she feels comfortable with me."

"You know what I mean. You like Brian. Well, if you like him so much how can you stand to see him dancing in that fountain with his pants off? If Melissa did that, I'd go nuts."

"Melissa mitigates the attraction I feel to Brian."

"She's some woman," Julius added, watching as Melissa dipped her hands into the fountain. His other eye was somewhere else; I guess on Brian, who had climbed to the top of the statue in the middle of the pool.

"Have you told Brian how you feel?" Julius asked, his hand over his mouth as if the words would be picked up by electronic eavesdropping.

"I can count the number of words I've said to him."

"Do you think those two have fucked yet when we weren't looking?"

"Julius, I don't know. Melissa's with me most of the time, and you and Brian have been together most of the time."

"Is that how you really see it?" Julius said, with an exaggerated look of surprise.

"Last night you two went off together. This morning you slept late with him in the wagon. And what's this soiled T-shirt thing?"

"What are you trying to say? " Julius put his hands on his hips like a boy accused of stealing.

"Just the obvious, you fool. You are spending most of your time with him. Things have just worked out that way, that's all."

"Well, we have to change that. I mean, if you like Brian and I like Melissa, I'd say we're going about this wrong. When they come back, you go t to Brian and I'll do my thing with Melissa."

"Forced attractions never work."

"They are the only things that do work."

When Melissa and Brian came over to the bench, we made sure that Brian sat next to me and that Melissa sat next to Julius. Brian had goose bumps on his skin, and his wet hair was dripping on my trousers.

"I wish I had a towel to give you," I said.

"Man, I could use a 100% cotton squeeze."

On the other side of the bench, I heard Julius whisper to Melissa: "I've had it with cotton. There's nothing like a pair of strong hands."

Melissa uttered a cursory "Awesome," then leaned back to get a view of me. "Dennis, you know…"

Julius cut her off. "Brian told me something about you fishing for clams with your feet from your Father's pier; wow, I mean how did you do that?"

"The whole family used their feet," she said.

Brian slouched down on the bench. Not only did he have a seductive look, there were droplets of water on both his nipples.

"Melissa told me about your walk on New York's wild side," I said.

"Yeah, I was once one of Allen Ginsberg's boys."

"'Who lost their love boys to the three old shrews of fate, the one eyed shrew of the heterosexual dollar, the one eyed shrew that winks out of the womb,'" Melissa quoted Ginsberg, laughing.

By the end of the conversation, I could see that all our necks were strained. We were relieved to get up from the bench and begin a leisurely walk around the city. We went back into our usual grouping, which seemed unavoidable. Melissa had an idea to tour some art galleries, while Brian wanted Julius to accompany him into a sports equipment store.

"We'll wait for you guys," Melissa said.

Together we went into the gallery, stepped over the dead sales clerk, and studied the first painting.

I put my hand on her shoulder and started squeezing. "Look at this, pure Philadelphia – scenes of barns, cows, and old country homes." I found myself stroking her left shoulder and pulling her towards me as we stood looking at a watercolor of City Hall in the snow.

I could smell something in her hair. I looked down at her breasts. They were small and firm, not much bigger than a boy's, but better, I thought, as I tried to turn her towards me full face. Before I knew it, we were kissing. I ran my hand over her hair and down the back of her buttocks.

"What would Brian do if he walked in on us, now?" I offered.

"He would clobber us," she said, "But what do you think those two are up to you, anyway?"

"I bet every hair on my body they're rubbing their hands all over sports equipment," I replied, my tongue headed for her ear.

Melissa and I wound up waiting for them on the steps of the gallery. When they appeared, they were carrying a rubber raft so that only their legs were visible as they crossed Walnut Street with the raft on the top of their heads.

"Where were you two doing?" Melissa inquired, exaggerating 'doing' in such a way that Julius took the raft off his head, somewhat panic stricken.

"We thought maybe you two decided to run away to San Francisco," I said.

Julius' embarrassment was obvious; he did not like it that he and Brian were being referred to as a couple even as he noticed that Melissa and I were beginning to do just that.

"What do you guys have under your arms?" Melissa pointed to some horseshoe-shaped irons.

"Quoits," Brian said, "we can fix 'em up by the river."

"I hate Quoits," Melissa said, "they're not ecological because they dig up the earth. Why didn't you guys get a badminton set? It doesn't matter, I really love you guys. We're all a family now."

# # # # #

Brian had trouble sleeping that night. We didn't know what was wrong until he left the wagon in a huff, mumbling something. It woke all of us. Julius asked Melissa, who seemed troubled, what was wrong.

"He couldn't perform. He failed. He tried and tried but he couldn't do it. Nothing we tried worked, even the fantasies I used to tell him fell flat."

"Old Chinese proverb says, 'man with erection walking through door sideways is always going to Bangkok,'" Julius said, stifling a laugh.

117

"He's far from that because he's had this problem for days now."

"I had no idea you two made so many attempts."

"He thinks the flash did it. He thinks the flash contaminated him."

"I'm not contaminated," Julius said. "Are you, Dennis?"

"Well, how would I know?" I told him.

"We'll talk to Brian tonight," Julius offered.

Brian returned about an hour later. I wasn't asleep yet so I could see him get into his sleeping bag. He was mumbling all sorts of nasty things. I didn't want to disturb him, so I lay there in the stillness with him, knowing we were the only ones awake.

Things broke when, later that night, I awoke again. I heard Brian mumble in sleep, "Julius, Julius!" I turned and looked, and saw the poor kid all balled up in a fetal position with one hand over his eyes – the very same position in which I mumbled Melissa's name, very softly, two nights ago.

Very strange things are happening here, I thought to myself.

"Julius! Julius!"

Brian kept repeating the name in a sort of groaning chant that got louder and louder until it woke Julius up. I had to get up for this. I went to the side of the wagon and watched them in the dark.

The flash had done it. Brian was right. We were contaminated.

# # # # #

The next day when I had Julius alone, I asked him, "Julius...remember there are no people around and as far as we know we may be the only people in the world. Have you been thinking strongly about Brian the last few days? Try to answer truthfully."

"I feel for him like a brother," Julius said. "I might even love him like a brother. Is that what you're saying?"

"No, not that exactly," I said. "I know you're strictly a ladies man and all that..." I tried to humor him, but it was no good. His face reddened. "Julius, I think a very important thing in our lives has been changed. I don't know how to begin to tell you this, especially if you don't open up to me."

"I haven't had any Brian-related wet dreams if that's what you mean," Julius said.

"More specifically, are you sexually attracted to him?"

His reaction was a mix of surprise and anger. Finally, after some silence, he faced me. "You know?" he said calmly.

"Julius, I cannot stop thinking about Melissa, and I know that Brian cannot stop thinking about you. He says your name when he's asleep!"

"Yes, but, think about it, I cannot imagine myself as a homosexual, and you with Melissa – you, once the biggest fag activist in Manhattan."

We were silent a long time.

"So, what do we do about this?" Julius asked.

"As soon as we can, we'll bring everyone together and talk about it."

"When?"

"Tomorrow at noon."

# # # # #

At noon the next day, I got up in front of everyone and told them what I thought had occurred. No one seemed surprised; it seemed that on a certain level, we had all been reaching the same conclusion. When I had finished, Melissa came up to me and held my hand. "I love you," she said, "We are really a family now." Julius and Brian seemed to walk around one another. It was embarrassing to see. They did not have the courage to go "public" with their feelings. Every once in a while they would look at one another, but there was no touching.

I felt it was a proud moment, but I wanted Julius and Brian to loosen up. I looked Brian in the eye. "This is no time for passive-aggressive behavior. Tonight marks a new beginning. Tonight let's sleep in different sections of the camp to mark in order to establish boundaries as couples. We will light two separate bonfires and dance to mark the new beginning. In the morning, we will officially be couples."

Silly or not, Melissa shouted "Good start," and immediately drew me down to the ground where I felt something cold rise up from the bottom of my belly. I groped blindly for a minute because while I felt attracted to her, the idea of having sex with a woman wanted to interfere. I imagined Julius wrestling with the same issue inside the wagon with Brian. "What's the matter?" Melissa asked, "You're trembling."

"Relapse, maybe," I said. "I don't know. For a moment I felt as if I were falling into a big, black hole."

"Well, you are," she said, laughing.

"It's hard to explain, it's something deep and psychic..." But before I could get the rest of the words out, she drew me towards her and suddenly the fear was gone.

Later, I asker her, "I wonder how they made out." I called Julius' name.

"No, you shouldn't call him." She was pressing her body against mine and putting her hand over my mouth. "They must be in the thick of it. Listen, I hear them laughing. Julius is laughing. He's gotten over his gay panic. Hey, you guys! Come over here and join the party!"

"You're a prophet, Dennis" It was Julius. He was shouting, "Dennis, you're a prophet. It worked. Oh, Dennis, I feel like I could level the breakers in the ocean. I am on fire. Brian, let's dance a circle around Dennis."

There was a mad scrambling over the grass as a nude Brian and Julius began to dance in a circle around Melissa and me. It was a primitive, over enthusiastic display, their genitals and buttocks creating quite a memorable visual.

Chapter Three

Two months passed. We had time to settle into our respective relationships and Melissa and I were like an old married couple. In fact, she was pregnant and at night around the campfire, I would put my head on her lap and listen for baby sounds. Brian and Julius had also progressed; they now held hands in our presence. We all slept together in double sleeping bags, perfectly content and happy. Melissa and I were content to stay in Philadelphia and start a flower garden, but Julius and Brian wanted to move on. Decked out in theatrical buckskin pants and fringed suede vests – all from the local Army and Navy store – they looked like Lewis and Clark.

Their baby was adventure, going out together and coming back with the things they found on their journeys. They had taken quite a few rifles and guns from a gun shop and were anxiously waiting the day when they would spot live game. Melissa and I expected them to leave the city any day on a permanent expedition.

It was quite a day when they raided one of the museums in the city and came back with an authentic Conestoga covered wagon. It was a real beauty. With two wagons by the river, we had a real encampment. At night we played banjos, guitars, and rested our heads on each other's laps.

Summer passed into autumn, autumn passed into winter, and we decided to move into one of the many available apartments on Rittenhouse Square. We had not done so before because of the number of rotting corpses there, but now the process of decay had solidified many of the dead into mummified moveable bits. At first we wanted to move into the former home of Henry Mcilhenny at 1914 Rittenhouse Square. I wanted to soak up the history and the ambience there, since it was once the home of Philadelphia's most famous art collector. Andy Warhol, kings and queens, and notable actors had visited and stayed at the place. We didn't expect problem but were dismayed upon entering to find piles of corpses sunk into the floorboards. As an alternative, we took one of the more lavish apartments with three bedrooms and all kinds of books and corridors and balconies and decks. Oddly enough, I was able to ascertain that it was once the apartment of Philadelphia newspaper heir John S. Knight, a gay man who was murdered by two hustlers in the 1970s. The murder was international news and was later documented in the book, *Kings Don't Mean a Thing* by Arthur Bell.

The nice thing about the apartment was that we had a great view of the Square from our living room window. Gone, at least for the moment, was any thought of moving on.

# # # # #

Trouble came when the baby was born. Isn't that always the case? I don't know why, but nobody bothered to name it. It was also a flat out scary baby, and it would not stop crying. It screamed so much that Brian and Julius were forced to leave the apartment and take another one underneath us. I had a bad feeling about this development.

"Take the baby for a walk in the Square," Melissa was always telling me.

I would wheel it through the cold Square over mummified squirrel carcasses, and pass empty benches and bare bone trees. Brian and Julius would often see me and come out and we'd have a chat. "How's baby?" they would say, as if they wished they could have a baby themselves.

"Why don't you leave it with us some night," Julius kept asking.

After a while, I mentioned this to Melissa. "Julius keeps asking to borrow the baby for a night. What do you suppose he's up to?"

"Just lonely," I suppose, Melissa said. "You know, he and Brian only have one another, whereas we have a real family. We're moving up; they're staying the same!"

She was correct, of course. Yet I felt differently towards Melissa now than I did when we were joined together in the campfire ceremony back at the wagon. I felt that the baby was the apex of a triangle and that we were connected underneath, the two lines going up to meet it. I felt trapped in this prism, this magnetic geometry, and I felt a new pressure – a sense of jealousy – especially when I'd look out the apartment window and see Julius and Brian going about their business.

The baby grew fat and charming. As winter grew into spring, we left the apartment more and more. Our baby, as far as we knew, was the

122

first baby born after the flash. Melissa wanted to call the baby Adam. This was only natural. We discussed this with Julius and Brian when we brought the baby down to them and sat it on their sofa.

"I think if you call it Adam, you will come dangerously close to duplicating what had gone on before. Call it something else. This is a New Age. We will build Heaven on earth." Julius seemed perfectly adamant.

"If you go the Adam route, what about Eve?" Brian said when Melissa was out of the room.

I said, "I don't want to put too much importance on a name. Melissa has gotten very serious about our role in the universe. She lectures me every night on the mission she says we have to accomplish. She says history will record our deeds, and it is important that we do it right. When baby was born she said he would be a great leader, and that we had to watch out, and teach him well. At first I didn't believe her. I said, 'Look, he's just a normal little baby, like any other baby,' but then she said, 'No, look into his eyes at night, look into them for a long time and you will see."

Brian and Julius thought that Melissa had gone off her rocker. It was painful to have to sit and defend her. Every night she would go outside and gaze up at the stars. What was she watching – for some kind of sign? I said, "She says that on the eve of baby's birth, she saw two comets intersect and form a zigzag pattern in the sky, making an X directly over our apartment. Then she saw some forms in the clouds."

"And so she thinks X marks the spot and that was the sign?" Julius said, staring at baby, who had just begun to slump onto the arm of the chair.

"The baby looks like every other baby to me," Brian said, unable to mask a sneer. Since Melissa wasn't in the room, Brian felt free to sit next to it on the sofa. He took the baby's right hand into his own and began rubbing its fingers. He leaned over and spoke directly into the baby's face. "Hey, are you a real baby or what?"

Melissa returned, saw the smiles on our faces, and was not happy. I knew I was going to get it when we returned to our apartment.

"The new baby must not have the contamination of the Old World," she said, after which she said she didn't want Brian to roughhouse with it.

I told all of this to Julius, who took offense at the word 'roughhouse' and adopted a different attitude towards Melissa from that day on. I tried to act as a peacemaker but gradually, I could see that there was little hope of reconciliation. We had thought by now that we'd meet other people or at least be rescued in some way. We did not expect to be stuck in the same Limbo. Baby seemed a way out.

When I finally did look into baby's eyes, I saw, or thought I saw, a glimmer of something – a sparkle of light with a depth that convinced me of its divine origin.

"There's hope for the world in this child," I said

Melissa, who was in a nightgown and leaning in our bedroom doorway when I said this, moved into the room and put her hands on my shoulders. From then on I knew we were a team with a very special, world mission.

It was unfortunate that our relationship with Brian and Julius had begun to disintegrate since the appearance of the comet. Little by little, Melissa began to believe that Brian and Julius didn't fall into the Scheme; that they wouldn't matter unless they committed themselves to Baby as she and I had done. "If they come around and honor Baby then our heads and hearts will be unified. Until then, we will be fragmented and they will live in schism." Melissa also expected Brian and Julius to separate if they ever met up with women survivors. "Allen Ginsberg be damned. The race must continue; we cannot afford the luxury of homosexuality." Her new formalized tone, I decided, must have coincided with the comet. I knew it was no use arguing about the permanent change the Flash had instilled in our sexual natures.

Meanwhile, Baby was learning to talk. Melissa spent long hours with it as I combed the city for various baby things like bassinettes, cribs, high chairs, and play pens. Baby suddenly had become the reason for our existence, and Melissa wanted only the best, so she drove me to keep coming back with nicer and more imaginative artifacts. Since I also believed in Baby's mission, I helped with the alphabet lessons, and even went so far as to obtain cardboard and construction paper for a special drawing of the two comets that we placed over the primary crib.

Melissa would often stand at the apartment window and watch Brian and Julius walk through Rittenhouse Square. She had convinced herself that they were searching for an additional sex partner, a young male survivor they could take back to their bedroom. "How can they live apart from Baby's divinity?" she wondered, while pointing out signs of unhappiness all over them. "Look at the way Brian is walking – like he yearns to know, to release his mind to the spring." She always called Baby "the spring" and even referred to him as *The Great Thaw*. "When Baby is older, they will have to come to him," she said, shutting the drapes and returning to the sofa where she observed me giving Baby a bath.

Melissa was writing a Great Book. Pages and pages of it, all in longhand, and in one of those expensive leather bound volumes sketch artists used to use. She had one volume filled with a complicated Plan of Action derived from messages received from Baby. She had appendix chapters on rules and codes of behavior.

She had such tremendous faith; I don't think mine matched hers because sometimes I would become upset by little things Baby did, like the times it would crawl away from us in the living room to go off by itself and sit in a corner behind us where it would then proceed to stare. This was an unsettling development, especially since I always felt its little blue eyes boring a hole into the back of my head so that my only thought was turning around so that it would not be behind me. When I would do this, Melissa would shout "Don't" and I'd get so frustrated that I'd often get up and leave the apartment for a walk in the park or I'd sneak down to Brian and Julius' place. I could never be with them for long because not only would I soon begin to resent their not believing but I would feel Baby's vibrations begin to take control of my brain.

"I have to leave now, guys," I'd tell them. And then I'd run upstairs to our place quickly. Melissa would know instantly where I was no matter how hard I tried to hide it, and she'd give me Baby's secret salute, which was a raised thumb and little finger on the right hand.

What was Baby's mission? I asked Melissa this one night and, by doing so, admitted my lack of faith.

"Something like actualization and deliverance," she answered, "The building of a new kingdom on earth."

"Yes," I said, recalling all of my doubts in this area.

"You see there!" she said, pointing to Baby who had his fist in the air and was getting ready to slam it down hard on the high chair tray.

"Please tell Baby I am sorry, because I cannot stand that noise."

"I will this time," she said. After that all she had to do was look at Baby in a certain way and all would be calm. This sort of thing was nothing less than some sort of witchcraft, the result of a unique bond between Baby and Melissa. Baby liked Melissa much better than it liked me. Perhaps he sensed my lack of faith and knew about my periodic visits to see Brian and Julius.

Every so often I would get disapproving looks from it... Dagger looks – real soul depth searching looks – as well as a baby pout that sent its fat cheeks on a downward sag, so that underneath all the baby fat I sensed a powerful force.

The first time I saw this, I covered my eyes and mumbled "Oh no!" Melissa was fixing toast for the three of us when I blurted this out, but she dropped everything and said, "Did you know Baby knows everything? Your every thought and desire, everything?"

The thought, 'this is horrible' ran through my mind and even this communicated itself to Baby, who seemed to be smiling crookedly and communicating some terrible feeling to me. I knew then that whatever happened, Baby and I would always be at odds – no matter how much I tried to get along with it, and no matter what I did for it. Perhaps someday we'd come to terrible blows.

"Oh take this curse from me!" I called out in desperation one night in the Square, but no one heard me. I couldn't believe it when I heard a rapping at a window and looked up to find Melissa holding Baby out to me.

I wanted so much to talk to Julius, but I was afraid. Half of me believed in Baby, and half of me hated it. Finally I went down to Julius' apartment after Melissa left with Baby for a stroll in the Square.

"I have to talk to you," I told him. "Things are really bad. Sometimes I can't live with Baby. Melissa told me more or less that it is the world's Little Horn, the new savior; that it sees, hears and knows everything. Sometimes I think I will crack from the strain. I really believe that Baby has a hold on something…"

"What thing?" Julius said.

"The flash –everything. How we're living."

"How you're living, maybe," he said. "I've been happy, more or less. No people. Free access to stores, shops and houses. So whatever you want."

"It won't last, Julius. The time will come when the supply dries up. Then we'll be reduced to cavemen."

"Cavemen living in a high rise maybe. So what? They'll always be dried or smoked goods around. Consider the size of this city, all the canned goods…all the supplies."

"It won't last. She says so in her Plan of Action log. She gives it another year. She wrote that whatever radiation the flash dispelled will eat through canned goods and contaminate them."

"Melissa's Plan of Action?" Julius replied, walking over to his large living room window and looking out onto the street.

"She says that Baby will lead us to a new place. And she says that there are two women alive somewhere between here and Kansas City, that we will meet someday and that you and Brian will have to marry. She also wants you guys to stop canvassing the city in search of young male survivors to have sex with, because she says if you continue to do this she'll have no choice but to get Baby involved."

"Melissa said that?" said a shocked Julius, returning to the sofa. "Brian and I am a committed couple, but you know how men are after a while. Look, this is none of her business. We will refuse to marry women."

127

"I don't know what Baby is capable of doing. All I know is what's in her Plan of Action log. I'm satisfied here, like you."

"Dennis, I don't know how I can help you. The baby bothers you, yet you all but swear by Melissa's so-called plan."

I grabbed hold of Julius' hand. "No, please, I need your help. I've thought about this for a long time. I've made a decision. We have to get rid of Baby."

"Get rid of Baby?" he said, letting go of my hand and walking around the room. "So this would be the first infanticide in the new world! My advice to you is, just ignore the whole thing. When she talks about Baby's divinity, sit there and agree with her, but continue to treat Baby as you would any other baby. Her delusions come from the flash."

"No, I have to get rid of Baby, infanticide or not. I have to eliminate it or go crazy. Otherwise I would have to leave, but where would I go? Would you and Brian come with me?"

"You would walk out on everything just like that?"

Upstairs, I didn't know it but Baby was crawling around until it came to the end of the sun porch where it could pull itself up. When Julius and I went out on his sun porch below for a breath of fresh air, he heard it going and when we looked, we saw it crawling along the porch railing, a good seventy feet off the ground.

"Look at that," he said instantly, and for a frozen moment I studied the scene of Baby inching along.

I looked up and, despite what I had said, experienced a spasm of horror myself. I immediately ran upstairs to get it off the railing but the door to the apartment was locked. As I yanked the knob and shouted for Melissa to open it, I heard Julius scream and knew in my heart that Baby had fallen.

I kicked the door and tried to ram it, but it was so solid I couldn't open it. I did the nest best thing and went into the apartment next door and headed for the sun porch.

Once out on the porch, I didn't see Baby on the railing, but saw it – after Julius pointed to it – hanging onto a railing with one hand, about to fall. It only had its diapers on and hanging there, I saw it wasn't crying but hanging emotionless like a rubberized doll.

Julius had his arms out to catch it if it fell and I went over as close as I could to it before attempting to jump the space between this porch and my own. I couldn't; the distance was nine feet, so I leaned down and prepared myself for the most horrendous of scenes. Baby started swaying sideways as if on a vine, and then started to exert its muscles – little infant muscles that appeared from nowhere – and it seemed to pull itself up, and then down again – doing chin-ups!

Chapter Four

Both of us watched, aghast, as it pulled itself all the way up finally and crawled between the cracks in the railing. Then it started this ordinary baby waddle towards the apartment. But just before it entered, it turned around a flashed a grin at me, and then made a growling sound as if it was calling me a name. Slowly the picture of it pulling itself up, those little muscles flexing like an adult man's, came back to me, and it was a full minute before I was able to face Julius, who also looked transfixed.

"He has unearthly powers!" he said.

"You see what I mean. I need help, Julius. This is no ordinary baby."

"Brian won't believe this."

Inside the apartment, I heard running water, and so went into the bathroom where I saw Melissa filling the rubber bassinet from a hose. Baby was already nude on top of two thick quilts on the floor, as if nothing had happened. I looked at it for signs of the growl it had given me moments before, but it was lost in Melissa's baby talk.

"Ahhhh, goochie goochie goo – goochie goo, yes! Mum mum mum yes, Mommy loves you. Yes, she does, Mommy loves you so much!"

There was a knock at the door. It was Brian. I stepped out into the hall.

"About the baby," he said. "Well, I know you have your hands full. I don't know whether you know it or not, but at night sometimes, I hear these scratching sounds above our bedroom...where your kid sleeps..."

"Don't be apologetic Brian, spit it out."

"Well, at first we thought it was a rat but then we realized there aren't any rats. Then, one night, I heard the scratching and baby noises coming from the ventilator. Well, I mean this has been going on for a month now without letup. Then one night, I heard something –I guess it was the baby –crawling through the ducts like he was really inside. When I took a closer look, I heard noises as if something was inside there. I listened and I'm sure it was your baby Dennis, inside the radiator tunnel trying to crawl out the end of it over our bed. Dennis, it freaked me. I wasn't dreaming, Dennis….How could he have gotten in there?"

I thanked Brian but told him he had to leave because Melissa was on the warpath.

I didn't sleep well that night. I tossed and turned while Melissa slept soundly. I got up, parted the bedroom curtains, and in the light of the full moon saw Julius and Brian sitting around a campfire in the Square. No doubt they were down there looking for young male survivors. Up in the sky, the same mysterious lights that had been flashing on and off for weeks were still going strong. They were long trails of light spinning in circles, Melissa was sure that they were signs that the name we had chosen for Baby, Beng, was correct.

I made my way into the kitchen, lit an antique oil lamp we retrieved from Antique Row, and poured myself a warm soda. When I returned, I saw Beng climb over into his crib and lay on his stomach as if he had been sleeping all along.

I so much wanted to find out what made him tick. I picked him up and carried him into the bathroom where there were two oil lamps already rigged up. I was surprised that he didn't offer any resistance, considering his muscle stunt on the patio. In the bathroom, I put him down on the lid of the toilet with a towel underneath him and brought one of the lamps near his face. To my amazement, there were crossing lines on his forehead that looked like fine wrinkles but which I knew to be an identical imprint of the lines and signs we had witnessed in the sky. I drew closer to him and, with my thumb, opened one of his eyelids. There was nothing but an eye. When I did the same thing with the other eye I found nothing unusual either. There was nothing to do but take him back to his crib, which I did, feeling a sense of frustration. When I put him back, I returned to bed and turned on my side in order to try to go to sleep.

Before I knew it, it was morning and Melissa was up writing in her Action log. She usually did this at her desk, which faced the window, and she always had Beng in his high chair by her side until she had the day's work completed. Often she mumbled things while she wrote them and this morning the first thing that greeted me was, "There shall be one wagon, and it shall be covered as wagons were covered in the Old West, and a baby shall lead them." The sound of it forced me to turn over and cover my ears with the pillow. How could I face another day of this? Surely, I could escape by going out with Brian and Julius, whether that meant hunting for male survivors or hanging out at the Philadelphia Museum of Art.

I went down to the museum that morning and walked around. I went into the photography exhibit area and took a couple of photos for the apartment after which I took the European miniature, *Saint Francis Receiving the Stigmata* off the walls and put that with the photos. Dead curators and staff people were piled up by the elevators; a few were lumped near the bigger masterpieces as if the onslaught of the flash had caused some to seek solace before a great work of art. But a work of art cannot save you when the world is ending, and prayers before a famous sculpture or painting are futile.

I sat on the outside steps, after having noticed for the first time a large group of bodies collected near the Rocky statue. People, in their panic, had all decided to pray before the wrong gods. Sitting on the steps, I put my hands to my face and prayed that I would come to know the answer about the lines on Beng's face. What did they mean? Who was he? I must have sat there for a couple hours because when I left the sun was beginning to set. On the way home I passed a newsstand and took several magazines just to have a reminder about how the world used to be. At the apartment, I saw Melissa holding Beng's hand as they both power walked from the living room to the bedroom. They were making marching noises as if parading themselves before a reviewing stand.

"What is this?" I asked,

"Our drill," she said. "While you were gone, I located some old police horses and brought Beng back on one."

I excused myself and went to Brian's place. Julius came to the door. "You here for more than ten minutes?" he asked. "Because if you are, Brian said he was getting some pharmaceutical memory and hypnosis stuff and some needles. We can use it on Melissa and the baby."

"Stuff is here!" It was Brian. He rushed in behind me with a bag filled with pharmaceutical supplies. He dumped the bag out onto the sofa: Needles wrapped in plastic, gauzes, alcohol swabs, bottles of Xanax, Thorazine, OxyContin, Diazepam, Percocet and Benzodiazepine Receptor Ligands, and more. The Ligands, he said, affected memory and was hypnotic, making the patient a willing subject. "The injected person will do almost anything you tell them to do," he said, holding the bottle up to the light.

"When do we begin?" Julius asked.

"Maybe tonight," I ventured.

"Bang on the radiator if you need help," Brian added with a laugh, "especially if Beng turns into a werewolf."

"This is no joke," I said. "Melissa thinks she is the mother of a prophet. This could spell doom for everyone,"

I had to wait a long time before Melissa finally went to bed. I leafed through magazines as she sat on the floor combing her hair. It was a tranquil setting. She even started to get romantic and this almost made me give up the plan. But I knew that even if I fell for the bait that things would go back to normal in the morning. When she asked me when I was coming to bed, I said no, I would wait up. But then she talked me into coming to bed where I gave her a back massage. I had to fight off a case of the erotic shivers because I knew that once I consented to an orgasm, it would be over for me. Orgasms turn me into silly putty and I am like wet clay in a woman's hands. "I'm saving myself for the eve of our move," I told her, "waiting will create the perfect storm."

When I was sure she was asleep, I got up and went to the white pharmaceutical bag and brought it into the bathroom. There I arranged the syringes, dissolved the appropriate drugs in spoons filled with water, and placed gauzes on the back of the toilet. I opened the syringes and let them soak up what was in the spoons. Next, I grabbed gauze soaked in alcohol and walked out of the bathroom. I entered the bedroom, went over to Melissa, gently pulled up her night gown, wiped her left buttock with the gauze, then injected and pushed the nozzle down. I repositioned the night gown and went over to Beng. I undid his diaper, wiped him with gauze, and stuck him. In ten minutes it was all over and I was cleaning things up in the bathroom.

# # # # #

I was awakened by a thrashing sound. Someone was moving furniture. Melissa was saying, "Get up, Dennis, immediately. We haven't time to waste. Now, Dennis, now!" I remembered the injections and sat up in bed. All around me were suitcases packed on tables; Melissa stood in a long pink dress and wore an historic nineteenth century bonnet. Beng was in a little rawhide outfit with fringe about the sleeves. "The horses are tied to the wagon; I got up early, before sunrise, and brought in the wagon from the river. Flash is out there too. We're leaving, Dennis."

"Leaving?" I wondered why she wasn't in the arm chair waiting to receive my commands. Even Beng was crawling around everywhere, throwing things aside, putting things into his mouth.

"We can't leave now. There's no notice, no preparation. I haven't had time to think about it. What about Brian and Julius? We just can't leave."

"There's going to be an earthquake. If we don't leave, we'll be killed. The earthquake will hit the Center City area and swallow everything up. That's what Beng told me in a dream."

"What about Brian and Julius?"

"I told them but they chose not to believe me. They do not believe Beng. We must evacuate."

That's when the ground began to shake. Although it lasted only a second or two, it was enough to knock over several things in the apartment, while outside I heard several things crash to the ground. "It's true," I said, with my eyes on Beng, who had pulled himself up on the foot of my bed and was staring at me. "Oh lord Beng, did you predict this?" Suddenly I wanted to hug the boy, despite his dark divinity. He was a savior! I went to hug him but he pulled away –a baby pulling away from his own father. I tried not to show it, but it hurt.

"Now's not the time for soap opera," Melissa said, "Make up with him in the wagon, and leave the drugs here."

Chapter Five

I gathered together a few of my personal belongings and was making my way out when I met Brian and Julius on the stairs. They had suitcases in each hand.

"We think that Melissa and the boy may be right," Julius said, "we're ready to come along."

"Not so fast, guys," Melissa said, turning around when she reached the bottom of the stairs. This frightened them considerably although I could see that Julius was coming close to losing his temper. Had Beng not been part of the scenario I knew that there would be no holding him back, but something about Beng scared us all. "If they come with us in the wagon they will have to put up a separation sheet, and promise not to make love when we are all together. I don't want to hear those sounds. We do not want Baby Beng to hear those sounds. Dennis and I are a family now, and as a family we have moved on from fun to seriousness. Guys, you know I love you, but if you cannot do this tell me now. You are free to go your own way. I say this with love."

"We will put up the sheet," Julius said meekly, more out of fear of Beng than Melissa.

Beng, it seemed, was allowing Melissa to share in his power. She was a changed person. There was an alien presence within her. I wanted to throttle her for what she had said. Put up a separation wall? I could see that Brian was especially angry. His cheeks were flushed and he was on the verge of lashing out. Again, Beng was the deciding factor here. There seemed no way to rectify this. As we walked from the apartment building, I whispered to Brian.

"Your Benzodiazepine receptor ligand, or whatever-it-is called,

backfired. It caused all of this, maybe even the earthquake."

"Maybe it saved our lives. You want to be one of those cadavers lying in the street? Look, man, I don't care how crazy she gets. Maybe she's on the rag. She'll change, and then she'll want to do everything for you. It's that Beng baby I hate. That baby opened its mouth while

Melissa was talking to Julius just now and stuck out its tongue at me. It was a red tongue too, and long. I've never seen a tongue like that, Dennis. The baby's got to be from Lucifer."

All of us piled into the wagon, Melissa at the reins. I sat beside her. The guys did as they were told and went into the back section and put up a sheet to section themselves off. Melissa produced a whip, lashed out at the horses, and off we went down Walnut Street until we came to Broad Street. Finally we arrived at the freeway entrance and, galloping as fast as we could on the asphalt, felt another rumble of the ground.

"You see," Melissa said, turning in my direction. Beng was in a portable cradle just behind us, and the quake caused it to rock back and forth. When we were about five miles out of the city, another quake led to an explosion that leveled the skyline in one fell swoop. Down came Billy Penn and the Comcast Tower; all of Ed Bacon's and Vincent Kling's hard work up in smoke; historic architecture blown to bits, Frank Furness and William Strickland buildings now a pile of rubble. I thought of the Liberty Bell and Independence Hall zapped out of existence; the Betsy Ross House as a pile of rubble. Although Melissa advised against turning around so I wouldn't see what was happening, I could not resist and saw the PSFS building collapse like the twin towers on 9/11. The entire skyline had come down like faux stage scenery.

"Mother of God," I said, holding my ears. Beng, however, had a broad smile on his face and seemed to be enjoying himself, even if at the words Mother of God he shot me a dirty, threatening look.

"Where are we going after this?" Brian shouted from the back.

"Only Beng knows," Melissa replied.

For a long time nobody said a word, but finally Melissa ordered the horses to stop. It looked as though we were on Lancaster Pike somewhere on Philadelphia's Main Line. We were stopped at a roadside diner and got out to stretch our legs. Melissa took Beng out of the cradle and held him against her chest before kicking in the door of the diner. We went inside, helped ourselves to what was salvageable, and began opening cans of things and pouring them into bowls.

On the counter was the last edition of The Philadelphia Inquirer with headlines announcing the passage of The Military Detention Act, and a massive corporate takeover of the Internet.

"What's that?" Brian asked, cocking his ear.

We heard the sound of a guitar, and a voice singing a ballad of some sort. It was coming from the back of the diner. Brian left to investigate.

"We've run into Joan Baez," Julius said. "Maybe there's hope after all."

When we caught up with Brian, we saw a girl about twenty years old. She had long blond hair, freckles, and John Lennon-style spectacles. She continued to strum while she looked at us through a stream of tears. When she could no longer control herself, she dropped the guitar and ran up to Brian and embraced him. Next, she embraced Julius, then me. When she got to Melissa, Melissa nodded her head knowingly as if she had expected to meet the girl all along.

"Your baby!" the girl said, indicating Beng.

"My baby – the world's baby," Melissa exclaimed, holding Beng out like a statue in a religious procession, and as if she was expecting the girl to kneel down.

In a couple of hours, we were on our way again with our newfound friend, Tiffany. Our wagon was slowly winding up a narrow road in the country. There were farms on the horizon and fields of corn and wheat. The only ugly sights on the landscape were the cow carcasses and farmer cadavers hanging off tractors, but otherwise the view was idyllic. Even a fresh country smell was evident.

Melissa stopped the wagon at a little log cabin next to a brook in a most picturesque spot. Behind the cabin was a high green hill, and behind that, more rolling hills that led to Pennsylvania's Blue Mountains. A blue onion domed church with a three bar cross could be seen among the tall trees. Melissa got out of the wagon, held her arms out wide and sniffed the air. "This is the place – for now!" she said. She pulled Beng out of the wagon and held him up so that he could view the landscape. She stood that way for some time, and put him back in the cradle only when he made a gurgling sound.

139

"Yes," she said again. "This is the place. Disembark. We will live in the cabin until Beng finds the Golden Parchment."

Julius, perplexed, whispered, "Golden Parchment?"

Together we went into the cabin. It was small, with a fireplace and various stuffed animal heads protruding from the walls. There was a rabbit's head as well as a boar's head mounted on the kitchen wall. The beds were bunks, three of them, with nine bunks altogether. With only three rooms, everything seemed cramped.

"We will live here," Melissa said, "until the boy is nineteen."

"Twelve!" I said, imagining eleven years in the small cabin. Everybody sat down on what available chairs there were and considered the proclamation. I know what they were thinking: they couldn't stay and they couldn't run away, for the baby had proved himself to be more than a baby and, in every sense, we needed each other.

"Wouldn't it be easier," Julius said, "to go to a city, where we would have lots of room to spread out, and access to materials? What about Pittsburgh? Pittsburgh can't be far away. Here we have to live like pioneers. We are inviting extra hardship when there doesn't have to be hardship."

Melissa spoke up, nonchalantly taking out a breast and nursing Beng. "We have to follow the Plan to stay alive. Julius and Brian, you two will work in the fields. There's a horse drawn tractor by that farm over the hills behind the cabin and you two are to go fetch it. Tiffany, you will be my helpmate. You will mainly do domestic duties; clean the cabin, prepare dinner for the men, do the laundry at the stream, and see if you can find live chickens and eggs. Beng told me you have a little problem with men; you can't keep your hands to yourself, so I'd advise you to keep your hands off Dennis. And please don't steal from us. We are in this thing together."

Tiffany's eyes widened in their sockets, and she broke into tears. She quoted a passage from Scripture and told Melissa she had her figured out all wrong. "I am a God-fearing girl," she said, putting her head in her hands and doubling over in such a way that put her ample cleavage on center stage.

"And you, Dennis," Melissa added softly, squeezing her right breast so the milk would flow more freely, "you will always be my lifelong husband. You will assist Beng and me in our search for the Golden Parchment. You'll also help Julius and Brian any way you can – and Tiffany too. But your main job will be to translate the Golden Parchment when Beng finds it. Since you have beautiful penmanship, there should be no question why I chose you for this job. This will not be easy. It may take several months to translate after the angel tells Beng where it is buried."

"I think I'm going to go out and look around," Julius said, standing up.

"No," Melissa said, "you will stay here. Brian will take Tiffany as his wife. They will be married tomorrow at sunrise." With this, she got up and walked out of the room with Beng.

Brian glared at Julius, then at Tiffany. Julius looked at me as if for help. It was a tense moment that called for some kind of reaction from Julius but that did not happen. I expected Brian to get up and follow Melissa into the kitchen but he sat there, staring at the wooden floor. There was a feeling of real helplessness all around.

"You don't have to do it, Brian," I said. "You and Julius are a legitimate couple. You can take off tonight. I will help you. You can have one of the horses."

"Why don't we work out a sperm donor situation," Julius wanted to know. "Marriage isn't necessary. We all know the planet needs repopulating, so just have Brian do the nasty and then have Melissa transfer it into Tiffany. Tiffany doesn't seem like the kind of girl who would marry someone she barely knows. She seems like she deserves something better than a bisexual guy who has to have sex with men periodically in order to feel like he's alive. Isn't that so, Tiffany?"

"I kind of like Brian," Tiffany said, looking at the ground and then slowly raising her head, her eyes wet with a Teddy Bearish glow. "Sometimes all a bi guy needs is a good woman. I know what men want. I'm no penis-indifferent woman, that's for sure. You don't mind marrying me, do you Brian?" Tiffany, suddenly, was wrapping her curls of hair around her fingers and winking at Brian as she did something with her lips.

But Brian, managing an amused half-smile, indicated with his thumb that Julius was "really the best." Then he asked if anyone had a cigarette.

# # # # #

The next morning Melissa was in a major tizzy, rearranging tables and chairs in the small living room. The night before she had cut up a white sheet into long ribbons, and these she hung outside the cabin, draped from tree to tree. She found a large silver bowl and poured a bottle of cooking wine into it. Because the cabin had no running water, she saw to it that Brian bathed in a nearby stream. She found a man's black suit in one of the closets and told him to put it on. She did not have a bridal gown for Tiffany but she improvised, again with sheets. For their bridal night, she arranged to have everyone sleep in the wagon and to stay out of the cabin for a day.

She at least had the good sense to make Julius the best man and have him walk under the canopy with Brian, with myself behind them. Melissa stood behind the presentation table with Beng, who was dressed in white as he sat in his portable chair. When the procession began, Tiffany walked up the opposite side of the aisle Melissa had decorated with logs she found behind the cabin. Face to face, Brian and Tiffany followed Melissa's instructions to stand closer together, not the way that they were doing it, "like two companies signing a merger agreement."

"This is a magnificent moment," Melissa said, as Beng began to cry. "This is more than a marriage of minds and of bodies; it is a union that will repopulate these United States. This girl, discovered by us behind an old diner outside Philadelphia after an earthquake brought that city tumbling down, this girl was sent to us in order to meet and join hands with Brian, the confused Irish boy, a former runaway, heroin addict and common street hustler who now stands on the verge of a new life. He stands with Tiffany, and together they will build a solid life, moving on from and forgetting what in their lives came before, all the confusion and sexual anarchy that caused them so much grief and misery. Together they will build a solid life, and a deep and abiding love will grow between them. Brian, take Tiffany's hand and repeat after me:

"All knowing lord of subterranean things,
Who remedy our human sufferings,
You give to the doomed man that calm, unbaffled
Gaze that rebukes the mob around the scaffold.
O Prince of Exiles, who have suffered wrong,
Yet, vanquished, rises from every fall more strong.'
Bless these two in the manner according to Beng
And so be it...."

Chapter Six

Afterward, a short reception followed. We sat around the kitchen table and Melissa sang. There were no more readings from poems by Baudelaire, and the mood was light, especially after we drank all the cooking wine. Through it all I kept wondering how Brian would fare with Tiffany. Obviously Julius was wondering the same thing. Tiffany, however, seemed genuinely enamored of Brian but, what with his good looks, it's no wonder. I chalked it up to a superficial attraction, nothing more. Once Tiffany became pregnant, had her first baby and gained weight, I was certain that Brian would turn away or find his way back to Julius. He would no doubt come to dislike the suffocating style of loving that Tiffany had to offer. Tiffany needed men who need an extension of Mama but in a hybrid sexual form.

I admired the way Julius ate in silence, offering no malicious or snide comments to either Tiffany or Melissa, though I knew he would probably react in time.

But when the bride and the bridegroom got up to begin their little walk to the bedroom, that's when Julius lurched forward in his chair. His eyes became two piercing daggers. I knew it was only a matter of time before he did something. Tiffany, I could tell, was in seventh heaven. Soon she would be moaning under Brian's writhing, muscled body. What would Julius do? I went up to him and put my hand on his shoulder. It was a gesture I'd seen many buddies do, especially in the movies, when one of them was troubled. I didn't know what to say to Julius, was almost afraid to say anything because Beng was looking at me. Yet finally, as we left the cabin, this came out: "Look, just wait this thing out; time is on your side."

That night, their wedding night, we heard Tiffany playing her guitar. She was trying to sing like Joan Baez, then she'd switch to Judy Collins, then she'd alter the beat and come on like somebody else. She was all over the musical map, forgetting lyrics halfway through a song although she managed a bird like rendition of "On Eagles Wings" in honor, she shouted out to us, of her home Catholic parish, where the much beloved priest, "a really cool guy," would usher in the altar girls in baseball caps carrying balloons and incense bowls. Her songs kept us awake, with Melissa making comments about how lovely it all was. At one point, Melissa asked me to come to bed so that we could snuggle, but this meant that Julius would be all by himself in a corner of the wagon; I said no. I could see she didn't like this, but I knew Julius needed comfort more than she did. I was sitting next to him, my legs astride his, and just kind of dozing. I suggested that Melissa come and sit next to me, but she just looked snake-eyes at me and then watched Beng sleep on his stomach in the cradle.

The sounds of the newlyweds' lovemaking sent Julius out of the wagon and into the forest. Tiffany's symphonic high notes and prolonged mantra moans were insensitive and overdone. It was pure erotic overkill, given Julius' situation. I went outside to search for him but didn't find him in the area surrounding the wagon. Then I saw him peeking into the windows of the cabin, ducking and keeping out of sight as well he could. In the real world that had just passed he would have been arrested for stalking and voyeurism and leveled with a bail totaling some $150,000, but this was the woods and a new age. My own erotic curiosity got the best of me. I went up behind him, tapped him on the shoulder to show solidarity, and asked him what they were doing.

"She's on top of him flapping her arms, riding him for the fifth time," he said, in a tone of a man who has been beaten. I snuck a look. There in the shadows of the oil lamps, Tiffany completely covered Brian, her blond curly hair brushed over her head so that she looked like a mad horsewoman galloping in the wind. Only Brian's feet were visible, the toes curling and the rapid pumping of his thighs.

"In the old world, this kind of thing would be on X-Tube. What an appetite she must have," I said. Tiffany then had Brian take her standing up, but the sight of this was just too much for Julius, who turned around and walked away.

"She's using him up like an exhaust engine," I said, trying to be consoling. "He'll come to you when he needs attention. She cares not a whit about working on him!"

From the direction of the wagon came Melissa's odd and incessant chanting.

# # # # #

The next morning Melissa was up at the crack of dawn walking around the perimeters of our property. Beg was outside crawling around on some logs and poking things as any child might. I was up too, cooking oatmeal and raisins over an open campfire. There was a crisp, autumn smell in the air. It seemed like a good morning.

Julius was still asleep, however, and when Melissa came back to the wagon she told him to get up. I argued with her, telling her he had had a rough night and because of this he should be allowed to sleep late. But, after a short time had elapsed, I heard a scream from the back of the wagon. When I turned to see what had happened, I saw Beng crawling out from behind the wagon as fast as he could, and Julius chasing after him with a stick.

"He bit me, he bit me," Julius said. "Your baby bit me on the arm and drew blood. Look at this!" He held up his bleeding arm.

He had no intention of hitting the baby, but he thrashed the stick at him just the same and Beng, apparently forgetting that he was to usher in the new Earthly Kingdom, became just a baby again and was actually frightened. Beng's dual-nature perplexed me; it apparently could only act like a god at certain times, and at other times it was as helpless and dependent as any other child. I went over to Beng and stood there with my arms crossed.

"Dennis, I wasn't going to hit Beng, I swear. But he turned on me just now." Julius threw the stick away and pondered Beng, who had turned on his back and smelled like he needed a diaper change.

"You're bad, Beng, you're bad. That is unacceptable!" I shouted like I had never done before, and at my harsh words, Beng cried.

I invited Julius to sit by the fire with me and have some oatmeal. We just let Beng lie on his back in the grass in his dirty diapers until Melissa returned. She often disappeared in the mornings to watch the skies for signs and wonders. The grass was wet; Julius and I hadn't realized this because the area around the campfire was dry. Nevertheless, when Melissa saw us and picked Beng up, his clothes were soaking wet and he had developed some kind of sniffle. There's no need to describe the temper tantrum that followed. I was upbraided for my irresponsibility and Julius was given a scolding also. Melissa disappeared with Beng into the wagon, where there was considerable silence for a long time.

# # # # #

Tiffany emerged from the cabin first, smiling victoriously. She said Brian was still asleep, but she was going to take coffee to him in bed. There were circles under her eyes and her voice was hoarse. She leaned over the campfire, rubbed her hands over the flame, and then looked up at Julius. "I saw you looking," she said.

Julius dismissed her with a wave of his hand. With a cup of coffee poured for Brian, she started back to the cabin when Melissa called to her from the wagon. "Where are you going with that?"

"To my baby, he needs his brew," Tiffany replied, her tone suggesting newfound familiarity and confidence.

"No, you're not. Tell him to get dressed and come out here. We're having a meeting. Everybody eats together...your honeymoon is over."

# # # # #

Months passed and many things happened. Melissa became pregnant again –she no longer had to help seed and plant the huge field that bordered the cabin. She helped Tiffany inside, and fixed lunch for Brian, Julius and myself when we worked. Beng could walk now. He ran around by himself, often coming up to us and watching us work. He wasn't a bother during this time. In fact, he was more a child than ever and for a time we forgot that he was a prophet and just treated him like a normal kid.

Brian's new life changed him somewhat; he was more introspective and less able to share his feelings. Tiffany had changed his personality. His spontaneous gay self seemed to be tucked under one of her mattress folds.

It was odd to see. Julius, being so passive, did little to win him over again. He seemed content to float along, absorbed himself in his work, part of which included painting landscapes and taking long walks into a neighboring town since he still hoped to find a suitable male survivor.

Unfortunately, Tiffany was becoming like Melissa. The day-in and day-out association with her was rubbing off. It seemed they had decided that our second baby was to be somebody too –a disciple who would take the translated Golden Parchment to Europe, where he would start a colony. This, of course, was predicted for his mature adulthood, and no doubt we would all be dead or incapacitated when this happened. Melissa's seriousness about life and her mission, and the world goal of her children, changed her into a humorless person. She had objected to my housing the small icon of Saint Mark that had been a source of comfort to me since New York, in the nook of a large tree not far from the cabin. I often went to the icon to meditate but Melissa insisted that Beng had made icons and the religious ways of the old world, "irrelevant." I didn't fight her on this but I went to the icon anyway.

The night the second baby was born, we were all gathered around her as she lay in the cabin's only double bed. This was the way she wanted it. The labor pains seemed unusually harsh: Melissa would push and scream, faint, then wake up screaming. Her body was covered in sweat and she shook as if in the thrall of a great fever. Tiffany was in tears. The agony went on for two hours or more, and when the head finally showed, I prayed that it might be a girl to offset Melissa's prediction. But when Tiffany held the baby up, I could see the tiny penis and my hopes were lost. We quickly washed it and presented it to Melissa, who cradled it and told Julius in no uncertain terms that he should paint the scene as a kind of Madonna and Child for the new world.

Brian, looking like he was sleepwalking, came over to examine the baby. He seemed curiously happy despite the fact that Melissa's labor pains had affected him the most. At one point he covered his eyes and for an instant it looked as if he was reaching for Julius' hand.

Melissa had a name all picked out. She calmly said, "Metatron," and that was the end of the discussion. In my mind I tried to reconcile the names Beng and Metatron with out backwoods life, our strict discipline. I could not. I would have been satisfied naming the baby Jimmy, just a plain name from the old America. It might even make for a smooth continuation of that time. But, as always, Melissa was adamant and I lost. I was always losing. Julius and I were both losers in this new world.

I asked myself: what made us pick up Melissa and Brian, anyway? I asked Melissa this one night during a heated argument. I said to her, "Look, I regret the day we stopped our wagon for you!" She just said that she and I would have found each other anyway, in time.

Metatron was an ugly baby. I don't know why. I was always thought attractive, and Melissa wasn't bad looking either. But Metatron looked, well, misshapen. With an oblong head and hardly any chin, and with eyes that seemed to indicate a thyroid condition, he was no pretty picture.

Every morning, we took turns digging for the Parchment. We had been doing this for some time now, each of us without success. It had gotten to be a big bore, and most of the time our hearts were not in it. That is, until Melissa came around on her periodic checks and told us that the future of the planet depended on our actions and commitment, and that what we were doing was "the new Green." But since we had until Beng turned twelve, there seemed to be no hurry. Melissa said that we should have found the Parchment by now and that once we did, it would take a long time to translate.

Finally we men rearranged the work schedule to give it more flexibility. If I was out all night hunting or trying to find other survivors and had to sleep late the next day, well, I just moved the work up till dusk or whenever.

But things weren't right. Melissa was losing weight. Some days she refused to get out of bed – would lie in it all day, and just have Tiffany nurse her. We men wouldn't be allowed in the room except when she wanted us. There was a general feeling of sickness and apathy all around. That was bad, because it depressed everybody, and suddenly there didn't seem to be any reason to live here anymore. If we had only stocked up on pills to alleviate the depression, perhaps life would have been better. To wait until the Parchment was found and translated seemed a foolhardy plan bordering on lunacy.

All of us, I think, except for Tiffany, were beginning to feel the itch to move on. Brian just sat up against the cabin after his share of the work and chewed on grass and sticks. Julius said he had a secret tree house out in the woods where he could be himself and he went there to escape. I generally acted as a go-between and kept communication flowing among the group. But I didn't like the way things were going.

Something was lost as a result of Melissa's withdrawal. Even Tiffany, who tried as hard as she could to be a carbon copy of Melissa and keep us informed as to the instructions she wanted carried out, soon fell victim to her own depression. Pretty soon, of course, less and less of the work was getting done. Julius would disappear for days at a time, isolating himself in his tree house. Brian would sleep a lot, waking up and then searching the forests and fields for something to roll up and smoke.

I decided to let things hang out, or pull the strings. I went to Melissa.

Chapter Seven

"Can I come in?" I asked.

"Please Dennis, I don't want to talk."

"It's about the Parchment and our life here." She sat up a little and expressed an interest with her eyes. I went over and sat on the edge of the bed. I took her hand, something I hadn't done in ages. "I'm slowly beginning to appreciate what you, Beng, and Metatron stand for. I can see the destruction all around us, Melissa. Julius is dissipating slowly in a tree house, sinking in the mire of Ayn Rand individualism. I don't know what he does up there but whenever I go over, he always yells, 'Do not come up yet, wait till I tell you!' I can't get him or Brian to do any farm work. Our camp, Melissa, is slowly falling apart. Have you noticed the decrease in the portions of your food?"

"Oh," she said, reaching for a miniature copy of the *Bhagavad-Gita* she had carried with her from the beginning, "There is no possibility of one's becoming a yogi, O Arjuna, if one eats too much or eats too little, sleeps too much or does not sleep enough." She found another passage. "He who is regulated in his habits of eating, sleeping, working and recreation can mitigate all material pains by practicing the yoga system."

"Thank you, honey," I said, knowing how important this was to her. She shook her head, spooning some of the leftover oatmeal, now cold, and bringing it up to the brim of the bowl. Her eyes widened, and she seemed to be on the verge of scolding me.

"Take the *Bhagavad-Gita* and learn from it," she said, reaching for the book. I did as I was told, holding back an urge to remind her that two weeks ago she had quoted from The *Tibetan Book of the Dead* and a month before that it was the *Upanishads*, the *Vida*, and then the *Talmud*.

She opened her mouth as if getting ready to speak, but then turned her head to the side as if giving up. "Yes, what were you going to say?"

She rested there with her eyes half closed, as if I had asked a stupid question and could never understand, but I edged her on. "I'm serious. Things have gone far enough. For the last few mornings now, I've been digging for the Parchment all by myself and have started a new rectangular line of dig which I plan on following through."

She really concentrated on me now, her eyes strangely illuminated. "You have?" she asked, looking at me for signs of trickery. Sensing that I was being sincere, she said, "I had a dream that someone took the Parchment. In the dream I saw a figure inspecting the first rectangular dig and unraveling an ancient scroll. Then he took it with him into the forest."

My first thought was Julius. Suddenly his isolation in the tree house made sense. Julius had found the Parchment during one of his morning digs and decided to work on it away from us.

"Have any survivors wandered into the camp?" she asked, scratching the corners of her mouth.

"No, it is still just us. But your dream says something to me. It must have been Julius who took the Parchment because Brian is too lazy to care and Tiffany is devoted to you. I think I should go to Julius and find some way to examine where he's living, don't you think?"

"Be careful, Dennis. There's a dark cloud over the old plan. I hadn't anticipated it. I didn't think anything like this would come about but just be more subtle than I was. That was my mistake, I think. I was too forceful. If Julius has it, he could be altering what it says to suit his view of the universe; he could be adding same sex ceremonies and legitimizing anal sex and sodomy with high minded quotes from make believe deities. He could be up to anything. Yes, I think you should go there."

I crept up to the tree house, climbed up the makeshift ladder silently, and looked inside. Julius was hunched over an old table. He was writing, in fact dipping a pen into ink and making what looked like elaborate scrawls on a large sheet of paper. I was carefully ducking underneath a crudely fashioned window, my head level with the base as the sun was coming up over the horizon. I knew immediately that he had the Parchment and my guess was that he was translating it. He was holding an odd stone in front of his face while he wrote but then bringing it down close to the script at various points. My heart beat fast.

I didn't know how to approach him; what to say. If I walked in on him he'd put the paper away and pretend to be doing something else. The stone I recognized as a Seer Stone, the same device Mormon prophet Joseph Smith was said to have used when he translated *The Book of Mormon*.

I decided to chuck it all and just go in and confront him. How dare he, how dare he hide the Parchment and keep civilization from advancing onward. Consumed by this passion, I put my right leg over the windowsill and, at that, Julius turned around. His face was flushed and it was as if I had entered the Holy of Holies without knocking.

"Dennis, you scared me half to death!"

"I'm sorry, Julius. It's just that I think you know something the rest of us don't. I think you are hiding something."

"I am," he said after some hesitation, "I don't want Melissa – or anyone – to see this work."

"Then you do have the Parchment?"

"The Parchment?"

"The Great Parchment, the text that tells us why we are here and what we have to do now in this new world."

"Dennis, the Parchment Melissa talks about may be 20,000 leagues under the sea. I'm writing my own Parchment and starting my own tradition."

"Then it's a manifesto of some kind, not a scared book."

He held the sheet up to me. Drawn on it was a beautifully sketched wagon with suburban homes in the foreground. Underneath it was another sheet, and on that was a sketch of Melissa nursing Beng. Still another sheet showed Beng hanging from the patio rail in Philadelphia with a sickly grin on his face

"It's just a sketch diary. You've decided to become the Anais Nin of the new world."

"Somebody has to keep a record of this."

"Yes, but Julius…" I had just seen another drawing where Melissa and Beng both had horns extending from their foreheads. The

155

expression on their faces was horrifying. Even the sun, above their heads in the open field in this particular drawing, was covered by a dripping brown substance. "So you think there's something demonic about Melissa and Beng? That's a harsh judgment, don't you think?"

"Beng is an agent of some sort, yes; and Melissa is tied into that as well. Tiffany might be a saccharin version of something bigger and more terrifying, I don't know. As for Metatron, well, I think we may be able to save him."

"When Melissa finds the Parchment, your zine will be reduced to ashes. Come back to the cabin and stay with us and stop wasting your time on a comic book."

"From time to time I will," he said. "Melissa is a believer; I am not. I'm a realist. You once wished Beng dead; remember that?"

Julius is a heretic, I thought; a renegade. He has made himself an outcast. And his drawings seemed to cement him from the group even more; there now seemed little possibility that he could ever live among us again.

I admit I didn't know him anymore. He had become a stranger. I had no choice but to leave. So I did just that, taking the ladder exit and walking very slowly back to the cabin.

When I arrived, Tiffany and Brian were talking by the tomato patch under Melissa's window,

"Look, boy, calling Julius' name in your sleep is a little weird. You haven't been paying attention to me at all. I lay awake right next to you giving you little signs that I want you to love me, and all you do is turn your back and go to sleep. I am your wife. I am supposed to be your number one. You are supposed to fulfill my needs. That's not the way you used to be. You're not the same Brian and I want to know why. Night after night it is the same thing: me waiting for you. I am not going to make the first move anymore because when I do I always feel like I am forcing you. You should want me, but I don't think you want me." Tiffany began to cry. She composed herself and shook her head. "You're always lying on your ass; always eating things from the garden, always taking walks. Where do you go? Don't you know that this is the most important time in history and that we have to work?"

I stepped right in. I thought I assumed great confidence and leadership. "Tiffany is right," I said, pointing my finger at him and shaking it a little. "We don't owe you a living and getting by on your good looks alone doesn't cut it. Maybe it does for hustler heroin addicts. That worked in the old world. Here we all pull together or die together. You can't survive in this world alone."

My words had little effect. Brian merely looked at the ground as Metatron, crawling on the grass, seemed to appear out of nowhere.

"Consider our little family," Tiffany said. "Even Metatron loves you."

Brian, still in a daze, put his hands in his pockets. It was obvious he was on something. Perhaps he had walked into the nearby town and raided the CVS pharmacy. I could see that his eyes were glazed, and he was beginning to nod. Tiffany went over to him and pulled both his hands out of his pockets.

"You're not even presentable. You need a shave. You smell...when was the last time you took a bath?"

I waited for him to do something, but he only looked at the ground. In my heart I knew where he wanted to be, but I hoped he would have the strength to fight it and stay with us and work something out with Tiffany. It was at this point that Melissa came out of the cabin after weeks of lying in bed. I didn't want to come down too hard on Brian, but what could I do? I told Melissa that he wasn't pulling his weight and that he was walking away from his marriage.

"Does this have something to do with your wanting to be with Julius?" she said. "You're free to do what you want, you know we love you, but it would be nice if you at least tried to make it work. Tiffany is a wonderful woman. Just look at her. What man wouldn't want to be with her? Julius with his scraggily beard and hair – what do you see in that? Has he found a stash of heroin somewhere? Is that it? You're taking the easy road instead of living responsibly?"

"You don't know anything," Brian said, throwing his arm down as if pounding a gavel. "I'm clean. I just get...tired. Tiffany thinks because she's beautiful I have to be her lap dog. It's 'do this' and 'do that' and 'come into bed and make love to me.' It is always about her.

157

Rub my feet. Rub my legs. If you love me, you'll do this for me. If you love me you'll go the extra mile. I ran out of gas, way out of gas."

"He's drunk!" Tiffany gasped.

"Damn right. I'll drink all day till I'm out of this place. All this talk about 'us' as if we were a family when we are not a family at all but some kind of new cult being built around a creepy baby who gets messages from the devil or something. I think I'll go into a trance and start my own cult and write up my own rules. You are all whipped...she" – Brian pointed at Melissa –"controls everything, and you follow her like snails. Even Dennis is her dog. You are all dogs. Beng should be tied to a log and sunk in the creek. Metatron, he should be tried to a tree and..."

"You stop it!" It was Tiffany. She threw her shoe at him. Beng walked out of the cabin in his diapers, holding a walking stick. There was a pout on his face. He looked at us, and we, turning around and staring at him, knew that something was about to happen. I swear I saw a little light appear above his head. After months of being a normal child, whatever was other worldly in him was shedding its skin. He pointed the walking stick at Brian and charged at him, holding the stick out like a lance. Nobody did anything to stop him. None of us thought that he would really hurt Brian; after all, even if he had charged into him, the stick would have only rammed into his knees. But just as the baby was about to make contact, he tripped in the grass and fell on his face. He then let out a typical baby wail as Tiffany scooped him up in her arms.

"Does devil boy want some booby milk to feel good?" Brian shouted, before running into the woods.

Tiffany, in tears, soothed an angry Beng who was now throwing his arms around in a tantrum, resistant to soothing words and smiles but throwing punches at his mother and even reaching out violently for Melissa when the latter attempted to pat his forehead. It was odd to see such an angry look on a baby. The scene went on for a long time, with Beng hitting Tiffany in the face before jerking himself out of her arms and throwing himself on the ground where he proceeded to roll on the grass.

Brian did not return. I assumed he went to Julius' tree house. Now I was busy with two wives. That's how it had to be because we had to populate the earth. It wasn't easy since both women had enormous sexual appetites. Melissa, being more cerebral than Tiffany, was better able to accept sensual cuddling and let it go at that, but Tiffany wanted athletic style lovemaking as if we were making adult films. She wanted it standing up in the woods; she wanted it by the creek in the water; and she was always managing or surveying the state of my erections, saying "It was bigger the last time we did it, are you less turned on?" She was obsessed with me losing interest in her as a sex partner, and she thought nothing of asking me if she was better than Melissa. In bed, Melissa was able to reciprocate but Tiffany had no such interest. Her mantra, "Your job is to please the woman," gave me insight into Brian's old dilemma. Over a short period of time I grew to dread making love to her because afterwards she would review the performance. I very quickly came to the conclusion that polygamy is a very special kind of hell.

Very soon I was craving, and even starved for, the company of men although I still maintained my commitment to the family and avoided going over to the tree house.

During this time the only sounds we heard from the tree house were hammering and sawing sounds as well as an occasional howl. It was hard to figure out what the howls were about unless they were tributes to Allen Ginsberg. Melissa was quick to assert that Julius and Brian were into conjuring adverse spirits, and so a little fence was built around the cabin so that Beng and Metatron would not go exploring. When Beng was not in prophet mode, which was the majority of the time, he acted as any normal kid and would get lost walking in the woods. Therefore we felt it was our duty to protect ourselves as well as him and Metatron.

Months came and went. We never saw much of Brian and Julius, although occasionally we would see them down by the creek. I would say hello to them and we would exchange polite conversation, but it ended there. Everything deep and abiding about our old friendship had died. They were heretics, this I was sure of, even if I wavered in this belief from time to time. The important thing for me then was to raise my boys to live on the earth as sons of the new world order.

# # # # # #

When Beng was fifteen he had a strong manly build, and Metatron, barely a year younger, was just as strong. I exercised them in the yard right outside the kitchen window. Perhaps I loved them too much. I let them have one set of bunk beds and I made a new double bed for Melissa and myself, while Tiffany slept on a bunk above us. It was an ideal setup despite Tiffany's power plays and the sexual exhaustion I had come to accept. In the morning, the boys would start throwing pillows or we'd hear them racing around the cabin or outside, sometimes taunting Flash, the horse that would not die, in a good natured way.

This was the time when the boys started asking me serious questions about Brian and Julius' colony of tree houses which the boys had stumbled upon some time ago. Despite our best efforts to keep them within the fence, boys being boys we could only do so much. "Who are they?" they kept asking, and we had to tell them that they were The Others and that they were never to go near them.

Melissa came right out and called them pedophiles, which I thought grossly unfair since, even if it was true, would pose no danger to the boys who were no loner prepubescent children, but teenagers. But there was still a risk to the boys; that much I acknowledged, at least in my talks to them. "These are men who like men, and as such they would naturally like young men or at least present their unnatural lifestyle as normal, in effect getting you to change your concept of homosexuality over time." As far as I could see, homosexuality was just a mine field of moral anarchy, a Do What You Will world of moral relativism.

"Just trust your mother and me," I said, sounding like Pat Boone. "They were part of us once but they fell into schism –they did badly, and now they are in the trees." Naturally, as Beng grew older, his prophetic powers increased despite months and months of ordinary teen angst. We never knew when he'd switch modes and start performing small miracles or say something important. It was queer to watch an average fifteen year old boy chopping wood and joking with his brother, then suddenly jerk upright and come out with some parable. Melissa always ran into the cabin when this happened and scribbled

160

down whatever he said. We had three thick notebooks filled with his quotations.

Quotations from Beng

1. Never was there a time when I did not exist, nor you, nor all these kings; nor in the future shall any of us cease to be.

2. The blowing of all these different conchshells became uproarious, and, vibrating both in the sky and on earth and inside Tiffany, shattered the hearts of the sons of Melissa.

3. The humble sage sees with equal vision a learned and gentle brahmana, a cow, an elephant, a dog and a dog-eater like Julius and the homosexuals.

But the fact that we still hadn't found the Parchment tested our patience. It seemed as though Beng was just juicing up, as they say, for his big Spill-over or whatever when he reached adulthood. The big Spill-over would be Beng's coming off as a prophet, when according to Melissa there was a good chance that he'd pull up roots and travel on, as prophets are wont to do. That seemed unlikely, however, considering that we had not met any other survivors for many years.

# # # # #

At last it happened. One day, while walking back from the creek, Beng stumbled on something hard sticking out of the ground. When he went to examine what it was, he saw that it was a leather encasement. Pulling it out of the ground, he held it up and waved it at me.

"I've found it. I've found the Parchment!"

The prophecy had been fulfilled. Together we opened the case and saw the silver plates. Although Melissa said it would be a golden text, no human prediction is ever one hundred percent accurate. Paper thin with an Arabic sort of writing on the many sheets, I knew not to touch the text as this was Beng's province. I reluctantly stepped aside while I let him carefully lift each plate and hold it up to the sun. The fact that they were in our yard all along, right in front of our eyes albeit under the earth, seemed incredible to me. Here we had been digging large elaborate holes far into the woods and had only arrowheads to show for our work. The impromptu, almost miraculous protrusion of the plates through the ground, suddenly and with no warning, seemed to be the work of a super force. I then did what I promised myself I would do if Melissa's prophecy came true: I grabbed the icon of St. Mark in the tree, and threw it in the creek.

"I wish there was a girl around for Beng," Melissa said a few weeks later. "He'll soon be reaching that age when he needs a girlfriend. I worry about that. What will he do, Dennis?" I honestly couldn't answer that. I didn't know where the boys were going to get girls when the time was right. I dreaded the thought that they would be forced to mingle with Melissa and Tiffany in order to further the race. That would open us up to the dangers of inbreeding. Incest was out of the question. They could be celibate like Latin priests, but this was hardly realistic. What was coming was not a pretty picture, and I immediately thought of an old Samuel Butler quote: "Morality is the custom of one's country and the current feeling of one's peers. Cannibalism is moral in a cannibal country." Masturbation as a chronic lifelong option was also unattractive. Situational homosexuality was a real threat, since most men, if not all, will find an outlet in that world if the possibility of meeting women is next to nil. Clearly, something had to be done, but what?

We saw the beginning of this crisis when the boys flung themselves into that teenage vice that never occurred to me as being anything much until I cemented my relationship with Melissa. I now had a new view of sexuality, and it frightened me. Where did this new 'me' come from? I was always about sexual liberation and doing your own thing, and now here I was standing up for what I used to call old fashioned morality, or codes of conduct as outdated as a pair of well worn shoes. I was also worried because I found it hard to reconcile Beng's spiritual mission with his penchant for exercising this vice. Prophets don't jump from a *Portnoy's Complaint* state of mind to Krishna consciousness in the time it takes to peel potatoes. Or do they? There was much that I didn't know; it occurred to me that perhaps my concept of prophecy and how a prophet should be was wrong. If prophets are real people like everybody else, then the notion of a spotless, saintly unblemished life untarnished by human passion and fallacies is nothing but a myth. It occurred to me that perhaps Beng had something to teach me.

Melissa dealt with the teenage vice thing better than I did, probably because she refused to recognize it. She trained herself not to see it. "Beng has work to do," she said. "You have too much time on your hands. His life right now is taken up by spiritual matters. Stop spending so much time in the gutter, Dennis."

She asked me what I feared the most, and I told her that I was afraid that if they didn't find wives they would latch on to substitutes. Being well versed in the literature of substitutes, I mentioned the possibilities to her and her reaction was as I expected: negative. "When I was an adolescent, I had neighborhood outlets. I won't shock you with stories of my immorality," I said. "But it was a time in my life when I went...everywhere."

"Remember that these are good boys. Beng is working hard on the Parchment and his days are spent reconstituting the word." With that, she walked away. She didn't want to talk about it anymore. "Not another word about this," she said, glancing back at me.

She was right. During the day, Beng worked at his little wooden table with the diligence of a medieval monk. When he ran out of ball point pens, we would walk to the town CVS and replace them, along with paper, tablets and binders so that the work would be protected. In order to give Beng a psychological push, we had him sit with his bare feet in a saucepan of cold water. When he needed lunch, Melissa served him his favorite bites, peanut butter and jelly on campfire baked bread. Beng ate like a holy man, not talking, not smiling, his mind and body on the Parchment. It was quite a spectacle to see –this strapping golden-haired boy doing a scholar's job, translating symbols we had never seen before with the aid of a seer stone he said had come with the Parchment.

We were so proud of him. Every day without fail he would get up before dawn and sit at the table and write, sometimes for hours until the skin alongside the nail on his writing finger was pressed down so far it looked like a disfigurement of some sort. Metatron would help him number and arrange papers; they would rarely talk but worked together as if in a trance. They were, I could see, the angel inheritors of a New Age and I was the father of a prophet! During times of depression I would remind myself of this and then I'd start to feel good again. On starry nights I would go outside and stand on a hillside and wait for divine messages to come to me, thinking every comet or object in the sky might be a sign. Then I would look at the light in the windows of the cabin and think, someday people of the earth will look back on this moment and revere it. They will try to conjure it up in their own minds, how it must have been, and so forth, but I am living it, now.

Spiritual overload can be a dangerous thing; that's why after obsessive high mindedness, Beng would inevitably suffer a relapse and turn into an ordinary fifteen year old boy, running, cursing, staying out late in the abandoned town, spying on Julius' tree house, and going whole hog with the *Portnoy's Complaint* thing. He'd forget his table manners, hide peas in his napkin, steal altar wine from the onion domed Russian church, and forget to say excuse me when dinner was through. There also seemed to be some sibling rivalry between the boys. Beng was suffering a very early form of male pattern baldness, a condition we attributed to the flash, but Metatron had a thick, voluptuous head of hair. Beng, thinking if he had to go bald then his brother should be bald too, would squeeze motor oil into Metatron's hairbrush hoping that the oil would corrode Metatron's scalp and make his hair fall out.

There were times when Beng would roll the translations up and leave them near the toilet. This exposed the Parchment to the cruder elements, so that Melissa was always hanging out the pages to dry so that they would not be lost. Why Beng's translations kept turning up in the bathroom was a mystery to us. In the meantime, I was still piecing together the relation between Beng's imperfections as a human being and his role as a prophet, especially when he'd suddenly and without warning go in and out of divinity mode, such as when he'd announce at dinner, "Tonight I will work on the Parchment. Please give me quiet. I do the work of the holy Avatar."

"The Holy Avatar?" I babbled out once, still telling myself over and over again that he was just a kid. But he gave me a look that shook me in my shoes. I don't know what kind of power he had, but it clicked the silver on the table and it magnetized our eyes, for we all stared at him like mounds of silly putty waiting for molding. It was scary; then I'd feel the Presence, and I'd lower my eyes and think, "I am in the Eye of the Universal Maker, in the Eye of the Storm, in the Eye of Everything!" And I'd look up at Melissa, and she'd have tears in her eyes, and Tiffany would be beaming and ever ready to assist him, and in would run Metatron, solemn and serious like the first assistant he was.

We were curious what the Parchment said. I knew it had to mean something important because of the way Beng transcribed it. I asked Beng what it said one morning while we were both shaving, me feeling weak and insignificant next to him with his magnificent physique.

"I can't tell you, father," he said. Apparently he was still in his Prophet cycle.

"But can't you give me a hint? Does it say anything about the place we have to migrate to?"

"We have to migrate, yes," Beng said. "But whether it is a physical place or a mental state, well, father, that has yet to be determined."

"…A mental state? You mean there's no hope for us here, no earthly kingdom?"

"I didn't say that," Beng said.

"At times I wish you weren't a prophet, Beng. Why don't you give your mother and me what we are looking for –something to believe in and a code to live by?"

"Father," Beng said, changing the subject, "Meta and I want to go backpacking. We want your permission to be gone several days. Do you mind?"

This caught me by surprise.

"Don't worry; it's just a spiritual journey."

I watched Metatron and Beng pack. They took cooking utensils, changes of clothing, and maps of the area and writing supplies. When they were ready, they said good-bye and Melissa and I watched them head into the forest. The Parchment was in the cabin covered over with a linen sheet. It was not to be uncovered until they returned. As they went into the forest, I heard them laughing and joking; they were also headed in the direction of the tree house. Melissa instantly regretted allowing them to leave.

"What did we just do? What just happened? Do we even know why we said yes? You know where they are going."

Later that night, as Melissa, Tiffany and I sat around the kitchen table picking at our food, we fell into the doldrums. I guess I hadn't realized how much I would miss my sons, for I had to force myself to eat.

"Melissa, don't worry," Tiffany pleaded. "Beng's got the divine spark. He knows what he is doing. You're much too negative."

"It's just that," Melissa paused a few seconds, "there's been so much deviation from the original plan of action. There are so many mistakes. Half of my calculations were wrong. I'm scared, frankly. Only this morning we learned from Beng that life may not change for any of us. Beng talked about a mental state."

"Well," Tiffany offered, "maybe we'd be smart to sneak a look at the Parchment. I know that would be trespassing, and if Beng found out, and he will know no matter what, who knows what he would do. We have to do something."

"I never said things were as bad as this," I said, feeling nervous about looking at the Parchment.

Life was dull in the cabin while the boys were away. Melissa and Tiffany spent most mornings washing their hair and the afternoons drying it while they picked string beans apart or shredded potatoes. I missed their assistance in the field, and so found it hard to work myself. A streak of laziness had come over the camp. Despite the fact that Beng told me to use this time as vacation time, I stalked the area around the cabin in search of things to do. I weeded the tomato patch, spotted a fox in the woods, fed Flash and the rest of the horses, but the whole time I was severely tempted to sneak a look at the Parchment. Tiffany caught me looking at it a couple of times and I got the distinct sense that she would have joined me in reading the document.

One night Tiffany came into the kitchen, slammed the door shut, and went over to the kitchen cabinet where the canned goods were kept. She took out a can of baked beans and applied the manual can opener to it, but so frantic were her movements that the can slipped out of her hand and onto the floor. Melissa and I, who were playing a game of

166

Scrabble that we had hoisted out of a suburban Philadelphia home, looked up and asked what was wrong.

"I was over by the creek, you know the deepest part, near the tree house, and I was stooping down to wash some laundry when I heard voices and all this prancing about. I looked up, and through the bushes I saw Julius and Brian, both naked. Then, I swear by the Parchment, I saw our boys, Beng and Metatron, both of them on the ground, naked, their bodies coated in oil, squirming around on top of each other like snakes. Somebody was beating a drum. I couldn't believe my eyes. I turned away as fast as I could and came here. That's the story, honest..."

"I knew it," Melissa said, slapping a towel she was holding against the sink. "Going after the children; pedophiles. They are molesting our sons. Scum of the earth!"

My heart sank. I knew they had found the substitute, the safety valve release that I had spoken of earlier to Melissa. But something told me to take it all in stride. "When the prophet comes on again in Beng," I said, "he'll be out of there so fast you'll hear a wind roar over the trees,"

"He's not a prophet," Tiffany said. "I wouldn't think twice about examining the Parchment now. What do we have to lose? He may be secretly working against us. Oh Dennis, if I were you I'd go and bring them back," she said as she dragged me out the door.

"Look," I said, waving my hands, "when I was a boy I did all sorts of weird things too. I played doctor with all my friends: stethoscope up, stethoscope down; thermometer in, thermometer out!"

"Must you!" Melissa interjected. "Look, maybe I shouldn't have jumped to conclusions. As weird as it sounds, maybe the boys need this experience. Let's join hands and form a meditation circle." Together we closed our eyes and concentrated on Beng and Metatron. We sent out positive thoughts and made the Om sound. Melissa grabbed the *Bhagavad-Gita*, and read a passage: "By meditating in this manner, always controlling the body, mind and activities, the mystic transcendentalist attains to the kingdom of God through cessation of material existence."

"Amen," Tiffany said.

"There's no Amen, this is not a Christian prayer," I told her.

"Now let us open our eyes slowly," Melissa intoned softly. "Breathe in; exhale."

"Om," Tiffany chanted, drawing a circle in the air.

We did not feel any better when we opened our eyes. I feared this would be the case, despite having a little faith. If the purpose of the chant was to draw the boys near, it did not work. Melissa, however, kept looking into the forest for signs of them.

"No," Tiffany said, shaking her head "It's no good, Beng is just an ordinary person and this Avatar is fiction. We've been fooled. History is not going to be rewritten. This is just a case of teen rebellion."

But there, above us in the sky, in the aerial realm of spirits, was something the likes of which I have never seen. It was a gigantic rectangular cloud of a glossy silver substance, resembling tin foil, which covered half the work fields and the woods. It glittered in the sun and seemed to waver slightly in the wind, and the sparkles and light reflecting off it were so bright at times I had to turn my face away.

I remembered an old line from the Gospels that warned against false prophets showing "great signs and wonders, insomuch that, if it were possible, they shall deceive the very elect." I quickly discarded the thought because I was feeling very confused.

"Oh Melissa," Tiffany said, getting on her knees to pray, "Look at that!"

Melissa pretended to act as if she knew what was happening, but there was confusion in her eyes also. Tiffany jumped up and ran to the woods, as if that would give her a better view.

"What is it?" I asked.

"It is," Melissa pondered, trying quickly to invent a name but, obviously stumped, reached for her *Bhagavad-Gita*, "It is…"

"It's the spirit of the Avatar," Tiffany called out in a tremendous turnabout of feeling, putting her right hand over her forehead in order to shield her eyes from the light.

Chapter Eight

I didn't like the way the spirit cloud, or UFO, was just floating in midair. Tiffany seemed to interpret it as a good sign, while I had mixed feelings. The odd thing about the object was that we could see ourselves reflected in the tin foil. It also seemed to have a tranquilizing power over us. This feeling of being watched, of the object's being possibly, a sign from Beng's Avatar, was unsettling.

Then something extraordinary happened. It went dark for three days.

This occurred after the earth shook and sent us, screaming, into the cabin. Then the sun disappeared or blacked out, I am not sure which. A terrible wind kicked up and blew a lot of the farming equipment some distance away. We felt a fear we hadn't felt since after the flash. Tiffany completely lost it during this episode. She cried many times, thinking that the sun would never return. We were afraid to venture outside because of the winds and storms. We were so frightened we refrained from looking out the windows. We passed the time huddled up on the kitchen floor, alternately sleeping and holding one another until the worst of it passed. When it ended the winds stopped and the sun gradually began to shine. It was like the dawn on a summer's day. We left the cabin and went into the yard to look at the sky. The object was still there, which did not help settle our fears and which had us thinking that the episode might start all over again.

Tiffany was afraid that we were in hell, but I would have none of that. That notion was permanently put to rest when we saw Beng and Metatron walk out of the woods. They were both in loincloths and their bodies were covered in tattoos. Nearly every inch of their skin – face, neck, legs and feet – had been inked. They were almost unrecognizable as human beings. Seeing them, Melissa lost her composure.

She told the boys to stand close to her while she inspected the elaborate webs and colorful drawings. They stood and stared. I guessed that they were on some drug, or that Brian and Julius had hypnotized them, for their eyes were glazed over and they seemed not to know us.

"Your role as holy prophet has gone right down the drain!" Tiffany said. "It's ruined."

Hearing this, Beng spoke to Metatron , and the two consulted. Melissa was upset that that the boys didn't seem to be themselves.

"Dennis, go over there and drag them here by the hair," she said.

I felt the corrective urge of a father, and walked over to them without thinking. After all, they were my children, and I was responsible for them. Standing before them, I could smell the fresh ink from the tattoos and the body oil. The oil had a mint aroma. They also had several body peircings: large ear lobe holes with stone inlays; miniature hoola hoop nose rings; and crossbars through their chins. They looked like a race of white urban cannibals or Matrix inhabitants of the old world just before its destruction. The symbols and ink drawings meant nothing. It was the art of Nihilism and nothing more. It took me several seconds before I could speak.

"As your father, I say we remove all the ink…"

"You do not understand the ways of the Avatar, "Beng said, looking at me like I was a sixth grade ignoramus. The object in the sky began to rattle. The sound frightened everyone except the boys, who glanced up at it as if he operated it himself by remote control.

There were these miniature rings in his nipples. How strange that I hadn't noticed that earlier. They were rings within rings so that they formed a coil. I searched their bodies for other markings I may have missed. "Do you think your mother appreciates this?" I asked, giving the coil rings a flip with my fingers.

"You expect me to live by mother's rules of etiquette?" Beng said. "Look, father, why don't you get the Parchment and the translations?"

Melissa walked up to us. "You," she said to the boys, keeping her eyes off the nipple rings, "have turned yourselves into fools. Don't you know that a continual struggle must be waged against the powers of darkness, especially in the realm of hearing which conceal the spoken words much as a cloud conceals the sun? Beng, you told me yourself years ago, when quoting from *The Mystery of Love*, your first notes from the underworld, that it is only by retreating within ourselves and giving reign to the spider-like threads upon which the words are strung that these may be re-cognized again. "

"What language are you speaking, mother? It means nothing to us, or to you ultimately, since I doubt you know what it means."

"I know what it means," Melissa, said, raising her voice, "It is by the equilibration of Spirit and Matter that the higher realms of consciousness may truly be sensed. That is from *The Mystery of Love!*"

"What is your idea of civilization, mother?" This came from Metatron, who had stuffed something into his mouth, and who, before this, had never said a bold thing to her.

Melissa looked defeated. "You," she said. "Only yesterday you were in diapers."

"Mother," Metatron said, as he turned around to show her the tattoos on his back. He withdrew a paper from his loincloth and read a Nietzsche quote: "Will to power! We have killed him (God), you and I! We are all his murderers! But how have we done it? How were we able to drink up the sea? Who gave us the sponge to wipe away the whole horizon? "

"What about the miracles? What about –that?" Melissa pointed to the sky where the object had been, but suddenly it was no longer there. Metatron laughed. Was the vision was obviously a trick, a sort of fakir's "miracle," and not a sign from Heaven?

"It's not the business of a prophet to tell his mother the secrets of the aerial realm," Beng offered, as he scratched his balls.

"The aerial realm?" Tiffany let out a venomous laugh.

"Close that mouth," Metatron said, pointing a finger at her.

"Pervert!"

Metatron threw something at her. It wasn't a rock or a stick, but more like small feathers that floated out of his hand, fell to earth and then turned into small grasshoppers. Tiffany leapt out of their path but they quickly made their way towards her, some having already attached themselves to her dress. She went in circles, shaking her clothing, and then they all turned back into feathers.

"Your bag of tricks doesn't impress me," Melissa said. "Especially not when you still wet the bed."

I could see Beng didn't appreciate this remark. He looked at his mother sternly, but said calmly, "Please get the Parchment, mother."

"Don't get it, Melissa, I don't care what they do. They can turn us to stone for all I care. They are up to no good," Tiffany said, crossing her arms.

"Why did you even allow that woman to come with you, father?" Beng asked.

"We thought it was part of the prophecy," I said, looking to Melissa for reassurance. "Brian needed a wife."

"Brian needed a what?" Beng said. "Brian did not need a wife. If anybody needed a wife, you did."

I was ready to slap the boy. I was sorry I didn't drown him in his bassinet when he was a baby, or use the syringe to inject him with mind altering tranquilizers. Now here he was attempting to stage some kind of revolution. "Nietzsche died in a mental institution," I said, out of desperation. "For a prophet, you're way out in left field."

"The attribute of my godhead is self-will," Metatron said, quoting something else and stuffing something else into his mouth. He was all over the map. What was wrong with him?

The quibbling about belief systems seemed silly to me. What good was it except to build up tension? Why couldn't we just chuck it all and live together in harmony? So what if the boys wanted to walk around in loincloths and tattoos? What was so bad about that? We were the only ones in the world as far as we knew. We could make our own rules now. I toyed with this idea as I watched the two of them argue with their mother. With the world littered with crushed buildings and broken bodies, arguments about belief seemed truly absurd. Yet I knew it was Melissa who had built up an idea of Beng that was now being realized as a totally false one. While he was in diapers and training pants, it was easy for her to say what he wanted done.

"You heard what your mother said" was all I could manage. Metatron sneered. I had never seen him act so brazen.

"Has there been sodomy in the tree house?" Melissa asked, almost whispering, her hand on her hip.

"Paranoid woman accuses former good friend of pedophilia," Metatron said, sneering again. "Mother, Brian and Julius have sex with each other. I don't know about Beng, but I want a woman, a big woman with a crotch like that tree over there. Come see the tree I carved into the shape of a woman, mother, and you'll find what you are looking for."

Together we watched the boys depart. They walked slowly into the woods, arms around each other's necks.

We went back to the cabin. Once inside, we opened the Parchment.

"This is all pornography!" Tiffany said with a shriek, reading the fine handwritten translations wrought by Beng before he left.

# # # # #

It wasn't till two years later that I saw Julius again. When I did, it was along the outer string bean field, way up over the tallest hill behind the cabin. I saw a man with a black beard, beads or something around his neck, and dressed in a loincloth considerably longer than Beng's or Metatron's. At first I did not recognize him; I thought he was some other man, a newcomer or a survivor monk from the onion-domed church. He was carrying a staff in the manner of an elder hermit. As I drew closer I could see that it was really Julius.

"You've changed," I told him. "I did not recognize you. As the father of the boys, you know I am concerned about them. Melissa and I miss our sons, the way they used to be. They never talk to us."

The truth is that every other morning Beng and Metatron would make a brief appearance on the edge of the field facing the cabin and stand there until Tiffany and Melissa noticed them. They did this, I suppose, in order to ease our minds about their safety and whereabouts, although they didn't talk or wave, but just stood there, then walked off. The first couple of times the women ran out to them, but the boys raced away in a flash and, since the women darned not go near the Tree house, they didn't follow them there. Eventually Tiffany and Melissa learned to just watch the boys, while occasionally using that time to yell out comments or suggestions to them.

"You look like the heroin addicts we used to see in the city. Don't you ever wash? If you could only see yourselves – The Planet of the Apes!"

Gradually, the comments from the women became less hostile and a more loving tone surfaced, including pleas to visit "just once." At one point Melissa announced that she was ill and that a visit would make her feel better, but the boys just laughed.

Tiffany whispered to Melissa on at least two occasions, "My, but they're growing up to be handsome young men. It's a shame. Love wasted on a tree."

"Look," I shouted out to the boys one morning, "why don't you take turns. Spend a few nights here, and then spend a few nights there. Will to Power!"

I looked to the women for their nod of approval. Melissa, realizing she had to let go of the prophet legacy, shook her head reluctantly. "Well," I shouted across to them, "what do you say? Life here isn't so bad. We're opening up. Learning to be accepting and all that. In fact, there have been a lot of changes here since you left. We read the Parchment and although we didn't like it at first, we've come to accept it. It has enlightened us. Oh, which reminds me, I'll get it for you, Beng; it has taken us a long time to finally decide that you should have it but you may and we apologize." With that I went into the cabin to get the Parchment and, when I had had it, I walked across the field and handed it to Metatron.

But it was Julius who invited us to dinner. When I saw him by the bean field, he extended the invitation, and when I told the women they were excited. This chance at socializing, at breaking the monotony of our routine, was a welcome relief. The truth is, our life had become dull. We didn't even try for another baby and Tiffany stopped asking me to come into her bunk.

"Can you imagine a tree house dinner?" Tiffany said, who only a couple of months ago would have scorned the idea. She was not yet fully reconciled to the idea, and every so often she'd let a bitter comment fly.

"We should bring a plate of something," Melissa said, who had gone through a similar change herself. "Why don't you hunt down a wild turkey," she asked me.

I agreed and spent a full day hunting in the woods for turkey. It wasn't easy. Most of the turkeys were near the Russian church and I didn't relish stepping over all the skeletal cadavers strew about over the churchyard. Turkey was also a rarity, though squirrels and rabbits were abundant. I did see one, its great tail fan like an Indian headdress being dragged across the floor of the forest. I snuck up with the gun I had taken in the hunting supply store in Philadelphia, and aimed. When I fired, it fell over on its face, its tail-end up like an open fan. I carried it back to the cabin where Tiffany had a great pot over a fire on the front lawn. It was my job to de-feather and clean the bird. When I completed this, I brought it over to them and they baked it in water and olive oil over the open fire.

The bird cooked for hours. Then we wrapped it in a moist towel and put it on a board for carrying to the tree house. When this was done, we prepared ourselves. The women put on their best dresses and I sported decent clothes for a change.

"I have my doubts," Tiffany said, who had made a bowl of potato salad. "What will this accomplish?"

"Sometimes you have to do strange things for peace," Melissa said. "We might win them over, and they'll come back. I still believe Beng is a prophet and that this is just his rebellious stage."

We followed the zigzag path. The women had never gone over it before. It was so beautiful in the woods I felt a sense of the purposefulness of life. When we came to the tree house, we were met by Julius in his beard, staff and loincloth. He smiled and studied our faces intently, no doubt looking for the signs of aging we were noticing in him.

Brian came up behind Julius. I have to say that he was a most magnificent sight. His hair was long and in braids.

He went up to Tiffany. Although Tiffany almost dropped her potato salad, she let him kiss her and grab hold of her hand and lead her to the table that the men and boys had laid out in the middle of the camp. Everything was serene and peaceful, although seeing Brian again was awakening a latent eroticism in Tiffany. I could see that she wanted him again. She wanted the old times, when she would ride him high and erect, her hair in a Medusa whirl. I sensed that she would not be able to hold her tongue for long, and this caused me considerable stress.

I felt sorry for her at this moment. I remembered their wedding day, and the hot honeymoon night that followed. I knew she must miss Brian terribly and, in a way, it was cruel to have to watch this display of husband-turned-hermit-seats-former-wife with a pat on the back. I had to swallow my hurt and annoyance as well, and let Julius guide me to my seat at the head of the table. Melissa had the two boys beside her. I could see that they looked weak and undernourished. I wanted so much to ask Julius what they had been eating and doing to make them like this —it was only a day since we had seen them last and they were beautiful and vibrant then.

"Do you notice how thin the boys look," I whispered to Tiffany while passing a plate of corn muffins.

"They look thin," Tiffany said. She spoke to Metatron, who seemed to be staring past the food on his plate and into space, "Eat your dinner honey, you're thin as a rail."

Melissa was feeling Beng's thin arms. Just as I looked at her, she was pinching his elbows and examining his earlobes.

"Both of the boys are...Dennis, look," Melissa said. But Julius and Brian were not looking. They were eating their turkey like vultures finishing up a carcass. One passed the corn muffins while the other passed the string beans while the other buttered his corn muffins. They were not thin; both of them had retained their muscles.

"Julius," I said, elbowing him. "What's with the boys. They do not look healthy."

"Dennis," Julius said, biting into a breast, "let's not have an argument tonight. I invited you to dinner, now let's have peace. But if you need to know, we are Vegans here. Brian and I are used to the diet, but the boys' bodies still haven't adjusted. This is a holiday for us so we are eating turkey."

176

"Tattoos equal piercing equal Vegan – that was an old world philosophy," I said.

"It's probably something rectal," Tiffany said out of the blue, referring, I think, to HIV/AIDS.

"Can't help being yourself, can you?" Brian replied, biting into a leg.

Julius seemed to be eating at a very rapid rate. He stuffed too much food into his mouth as if he wanted to gag.

Melissa observed all of this without saying a word. She was doing the best she could to hold her head high and ignore the tension. Suddenly, Julius got up from the table. He pushed his bench from under him and walked, almost hunchbacked, into a back room.

"Did you see the way he walked?" Tiffany said, "He's falling apart. This whole camp is falling apart."

"Homosexuality does that to entire civilizations," Melissa whispered. "That's why my boys don't belong here."

I chalked Julius' condition up to his rustic life in the tree house, and to the fact that he'd become a forest ascetic. It didn't seem to me that he had any sort of sex life with Brian anymore. They had outgrown their passion for one another and had become like platonic roommates. My sense was that Julius just liked having Brian around. I couldn't be certain of this, especially since neither of the men confirmed things one way or another. It used to be that they would shout this sort of thing from the rooftops but now there was an eerie silence.

I compared Julius' look to Tiffany's look and the two were worlds apart. Her red face and her firm breasts were a sure sign of health; what a contrast she was to them all, except Brian maybe, who had retained his strength and beauty. "This is not good. I feel a sickness here. The boys have lost their color. They won't even talk. Brian, what is the problem? Why did Julius bring us here?"

When Brian didn't answer, I got him to agree to let us ask the boys if they wanted to go home, where there were soft bunk beds and woman-cooked meals. Metatron said yes, but Beng shook his head no' he was the most stubborn, anyway. Since we had left the remains at the table, we had nothing to carry.

That night, while I lay next to Melissa, we talked about Beng. Melissa hinted that his prophecy was doomed, that the Avatar had fallen into disfavor with him, and had withdrawn his special gifts.

I didn't know what to say to this. I hadn't seen Beng jerk or go into a prophet spasm at dinner, but then he may have been in a deep post-prophet relapse. I mentioned to Melissa, "Look, we don't how many times the Avatar visits him at the tree house. He could be doing terrific work all day long; his soul could be drained, and maybe it was drained when we were there."

"I don't know," Melissa said. "He says one thing, and then another. It seems he is a prophet of confusion." Although she wanted both sons under her roof, she was glad to have Metatron back again and wasted no time quizzing him about the goings-on in the tree house.

"What is your brother doing that makes him look so awful? You can tell me now. Here, eat this oatmeal!" Lazily, Metatron took his hand away from his forehead and spooned his oatmeal like it was poison as Tiffany, sitting across from him and eating an apricot, said she wanted to remove the earrings from his nipples. No one paid any attention to this, so I guessed she would do it at the first opportunity.

"Come here, you," she said to the boy, right after breakfast, and Metatron went over to her like a zombie, and she, toying with a pair of pliers, worked at the nipple earrings. "There," she said, breaking the bands and pulling them out, "You're officially one of us now."

Chapter Nine

Tiffany became convinced, evidently, that it was her mission in life to initiate Metatron into sex on his eighteenth birthday.

So it was that one morning Tiffany invited him to look at an art book with her while Melissa and I peeled string beans. They were sitting in our bedroom on the edge of the bed, with this big art book over both their laps. It was a book of erotic nudes, *Erotic Art of the Masters* by Bradley Smith, as well as a smaller book, *Sex on the Screen, Eroticism in Film* by Gerard Lenne. Tiffany was reading Henry Miller's introductory essay from the first book.

"'Among the more simple, natural feasts of the flesh which this body offers us is the physical union of man and woman, To it we owe not only the greatest emotional experience the flesh can know, but life itself...'"

The air was thick with sexual tension.

I knew I had to get away. I didn't know what I would do if this continued. I went into our bedroom and lay down on the bed. I closed my eyes and counted to twenty. Was it wrong to want what my son possibly wanted – to allow him to have a smooth and liberated sexual experience? In the background I could hear birds chirping and Tiffany moaning. Melissa had resigned herself that this was going to happen, so she was putting things away in the cabinets. When I opened my eyes I saw shadows playing on the ceiling. They were in the shape of two columns and were criss-crossing and bending into shapes, as if they were trying to tell me something. At first I did my best to ignore them, but then I realized they were trying to tell me something. The more I studied them, the more I became convinced that they had a message.

One of the shadowed columns formed itself into a person in a monk's habit. It had a hood over its head, and it was seeing somebody out the door. Beneath the monk's habit I could see an erect penis but an erect penis that had become a shaft of light because its power was contained or sublimated into spiritual energy. The person being ushered out the door was being transmuted from a lover into a platonic friend.

A change had occurred where the withheld sexual energy had illuminated everything.

What was this? I saw it as meaning that the Avatar would return soon, but who, exactly was the Avatar? Melissa suggested taking a walk to clear my head. That seemed like a good idea. I got up, looked at myself in the mirror, and went outside with her. I noticed the way that Metatron and Tiffany had disappeared into another bedroom. She was till making a lot of noise, and poor Metatron, in the throes of Eros, was whimpering, "What's happening? It won't stop, it won't stop – don't stop, don't stop, what's happening?" If the Avatar was coming soon then all this was ended anyway – sex, Flash, the tree house, all our little family dramas; all swallowed up in another flash. I was confused. As we walked along in the field, I thought how odd it was that I should be chosen for a new prophetic message. I was so unworthy, and yet all along I knew I always had an inkling of Spirit in me.

#

Ordinarily, I think Tiffany and Metatron's sexual antics would have annoyed me. There were no holds barred at any time of the day or night. They would slip off together in the woods, on the hill, near the church, and even in the creek, and we would know what they were doing.

The coming of the Avatar concerned me more now than sex. I wasn't much interested in sex anymore, and Melissa, although initially frustrated, came to understand that I had to concentrate on my vision.

I don't know whether I was prompted by the vision or what, but in no time I was making my way over to the tree house with the news that the Avatar was coming. I went in the early afternoon, when I knew all of them would be up and around. When I came upon them, they were in the middle of the camp lifting homemade barbells. Julius had no muscle at all but I could see he was hard at work on a weight five times his own. He grunted as he lifted it above his head and held it there while it shook. It looked as if his arms would break. Brian stood behind him, guiding the log with the two small boulders tied on each end. He was an Adonis in the flesh, that one. His chest muscles looked splendid as the sun coming through the treetops put a whirling color wheel over his body. He was in a bikini. His crotch bulge looked bogus; he might have had an avocado in there.

"Hello guys," I said. Julius made the mistake of lifting his head up to look at me and the weight he was holding swayed slightly to the right. Then his arms shook and there was a near collapse until Brian swooped down and caught the weight himself.

"Whew!" Julius said, fluffing up his beard. The weight was on the ground and Brian was busy rolling it behind a holding ditch. He looked awful. His face was thin. His beard was ragged. He had his hair combed over his forehead. Yet he had the look of a prayerful mystic who had not lost a connection to the sensual, what with his necklaces of feathers and beads, his bracelets of rope and stones and long, frilly things that dangled as he moved. On his head he wore a multicolored cap. His staff was decorated with animal skins, a snake's head, and a lavender boa. His look fascinated me, being the new receiver of visions myself.

I didn't know how to tell them the Avatar was coming. I didn't know where to begin, so I concentrated on Beng. I asked Julius how the kid was doing and he said "See for yourself." At that, Beng appeared, and what I saw was an entirely different boy. He looked glum; he looked at me with sad, puppy dog eyes. Clearly I saw that something was wrong. "Beng," I said, pulling him over. I could see he had taken out the earrings, piercings, and had even removed all the tattoos. His hair combed straight back and tied in a long pony tail. He was not the same person.

"Hello, father," he said, with what I felt was a feeling of new found respect. I could see that Julius was unhappy with him. There was tension in the air. I told him, "You know, if you want you can come home with me. Metatron is happy. Tiffany keeps him happy, if you know what I mean." But I wasn't getting through. At the mention of Tiffany, Beng frowned. "Just come back with me if you're unhappy," I said.

"Beng is leaving," Julius said.

I looked at this bearded surrogate father, who had become a mishmash of earth and spirit, a wearer of jewelry that purported to be symbolic of something deeper but which had no meaning deeper than the cosmetic. "He announced to us last night that he was ready to go. It's his nineteenth birthday. He's got to make his own way."

"Beng," I said, "I had a vision of the Avatar yesterday. I know that he is coming even if I don't know how." I don't know what I expected to happen but at least I expected more than the no-reaction that I was getting. My announcement didn't seem to affect him. He seemed to have known already, or plainly didn't care, for he turned his head sideways. "Look, Beng, think what this means. The Avatar will be here. I received the message."

He stood there as if hypnotized or drugged. "Dennis, I don't know what's wrong with him," Julius said. "He won't lift weights. He has forgotten about the Parchment. He won't do anything. He refuses to do anything. He's lifeless, as if he lacked a purpose."

So, I thought, his life as a prophet is over. I don't know what made me do it, but I reached for his hand and held it. "Give your old home one more try," I said, as Brian and Julius walked back to the tree house.

Suddenly Beng came towards me. It was a great scene. We embraced, after which Beng got his knapsack and we made our way back to camp.

We were greeted by Tiffany, who screamed "Oh baby!" She leaned over him and gave him a squeeze. I could see his brother Metatron poking his head up inside the kitchen window. Melissa came out too, and ran a hand through his hair. It was good cheer all around until later after dinner when Tiffany opened up after the boys went to bed.

"What happened over there is what I want to know. Something must have happened. I know those two abused them. You can tell. Look how quiet they are; they hardly talk. They have been molested. There used to be laws about this kind of thing, but now there are no police. What can we do? I say we have a trial. If we have to do it ourselves, I say we have a trial and bring them to justice. They corrupted these boys."

"The boys pretty much confessed that nothing happened," I said. "We have to go by their word."

"We need to talk to them and get them to release the truth. They say there is repressed memory. Maybe they drugged them, got them to forget. We have to get to the bottom of this. We need to keep asking the boys and get them to open up. They were abused."

I didn't sleep at all that night. It must have been in the middle of the night when I sat up in bed and slowly made my way to the kitchen table. I lit a candle, and sat down and looked out the window. A few moments of peaceful contemplation were mine, but then I heard the bed sheets rustling and when I realized that Melissa or Tiffany might be waking up, I blew out the candle as I was in no mood to be disturbed, even for polite conversation. I sat as quietly as I could, without breathing, slumping down in the chair a little so that I wouldn't be seen. Soon I was able to see a shadow. It was Tiffany; her pink Victoria Secret nightgown cutting right through the darkness and her long hair looking like a horses' mane. I got as close to the window shutters as I could, ducking under the table. I watched as she leaned over the sleeping bags examining *The Sleepers*. Soon she was looking at their faces close up, and for a split second I thought of Whitman's poem *The Sleepers* and experienced an almost spiritual moment. Then Tiffany sat down between the boys. I geared up for a spectacular show.

She was uncovering somebody. Yes, it was Beng. She unzipped the top of the sleeping bag and even in the dark I could see Beng's bare chest. Tiffany threw her hair back behind her shoulders. Then she put her hand down atop him before lowering her head. She no sooner made contact than Beng sprang to his feet, screaming some obscenity. He was standing on his sleeping bag, his arms swinging like he was getting ready to throw a punch. Tiffany had gotten up and stepped back, walking backwards as fast as she could to bed where Melissa and I slept. But the ruckus had woken Melissa. Tiffany had succeeded in crawling back into her bunk. I followed her.

"Hey, what was that?" Melissa said, lighting the oil lamp beside the bed. In the light, she saw Beng, red faced, still trying to clam himself. "Beng, what's wrong?"

"Tell that woman to stay right where she is," Beng said, "or we will have to bring her to trial."

"Why, Tiffany's asleep, Beng."

Melissa looked at me for answers. "Dennis, do you know anything about this? What's all this talk of trials?" Tiffany let out an exaggerated snore.

"She copped a feel; she tried to blow me," Beng said, pointing at Tiffany. "Put her on trial."

"Why Beng, you probably just had a dream." But just to check, she nudged Tiffany, who did not budge. Beng, however, was not having any of this. He made his way toward Tiffany's bunk.

"Oh, no you don't," Melissa said, getting out of bed and holding both her arms up. "You stay right where you are. Come to your senses, Beng."

Yes, come to your senses, I thought. Tiffany was just being Tiffany, and Beng had better understand it.

Metatron was up by now. He looked at his brother with fascination. Beng, to my disbelief, walked around the back of the bed where Melissa couldn't grab him and stood next to Tiffany. This precipitated a frantic jump-up on Melissa's part. She was headed in Beng's direction, thinking to subdue a knockdown fight, I suppose, but I could see that Beng held his arms out in a very gentlemanly fashion and sort of waved a magic spell, or at least it made it clear to us that nothing like the Battle of Germantown was about to occur. "Hold it all of you," he said, in his deepest voice ever. "We can't let this pass, she is pretending to be asleep, mama; her snores are fake. She is awake right now. As a prophet of the Avatar, I am not a liar, mama. She doesn't want to face up to me. She is sniveling like a snail!"

Beng had a point, for Tiffany had stopped her snoring and was laying there all tensed up, measuring each of Beng's words and expecting, I guess, to be dragged out of bed. I wondered whether or not she would wake up and defend herself.

"Back to sleep, everybody!" Melissa said, making chopping motions with her arms. "We'll talk about in the morning."

Somewhat reluctantly, Beng headed for the sleeping bag, since there didn't seem to be anything else to do. But the next morning, he moved his seat away from Tiffany's at the breakfast table and was careful not to look at her.

Poor Beng had to witness Tiffany's flaunting of her relationship with his brother. It came to him as a shock. He couldn't believe it when Tiffany led Metatron into the bedroom four and five times day. He would often leave the cabin when this happened and go for a walk.

When he returned from these walks, he was somewhat calmed. After one walk he took Metatron into a corner, and I overheard some of the conversation.

"Do you know the Avatar has forbidden it?" Beng said. As if he were trying to teach his brother the Arabic alphabet, Beng continued: "It is absolutely forbidden. We are not to copulate with women. That is the rule. I received it a long time ago, but didn't understand it. Then it was revealed to me in a dream, and now I know for certain." Metatron had nothing to say. I was tempted to break up their talk, but decided it was not my business, especially after hearing the unexpected news that the Avatar had declared opposite sex relations unlawful. This naturally, I found incredible. I wondered how it could be, especially since we might be the only people left on the planet. How would the new nations and the world progress? What would happen to the human race? The question stuck like a summer tick on a dog. I was also tempted to throw this question out at Beng.

Metatron, to my surprise, asked Beng, "Why?"

"There's another band of survivors," Beng said. "We are not the only living persons. There are others of a better quality, a higher intelligence, a better gene pool. These people may do all the reproducing. But we have to live and die out. We have to get it other ways. There are lots of ways to get it. Metatron, don't you know? There are shapely trees, and now that we are over eighteen, there's Brian, there's Julius, there's daddy."

"You're sick," Metatron said. "I don't want to live in a world like that. Do what thou wilt!"

What was he saying to my youngest son? What was this outrage? I had the urge to jump up and strangle him. We were to die out, like the Shakers? There were other people of higher intelligence, better genes? He was insulting us, his was insulting prophecy. What kind of Avatar, I wanted to know, would proscribe laws like these?

185

I came to the sad conclusion that our boy Beng was psychotic. He was, in every sense of the word, dangerous. He was dangerous to us, dangerous to his brother, and about the only people he wasn't dangerous to were Brian and Julius. Yet, as usual, on this as on the other issues that cropped up, I was really split down the middle. Hadn't I seen the Avatar as a cloaked monk figure? Wasn't this, couldn't this, be a sign that we weren't to copulate, because monks don't. But even so, there were holes in his reasoning. Copulation doesn't have to be vaginal; it can be oral, safe from the danger of pregnancy. Yet as soon as I thought this, I saw Metatron whisper something in Beng's ear, and I heard Beng say, "Oral sex with a woman is worse, because you are psychically teasing the vaginal walls. It is far better to walk away."

"We are in for it, now," I thought.

When I told Melissa, she asked me repeatedly whether I was sure I had heard it right, and when I said I had, she agreed that Beng was a was a mortal danger.

"He's already taking Metatron aside and feeding him this information," I added. "I don't know how it will work, but he's working on him," I decided this declaration on Beng's part was the reason he came back to us. Otherwise he could have lived his quiet life with Julius and Brian and nobody in the cabin would have given a damn. Now the only thing I could think of was when he would officially announce it, take down the rule on the granite tablet, as it were.

Chapter Ten

Beng made his announcement that night when Tiffany applied a mixture of baby oil and Vaseline to Metatron's navel with the intention of making wide circles with her hand, until she brought the lubricant all the way down to his privates. It was late at night, but Beng crawled into Metatron's sleeping bag and slapped the oil out of Tiffany's hands. Metatron, of course, his big brother's shadow, said nothing, but this time Tiffany blew up. "What do you think you're doing? He's mine!"

"You don't touch him," Beng said. "He's not for you to touch. Copulation is against the law of the Avatar."

"Eat brick, you fanatic," Tiffany said. "Meta and I are in love. He's mine."

"Do you love her?" Beng asked his brother.

Metatron paled at the question. I knew in my heart that a lad his age didn't know what he loved and it was a useless question.

"I like her…a lot," he said.

"The time is now. The Avatar is coming. There are other people in a far corner of the globe copulating freely." That is enough for the world at this point."

I couldn't take too much more of this argument. I was in bed with Melissa by now. Melissa had stuffed tissue in her ears, but since I heard everything, I had difficulty falling asleep. I leaped out of bed and went into the living room. There I saw him, standing. Every now and then he gave off little glimmers of light in the eyes that revolved like spinning wheels. But I wasn't afraid of the light. At least I wasn't thinking about that now as I lunged forward, grabbed Beng, and yanked him towards me. He loosened up like a straw doll and when I saw the look on his face –as if he were a dragon spitting fire –I lost my temper even more and slugged him in the shoulder, sending him a little way across the room. By this time Metatron was heading for the kitchen table, as Tiffany put her hands over her mouth and muttered an "Oh no!" I was amazed at my strength. The boy cowered in the corner, fearing that I would lunge again. Suddenly I was caught up in the drama of it; I was acting out what I had wanted to do for so long, and the release was almost sexual, like coming. It poured through my veins and a swell beneath my head tickled and I imagined white spurts popping out through the roots of my hair.

"Don't you ever, ever, say anything like that again in this house!" I threw my fist down on a cheap card table we had beside the sofa and it collapsed. The noise brought Melissa out and sent Tiffany up to me, where she tugged at my shirtsleeves begging me to quit, that the punishment was enough. "Promise!" I said, shoving a finger at Beng, who was holding his hurt shoulder.

"I promise," said a quivering Beng, and as I heard this, I could scarcely believe it. If he was the prophet of the Avatar, why wasn't he giving me a good thrashing? Now he was only a skinny little boy, his hard prophetic stance funneled down to a whimper and a little acne around his chin. "Good," I said, searching momentarily for a Divine Light twinkle. "Now apologize to Tiffany." Without blinking an eye, the boy looked in Tiffany's direction and mumbled, "I'm sorry."

"That's it, now go take a walk."

After this episode, I wanted to be alone. I lay down on the bed and stared at the ceiling. I wished for a replay of the Avatar's shadow, for I wanted to know the truth. "Avatar, Avatar," I whispered. I was doing everything I could to bring the vision about. I was glad when I saw some criss-crossing shadows, for that made me realize that my punching the boy had not made me any less of a receiver myself. Slowly then, the criss-crossed forms evolved into the monk-like figure.

"Avatar!" I called again. "Avatar! I must know if what Beng said is true. You must know whether or not it is true. Please reveal it to me." I lay there for what must have been a long time, sweating, concentrating so hard that I forgot about the others in the house, and when Tiffany knocked on the door, I didn't hear it at first.

"Dennis," she said, "Metatron and I want to use the room." Since I hadn't received any messages, I was not powerless to act. I interpreted their coming to the door as a sign that the Avatar approved of us —not Beng's philosophy. I gladly opened it then and did a sort of mock bow as Tiffany led Metatron to the bed. Again, she wasted no time in going about it.

But sitting in the living room, with Melissa sitting across from me, I felt very depressed. The scene reminded me of the last chapter from D.H. Lawrence's *Women in Love*. I was there with my wife, but something was missing. "Imagine a boy like Beng," I mentioned to Melissa, "saying that we are an inferior race of people? That we are so inferior that we have to die out?"

"You did what you had to do. If the boy was following the Avatar's law, then the Avatar isn't for us. We will have to promote schism and hope prophetic-spasms develop in Metatron. Personally, I think this will happen. Already I have seen a faraway look in his eyes, and a certain twirling of the pupils. He has, when he bows his head in meditation, a certain body aura. On certain days, I'm convinced that I can see it."

"You mean sex-drenched Metatron – a prophet? Right now, Tiffany is his commander-in-chief."

"Remember, all prophets have human weaknesses. Just try to notice him at dinner one night. You'll see."

When Beng didn't return, I kept my eyes on Metatron and made a special note of the things he did. As he ate sauerkraut, for instance, he bit his lip and stared deep into the design of the table cloth, and I thought that perhaps this was a spasm-trance and he was about to receive a revelation. At this juncture too, Melissa kicked me under the table, and I smiled at her. We were about to witness something special, I was sure, yet nothing happened.

I began to worry about Beng's disappearance. I was half sorry I punched the boy. And as I certainly had no intention of banishing him, I took a hike out to the tree house in hopes of winning him back. I just had one rule of thumb that I wanted to apply: keep your thoughts, when they concern the rest of us, to yourself, and let us live our own life. You do what you want, provided there are no shocking, theatrical displays. This, I thought, seemed reasonable, and so I followed the path and when I came to the tree house, I called but no one answered. I went up into it and knocked on the door but there didn't seem to be anyone around. I pushed the door all the way in. There was no one inside, but I saw that Julius' sleeping bag and papers were gone. I knew then that they hadn't left for supplies, but that all of them may have left for good.

This was a great shock, for while our tribes weren't linked in the closest brotherhood bond possible, just knowing they were there, that I could talk to them if I chose, and visit them for a glimpse into another world, was comforting in a way. Now the world had been narrowed down to me, Tiffany, Melissa and Metatron.

I left the tree house and called Brian and Julius' name, but no one answered. The weights were still there and these I imagined Melissa would confiscate for Metatron at some point. But to never see my own son again! This thought was the hardest to take. For there was just the slightest possibility, a chance in a thousand, that he was speaking the truth when he said the things he said when I punched him, and if he was gone, then that meant we were out of the Avatar's direct presence, maybe forever.

I ran back to the cabin. I called them all out of their rooms and told them the news. Melissa shook her head knowingly, as if she expected it all along, but Tiffany and Metatron took it like two dumb waiters; they couldn't have cared less. I went into the living room. Metatron followed me, lay down on the floor, and put his hands behind his head. "Do you have any idea where they could have gone?" I asked. Metatron looked at me' for a moment I thought I saw his pupils whirling, but I found that he was just thinking. "You're going to miss your brother," I said.

"Ahh," he said, "maybe –yeah, maybe I will."

# # # # #

The next day I went to the tree house again. There were squirrels running around inside the house, and I was sure they would never be back. It was very depressing.

I sat down on one of the rocks beside the weights and meditated on a lifetime of Tiffany, Melissa and Metatron. But now at least we could have babies and this nonsense about there being more intelligent beings somewhere in the world would fade into the background. That, at least, was a relief. But gloom, gloom, gloom was the order of the day. I knew I had to come kind of resolve regarding my life at the cabin; I would either have to become a pioneering father, cultivating a true tribe to inherit the earth, or just fluctuate, sail along until I grew old. Although I realized that the history of the new world was being written every morning I woke up, I could not sense the magic of the history taking place. History is drudgery while it is being lived, and so is everything else –prophecy, Old or New Testaments, or whatever. It seemed like a horrible condemnation, Beng's Rule, that I not touch my wife and that she not touch me. I had become used to this way of life. To force me to touch Julius, when not a bone in my body responded favorably to such a union, was unnatural. I hadn't thought of Julius in that way in a very long time. No, I couldn't have done that, and I was still fairly certain that I had done the right thing in refusing and in giving Beng a good punch.

I went back to the cabin. Tiffany and Metatron were preparing a gigantic salad in the kitchen, while Melissa paced back and forth in the living room. I went over to her. When she looked at me there was real love in her eyes –no tom foolery, no judgmental haze; just head-on, well-balanced love. I really liked it. "Do you think Beng will ever come back?" I asked.

Melissa didn't have an answer. She seemed a defeated woman in many ways. The great prophet she had raised had turned against her, had stalked out of the temple.

That night we prayed to the Avatar together –the four of us in the living room, sitting around closing our eyes and meditating as hard as we could, I presented them with the image and we concentrated until it appeared in our imaginations. I knew everyone was having it because we all held hands and I heard Melissa say yes, she saw a man in a monk's robe standing by an open door.

"What is he saying?" Tiffany wanted to know.

"Shh," Melissa and I said at once, concentrating to see if he would make another movement, but there he stood, looking in, not moving, and certainly not saying anything.

"Say something, goddamnit!" Melissa cried out in a moment of impatience. But nothing happened.

That night I couldn't sleep. I was kept awake by shadows on the ceiling I took as visions. I thought the Avatar was trying to communicate with me. I answered 'yes' or 'no' as various things were put across to me and, when the time came, I walked out into the living room where I sat in a chair and looked at the visions on the ceiling there. I could scarcely believe it when I was told I would have to leave the camp and take off on my own; that Beng's dictum had been correct and that if I persisted here, mingling with Melissa and Tiffany, I was a doomed man. I would have to pay for it in the other world. With this knowledge, a feeling so terrifying grew in my soul that it was all I could to keep from screaming. When dawn finally came, I was a wreck. I was weak in the head and frightened. I was afraid to move from the sofa and could only think of things pertaining to my exodus or to Beng's dictum.

When Melissa came in the room on her way to the kitchen to make coffee, she noticed me sitting there wrapped in a blanket.

"Is something wrong?" she asked. But the voices told me to keep it from her, otherwise my resolve would be weakened and I would not have the strength to comply. So I drank the coffee she handed and planned my escape.

I would take Beng's sleeping bag, all the instant coffee, the mess kit, clothes. I'd put them all in a knapsack. I would do this when they were all out in the strawberry fields. But I would have to be careful and do it fast. If they saw me, it was all over. And I would have to push all sentimental thoughts out of my head. This would take real discipline.

I planned to grab the icon of Saint Mark, of course, just in case I was fated to have a far more lasting revelation in the future.

Already sentimental thoughts were trying to weaken my stand, the tender faces of Melissa and Tiffany floating in my mind like the space capsules of old.

With a shake of my head I pushed them all out and the blank space I wanted appeared. I was okay –momentarily.

But where would I go? If I was lucky I could catch up to Brian and Julius, but that was unlikely. They could be anywhere. The thought of dying in the forests occurred to me. But I could find my way to a suburban development or city and inhabit the houses there.

Yes, I would have to dispense with my fears. Didn't the Avatar appear to me as a monk? Wasn't that, in a way, a signal to me that I would end my days as a solitary figure, between two worlds, with the door half opened, looking in. But only looking in! That was the clue.

The End

About the Author

Thom Nickels is a Philadelphia-based author/journalist, the author of nine published books, including: *The Cliffs of Aries* (1988), *Two Novellas: Walking Water & After All This* (1989), *The Boy on the Bicycle* (1991-1994), *Manayunk* (1997), *Gay and Lesbian Philadelphia* (2000), *Tropic of Libra* (2002), *Out in History*, and *Philadelphia Architecture* (2005). His novel *SPORE* was published in 2010. In 1990, Mr. Nickels was nominated for a Lambda Literary Award and a Hugo Award for his book, *Two Novellas*: *Walking Water & After All This*. He was awarded the Philadelphia AIA Lewis Mumford Architecture Journalism Award in 2005 for his book *Philadelphia Architecture* and his weekly architectural columns in *Philadelphia Metro*.

He has written a wide variety of stories, including celebrity and literary interviews, and columns for *The Philadelphia Inquirer*, *The Philadelphia Daily News*, *The Philadelphia Bulletin*, *City Paper*, *The Philadelphia Weekly*, *The Broad Street Review* and *The New Oxford Review*. His travel essays have appeared in *Passport Magazine* and elsewhere. His column, *Different Strokes* in the Philadelphia Welcomat in the early 1980s, was one of the first out LGBT columns in the nation. He is currently the architectural writer/critic columnist and feature writer for *ICON Magazine* (New Hope, PA), a contributing writer at Philadelphia's *Weekly Press*, and the Religion Editor at the *Lambda Book Report*. He has been listed in Who's Who in America since 2003.

earing any underwear. "Excuse me," I said, having a hard time look

linded by that bulge in his crotch, "but don't I know you?" "Maybe

ind of to   bout

with Ray   God,

t loser?   in?" h

aid. "Lik   s stron

ce body   e on C

lly, he l   I eve

1 up to t   any id

istaking   he sam

n, I coul   ery lor

ood raci   ne sw

ing with   e in st

we go   behin

vill see u   in pu

ed?" he   vent to

rivacy.   grabb

hard. I

k, traci   t, so f

ed it, ha

with m   bing

bbing, I   n cock

he sound of unzipping filled the small space. I don't know who's h

, but before I knew it, I had his rod in my hand, and mine was in hi

it to do?" he asked, his tone challenging. I knew exactly, and sank